HDL   BC

CAERPHILLY COUNCIL

Please return / renew this item by the last date shown above
Dychwelwch / Adnewyddwch e

D1346333

BLOOD TIES

The new Naomi Blake novel

When Alec and Naomi take a much-needed Winter holiday in Somerset, they encounter local eccentric Eddy Thame, a historian and metal detectorist obsessed with the Monmouth rebellion of 1685 and the alleged Kirkwood treasure. A few days after their arrival, Eddy is found dead. Reluctantly, Alec and Naomi become involved, but they soon realise that Eddy seems very different to the rather dotty individual they encountered in the local pub...

Recent Titles by Jane A. Adams
from Severn House

The Naomi Blake Mysteries

MOURNING THE LITTLE DEAD
TOUCHING THE DARK
HEATWAVE
KILLING A STRANGER
LEGACY OF LIES
BLOOD TIES

The Rina Martin Mysteries

A REASON TO KILL
FRAGILE LIVES
THE POWER OF ONE
RESOLUTIONS

BLOOD TIES

A Naomi Blake Novel

Jane A. Adams

Severn House Large Print
London & New York

This first large print edition published 2013
in Great Britain and the USA by
SEVERN HOUSE PUBLISHERS LTD of
19 Cedar Road, Sutton, Surrey, England, SM2 5DA.
First world regular print edition published 2010 by
Severn House Publishers Ltd., London and New York.

British Library Cataloguing in Publication Data

Adams, Jane, 1960- author.
  Blood ties. -- Large print edition. -- (A Naomi Blake
  mystery ; 6)
  1. Blake, Naomi (Fictitious character)--Fiction.
  2. Ex-police officers--Fiction. 3. Blind women--Fiction.
  4. Historians--Crimes against--England--Somerset--
  Fiction. 5. Detective and mystery stories. 6. Large type
  books.
  I. Title II. Series
  823.9'2-dc23

ISBN-13: 978-0-7278-9603-2

Severn House Publishers support The Forest Stewardship Council
[FSC], the leading international forest certification organisation. All
our titles that are printed on Greenpeace-approved FSC-certified paper
carry the FSC logo.

MIX
Paper from
responsible sources
FSC® C018575

Printed and bound in Great Britain by the
MPG Books Group, Bodmin, Cornwall.

PROLOGUE

He had read somewhere that the desire to put your affairs in order is a universal one. That death has a way of focussing attention on unfinished business and that the instinct of most people is to leave behind as little trouble as possible.

That had been his initial impulse and he had lit a fire, the intent being to burn the whole damned lot. Why should another generation be troubled by the things that had haunted him for the past twenty years?

So, he had lit the fire in the kitchen, worried a little that the chimney would not be up to the job and unable to recall the last time this hearth had been used. His wife had prettied it up with displays of dried flowers and candles and would never have dreamed of using the grate for its original function, but she wasn't around any more to tell him what he should and shouldn't do, and it felt oddly cathartic, tossing the dusty bouquet aside and chucking the candles into the flames. Catharsis aided by the now half empty bottle of single malt he had purchased just for this occasion.

He stacked up all his prospective fuel. Twenty years' worth of birthday cards written to a girl who'd never aged since her seventeenth, never celebrated any of those anniversaries. Twenty years of Christmas cards and tiny, carefully wrapped gifts. His wife had opened a few of them and accused him of having an affair when she'd seen what they contained. Pretty pendants and slender gold bracelets; one year a Hermes scarf, though the teenager who had died would never have worn such a thing. Once, a pink diary, covered in shaggy fuchsia fur and complete with a tiny lock, then a key ring, shaped like a small silver teddy bear. He planned to burn the lot, along with the newspaper clippings and the photographs and those letters. All of the letters.

Then, when it came to it, he was unable to do anything. He poured the final glass and stared at the sad little piles of possessions she hadn't lived to possess and he came to a decision. Bugger leaving nothing behind, sod being tidy and thoughtful and cleaning up after himself. What had that cost him so far?

Later, when the police attended the scene and the smell of alcohol was so strong even on his dead body that they were left in little doubt as to the cause of the crash, the wonder would be that he could have actually even made it into the car. Blood alcohol, the post-mortem told them, was so far over the limit he was lucky to have been able to stand up.

'The only good thing,' the attending officer said privately to his colleague, 'is the bastard just hit a wall and not another vehicle.'

But then, there was no way he could have known that the wall had been selected so very carefully. The distance from home was so short, the road so straight, the street so likely to be deserted. Oh, in that respect he had planned and set everything in order with the minimum of mess left behind, but the stacks of cards and letters and tiny presents would tell their own tale for those that found them, and the ending to *that* story would not be nearly so decisive or so clean.

ONE

They had stuck a pin in a map, or rather, Naomi had, though it had taken her three attempts to find anything appropriate. Attempt number one had landed her pin atop a rather large mountain in the Cairngorms.

'No,' Alec said. 'Not even if I could ski.'

Attempt number two had ended up in the middle of the Bristol Channel.

'We need a bigger map,' Alec said.

'No, three's a charm; I'll get us somewhere nice this time.'

Alec watched, willing her to at least hit land. 'Look,' he said. 'How about if I find a blind-fold?'

'I don't really think *I* need one.'

'No, I meant, find *me* a blindfold and I'll have a go.'

Naomi giggled; an empty wine bottle stood on the coffee table, with a second, open and half empty, next to it.

'I'm just not sure you should be trusted with anything sharp,' Alec added.

'Oh, and we both know you're stone-cold sober. There –' she stabbed at the map for a third time – 'how about that?'

Alec leaned forward. They had laid out the map on the rug and both knelt beside it. He peered closely at where Naomi had stuck the pin. 'Oh, better,' he said. 'Somerset. Somewhere called Chard. Sounds nice.'

'Even in November?'

'We'll pack our thermals.'

Naomi reached out her hand in the general direction of the coffee table. 'I think I left my glass over there somewhere.'

'You want a refill?'

'Please.' She felt behind her, finding the edge of the sofa and easing herself back on to the seat before holding out her hand for the glass. Alec placed it in her grasp.

'Got it? So, Somerset it is then.'

'Never been there, you'll have a lot of describing to do.'

'Flat, wet, big skies, how will that do?'

She laughed, groped for a cushion and threw it in Alec's approximate direction. 'So,' she said. 'Tomorrow morning we phone round and find somewhere nice and dog friendly and then we go shopping.'

'Shopping?'

'For holiday clothes.'

'Too cold for a new bikini.'

'True, but you have to shop before you go on holiday. It's the rule. I'll need boots and—'

'You've got boots. At least three pairs.'

'Not really warm ones for walking in. November, remember. I want something a bit

9

bright, cheer us up. Oh, and some wellingtons. Sam told me about some really great ones, all hearts and flowers and—'

Alec groaned. 'Can't she take you shopping? Your sister's so much better at it. I never know the proper colour of anything. She's all, oh, it's a kind of pinkish blue with a hint of yellow. To me it's just, well, kind of blue.'

'No,' Naomi told him firmly. 'I want you. You've been away far too much. Our holiday started yesterday and I'm making the most of it.'

Alec sighed. 'Shopping it is then.' He leaned back and closed his eyes.

Naomi, sensing the change in mood, groped for his hand and clasped it tight. Alec hadn't slept properly in weeks and last night, the first time he'd had the opportunity to get a full eight hours, he'd tossed and turned and dreamed and had been unable to find rest. Naomi, who had also been a police officer before the accident that had blinded her, knew the score. It could take a while to come down from the adrenalin of an intense investigation, and this one had been particularly messy, uncovering as it had a great deal of unfinished business and not just for Alec.

'Have you heard anything from Mac?' she asked. Their friend had been on secondment and had now returned home, under something of a cloud. She knew Alec would have mentioned it if he had, but it was a way of opening the door on those things she felt that her husband was trying to avoid but might really want to discuss.

'No, not since that text to tell me he'd got back. I imagine he and Miriam are as in need of a holiday as we are.'

Naomi nodded. 'What do you think will happen to him?'

'He'll be cleared, eventually. If anyone really thought he'd killed Thomas Peel he'd have been in a cell so fast his feet wouldn't have touched the floor.' Alec sighed and Naomi could feel the thoughts and questions jockeying for attention in his head. Thomas Peel the child killer, dead on a lonely beach, just like the little girl whose life he had taken. The investigation, the aftermath, the fallout that still implied their friend Mac may have been responsible. Not that Alec or Naomi or anyone that actually knew Mac believed that to be the case.

It would take more than one day and slightly inebriated evening to put all that out of Alec's head.

'So,' he said finally. 'Shopping it is then. To-morrow morning?'

'No, like I said, in the morning we find ourselves a place to stay. Shop, then pack and leave the following morning. How's that sound?'

'Good,' he said, but she could hear the doubt creeping in; the guilt that there was still so much going on here and he really shouldn't have given in to the impulse towards taking

11

time off.

'Alec,' Naomi said quietly. 'You've done your bit, and if you add up all the TOIL time you haven't managed to take, and the Christmas holiday you've already booked, we could escape until just after New Year.'

Alec laughed loudly. 'You've worked it all out, have you?'

'Oh yes.'

'I can just see my bosses liking that. No one manages to use up their TOIL.' Time off in lieu, widely viewed as being management's way of maintaining staff levels for overtime without actually paying for it. You were supposed to get the days off but no one ever managed to claw them all back.

'Well, you are going to give it a damn good go. Alec, we need this holiday, we really do.'

Leaning against him, she felt him nod reluctant agreement.

'You'll feel better when we're miles away.'

'I'm sure I will,' Alec agreed, but the doubt still tainted his voice. 'I promise I'll give it my best shot.'

Morning found Alec trawling the Internet and finding a couple of likely places, one of which finally offered what they wanted. Not Chard, in the end, but a small hamlet closer to Glastonbury. Afternoon, the purchase of walking boots and wellingtons that Naomi had chosen largely on the grounds of Alec's reaction to them.

Apparently they had stripes. Pink and green and blue.

'You can't be serious,' Alec said.

'Damn right I can. You want a pair?'

'Only if they're drab green and even then I'm not sure I'm a wellington kind of guy.'

Evening and they were driving south, the B&B they had chosen confirming that they could, in fact, accommodate them from that night.

'That's because no one is daft enough to go and stay there in November.'

Napoleon, Naomi's guide dog, snored softly on the back seat, and Naomi fiddled with the radio, finding a classical music channel and then, when the adverts annoyed her, a programme dedicated to folk and roots. She adjusted the volume so that the music lent ambience but still allowed for easy conversation, deciding that, if this holiday idea was to have any chance of success, Alec had to be made to talk, however reluctant he might be. He had tried hard to enjoy that afternoon, but had been only half there, despite the jokes and the amusement over her choice of footwear.

'So,' she said finally. 'You going to talk to me?'

'Sorry. I thought we had been talking.'

'Not talking. I mean *talking*. Alec, your mind is still back in Pinsent, back with the job. If we're really going to get away for a few days, I need to know it's here, with the rest of you, so

13

talk.'

He sighed. 'I'm not sure I know what to say. I guess, I suppose I'm just upset, pissed off with the whole world right now, present company excepted.'

'I should hope so. You feel Mac let you down, don't you?'

He said nothing for a moment or two and Naomi knew she had struck a nerve. 'I suppose I do,' he said at last. 'I thought he'd trust me. I can understand him not trusting Wildman.' Wildman was the lead detective on the case they had just worked. 'Wildman is a tick, an ass of the first order, but for Mac not to trust me. That hurts. Much more than I realized.'

Naomi nodded slowly. 'Alec, if it had been the other way around. If I'd been the one Thomas Peel had taken and not Miriam. If Peel had called you and said you had to come alone or I'd be dead, would you have trusted anyone, even though you knew Peel might kill me anyway? Would you have confided in Mac?'

Alec tapped impatiently on the steering wheel. 'I know all that,' he said, 'and, no. No, I don't suppose I'd have acted any different, but you know, I didn't say I was being rational about this, did I? Just that I was pissed off.' He laughed. 'OK, and I guess it's not just Mac – the whole affair was a mess, had been a mess from the start, and I know the flak will be flying for weeks to come yet; the local press are acting like a terrier with a rag and Wildman is looking for anyone he can push into the line of fire. I don't want to be there, don't want to be Wildman's sacrificial goat once Mac is finally cleared, and I feel guilty as hell for running away on holiday while everyone else is stuck in the firing line. I guess that's why my mind isn't exactly on flowery wellingtons and walking boots.'

'Flowery? I thought they were striped.'

'What? Oh, they are. Disgustingly well striped. Anyway, I'm on a guilt trip, not just a road trip, and I think it'll take a few days of ... something, I don't really know what, just to get my mind off what I've left behind.'

'OK.' Naomi nodded. 'That, I can understand. But Alec, you staying to be Wildman's whipping boy wouldn't have helped you or anyone else and I think you know that.'

'I know it; that's why I wanted out for a while. I know it's going to take me a while to settle, too, but don't fret, love, I am planning on enjoying this trip to the back of beyond. We'll just have to find plenty of ways to distract ourselves, won't we?'

Naomi grinned. 'Oh, I have plans for you, Mr Friedman, make no mistake. All of which are going to be very distracting.'

Despite the use of the satnav and the very good directions the B&B owners had given them, they almost missed the entrance to White Gate Farm. Alec spotted the pub, The Lamb, that

15

they had been told was next door and realized they must have overshot.

'Damn. Looks like a tight turn into the yard.' He reversed cautiously in the narrow road, rather too aware of the stone wall that he could see in his rear-view mirror and the ditch that he could not. 'OK, I've just got to open the gate, sit tight.'

He left the driver's door open and Naomi shivered in the sudden chill. She could smell the damp of recent rain, wet grass, cows, and a faint scent that reminded her of the ocean. Napoleon, excited by the sudden influx of unfamiliar scents, sat up on the back seat and grumbled, eager to get out.

'Hang in there a minute or two,' Naomi told him. 'How far from the sea are we here?' she asked as Alec got back into the car.

'Oh, fifteen miles or so, I suppose. Why? If you want a moonlit walk on the beach you're out of luck. Thick cloud and drizzle is all you'll get tonight.'

'No, I just thought I could smell the sea.'

Alec manoeuvred through the gate and turned sharply to tackle a stone arch that led through into the farmyard proper. He got out again to close the gate and Naomi heard voices calling out a welcome. She heard Alec chatting and then her door opened and a woman's voice told her to come along in and have a cuppa, that the kettle was already on.

'Lovely,' Naomi said. 'Thanks for staying up

16

for us.'

'Oh, no bother. Do you need a hand getting out? Oh, hello there,' she said to Napoleon who had thrust his head forward between the seats, curious about the new person.

'Napoleon,' Naomi said.

'I imagine he'll need to go out before he comes in, if you see what I mean. Let your man take him down near the cut and we'll go inside, shall we?' She took Naomi's arm and, with a confidence that Naomi found oddly reassuring, led her across what Naomi's feet told her was a cobbled yard and into the sudden warmth of a farmhouse kitchen. 'Here, sit yourself down and I'll see to the tea. Jim, this is Naomi Friedman, her husband's just seeing to the dog. Give him a hand with the luggage in a minute, will you?'

'Welcome. Did you have a good journey? We made you up some sandwiches in case you were hungry when you got here.'

'Thank you.' Naomi was surprised by the thoughtfulness. 'That's really nice of you.'

'Oh, no bother. Good to have folk staying this end of the year.' He went out, the door closing quietly. This was a big room, Naomi thought, but very full of stuff, sounds muffled and softened as though by heavy curtains and soft furnishings. If the chair in which she sat was anything to go by, there were probably a lot of cushions and hand crocheted throws – her fingers identifying the peculiar patterns particu-

17

lar to crochet squares. A fire spat and crackled and gave off the scent of resinous wood. The door opened again and Napoleon pattered in, followed by Jim and Alec in conversation; Jim seemed to be explaining the layout of the farm to Alec and telling him about the food at the pub next door, which, it seemed, had something of a local reputation.

'We'll give you a good breakfast, but we don't do the evening meals any more. Not worth it with the pub being next door, especially not at the back end of the year. Ah, tea, good. Sandwiches on the table, help yourselves now.'

Later, settled in the warm, lilac-scented bedroom, Naomi felt that this decision had definitely been the right one. Alec lay on the bed, flicking through channels on the television, and she could feel that he was already more relaxed. The room wasn't large, but the bed was comfortable, tea and coffee making facilities were to hand, and there was an en suite that could easily be found because the door lined up directly opposite the corner of the bed.

Alec had put their cases on the ottoman by the window, suggesting they leave the unpacking until morning.

'How old is this place? It feels really old.'

'I don't know. Old enough to have the original sash windows. Ones before they had the counterweights. Did you hear Bethan when she was telling me about them?'

'No, I missed that.'

'Ah, well, apparently these pre-date the ones with the box sides and counterweights. You open the window and then wedge a very special stick into a groove at the side to stop it falling back down.'

Naomi laughed. 'Sounds very health and safety.'

'Old buildings can get away with it. They have special dispensation,' Alec said. 'If you only want the window open a crack then there are these fellows.' He slid from the bed and she heard him cross to the window. He placed something glazed and heavy in her hands. Naomi felt it, guided by Alec's fingers and explanatory words. 'Look, there's a high bit at both ends and the window fits into that valley in the middle. It'll hold the window open a couple of inches and let the fresh air in. Bethan told me these are Victorian but she said the design is much older than that.'

'It has a face on it,' Naomi said, feeling the unmistakable shape of a nose and what felt like elaborately coiffed hair.

'It does,' Alec agreed. 'There's a pair of them, that's the female half of the partnership. Her old man's lost his nose. But I don't think he was ever a looker.'

'And is she?'

Alec took the window prop from her. 'Only if you like bright green glaze and rather bulbous eyes. I like this place,' he added. 'Not a straight wall anywhere but it's got that sort of feeling that it could be here forever, you know what I mean? I'd like something like this.'

She was taken aback by the announcement. Alec had never really been into old architecture. Their house, which had been his before they married, was standard nineteen thirties, with a bay window at the front and an extended kitchen at the back. He had never seemed to hanker after anything else. Recently, his uncle had willed his house to Alec. A large and rather beautiful Edwardian place that Alec had loved largely because of the happy memories it had held. He had thought briefly about keeping it, but in the end had sold it to a local antique dealer who had been his uncle's friend. It meant there was money sitting in the bank that they had yet to direct anywhere in particular.

'You'd want to move somewhere this rural?'

She heard the clunk as he set the ceramic lady back on the windowsill and then he flopped down beside her on the bed. 'I don't know,' he said. 'I suppose I've been thinking lately it might be time for a change. Time to do something new.'

'New? You mean, as in leaving the force?'

She felt him shrug. 'I don't know. Maybe. I suppose something Mac said got to me.'

Ah, she thought, so he was finally going to talk about what was really bothering him. 'And that was?'

'He said he was tired of putting himself and

those he loved at risk. Of not feeling settled. No, that's wrong. It was because he was settled, because he now had someone he cared about and people he felt at home with, and, well, I think Mac's like me. It's only after *we* got together that I started to feel I could ever settle down.' He laughed awkwardly. 'Late starters, both of us, me and Mac.'

'Alec, what's this leading to?'

He took a deep breath. 'Kids, maybe,' he said. 'You know we always talked about it, but ... well, I'm not getting any younger and...' He paused, clearly waiting for a response. Pushed on. 'But I want to be there for them, you know. Not have the job intruding every five minutes. Not have ... Naomi, do you think you could say something? I'm feeling a bit out on a limb here.'

She took a deep, steadying breath. True, they'd talked in the abstract about having children, and both of them loved spending time with her sister's two boys, but this was the first time he had seemed to be trying to establish an actual concrete plan for a family.

'So,' she said lightly, 'you want to leave the force, move to a house like this and have kids?'

She felt him nod. 'Yes,' he said, serious now. 'I suppose I do.'

She reached for his hand and held it tight. 'Sounds good,' she said softly, wondering how much she actually meant it.

Extract from Roads to Ruin *by E Thame:*

The night Catherine Kirkwood left her father's home, she knew, despite his assurances, that she'd never see him again. The last battle had been fought and the Kirkwoods had chosen the losing side.

Catherine's brother, Thomas, had ridden out ten days before to join the forces of the Duke of Monmouth as he headed north. He had taken with him a dozen men from the estate and, more importantly, gold, especially struck for the occasion. More of the same – little medallions in silver and gold commemorating a victory they had been so certain of – remained at Kirkwood Hall and now they had to be disposed of.

Henry Kirkwood knew he must stand his ground. He still had powerful friends at court, friends who might still be prevailed upon to protect him, to speak up for him. He must have known, anyway, that he was far too high profile a figure to get far should he try to run. Locally, everyone knew Henry Kirkwood; knew his face and his affiliations. He had nowhere left to hide. The best he could do was to limit the damage and retain as much of his wealth as he could before the King's men came to claim it, as he knew they would. Henry Kirkwood had committed something close to treason, backed the cause of James, Duke of Monmouth, in his play for the English throne. He knew it was an act not about to be forgiven. His friends might help him to stay alive, but he'd have nothing other than that: no land, no house, no wealth.

News arrived at Kirkwood Hall at about seven o'clock on the morning of July the sixth, 1685, just an hour or two after the battle of Sedgemoor had ended and Monmouth fled the field. Henry's son was dead. One man returned to the estate to give news, but the others were either felled or fled. The returning man, we know from Catherine's letters, was Elmer Grove, and he seems to have been a trusted servant and an educated man. It is possible he was even Henry's secretary or similar.

Whatever he was, Henry acted fast. He told Elmer Grove to change his clothes and burn what he'd been wearing on the battlefield. To get himself a fresh horse and saddle it with the pillion behind the saddle, and within the next hour, or so Catherine states in her letters, she and Elmer Grove, together with much of the Kirkwood wealth, were sent out to get as far from the scene as possible before the King's men arrived.

I don't imagine they were the only family to take such measures or the only people on the move that day, hoping to escape recriminations, but at that point no one could possibly have foreseen the widespread and callous blood-letting that would follow this little uprising or know that more lives would be claimed in the aftermath than had been lost in all the battles and skirmishes of the campaign, combined.

So, when Catherine and Elmer left that day,

they must have known that things would be bad, that they would have to use their wits and their skills to talk their way through the King's lines and reach safe haven in the Scottish lowlands, where the Kirkwoods still had close kin, but they could not possibly have known just how bloody and cruel events would be, and Catherine could, I'm sure, never have foreseen just how her father would meet his death.

TWO

They spent their first holiday day like tourists, Naomi in her new striped wellingtons climbing Glastonbury Tor and coming down breathless and windswept. The conversation of the previous evening had been set aside, almost as though Alec was now back-pedalling and the conversation had been the result of a momentary impulse. Naomi wasn't sure what to make of it, but she let things lie. Alec was happy, laughing, joking, describing the wonderful carving high on the walls of the ruined abbey, commenting on the prices of assorted crystal displayed in the shop windows, delighting in the wood panelling in the medieval inn, The George and Pilgrim, where they ate their lunch. The rain had held off, though the air was damp and chill and Alec said the sky was solid grey.

'What you said last night,' Naomi started as they waited for their dessert – a sure sign that Alec was in a happy mood; he rarely indulged in puddings.

'I meant it,' he told her, suddenly serious again. 'Naomi, I've enjoyed my life so far, loved my job, met you, have good friends in the force, but suddenly it isn't what I want any more. I want more of ... this. More of us. More of just being happy, I suppose.'

'Sounds to me like you're just feeling burnt out,' she said quietly. 'The job gets to you, we both know that. Even in a place like Pinsent, which isn't exactly crime central. Alec, you might feel totally different in a week or two, and I don't want you, don't want either of us, to...'

'Rush into things? No, of course not and I've thought of all that, about feeling burnt out and tired and just, as I said, thoroughly pissed off. And I know I'm reacting to what might have happened to Miriam. I know I'm wondering what I'd have felt if it had been you, but Naomi, love, I'm not just reacting to the fear, I'm ready for a change and I think, I hope, that you are too?'

Beneath the table, Napoleon harrumphed, and conversation paused as the waitress delivered chocolate brownies and cream. Naomi felt for her spoon and poked thoughtfully at the cake. 'I am,' she said. 'I do *think* I am, but Alec, let's take it slow. Decisions like this shouldn't be made in anger or out of frustration. Let's make a deal. We take this time just as holiday, enjoy it, and in a week or two, when we've both had time to think, we talk it all through again.'

'Deal,' Alec said. 'Eat your pudding and we'll drive to Wells. I want to see the cathedral.'

'You do know we don't have to do it all in one day,' she reminded him.

'Oh, but I have a list,' he said. 'You want to hear it?'

She heard him rustling about, exploring his coat pockets. Heard the sound of paper being unfolded. Several sheets from the sound of it. 'How long is this list?'

'Oh, long enough, a couple of pages. This is an interesting part of the world, you know. Abbeys and battlefields and fossils and—'

'Alec, when did you write this list?' Naomi felt caught between amusement and concern.

'Oh, this morning.'

'No, you didn't. We got up, had breakfast and came straight out. When this morning?'

Alec hesitated. 'I'm not sure what time it was,' he admitted. 'Naomi, love, I couldn't sleep. There were all these guide books and tourist pamphlets in the drawer and I thought, well, I didn't want to wake you up, so I made a list.'

'Alec...'

'Naomi, don't. Please. I just made a list. Just enjoy it with me and let me work the rest out for myself.'

'It shouldn't just be for you. Two of us in this, remember?'

'I know and I'm not trying to shut you out. I'm just ... I don't know what I am.'

Naomi hesitated, questions jostling for position, so many things she felt she ought to say. Instead, she closed her eyes and took a deep breath, a leftover habit from her sighted days.

She felt Alec tense, knew he recognized the ancient tic and what it meant. 'OK,' she said finally, trying to keep her tone light. 'No questions, no discussion, no mining of the psyche.'

'Glad to hear it! You probably need a license for psyche mining.'

'For now.' Naomi finished firmly. 'I'll go along with whatever you feel you need to do. We'll work our way through your list and we'll pretend nothing else matters. You never know, by the time we reach page three – Alec, I can hear the difference between unfolding two sheets of paper and three, so don't try and kid me. By the time we reach the bottom of page three, maybe nothing else will matter any more. But if it does, we have to talk. We really do.'

'Deal,' he said. He seemed to be using that word a lot lately, Naomi thought. She fixed her attention on her brownie, wondering where all this was leading to and what on earth Alec, a career police officer, could find to do that would fill such a massive place in his life.

THREE

Their days fell into an easy pattern. Leaving the B&B after a very substantial breakfast, working through the items on Alec's list, eating lunch in a rural pub and then returning to the B&B in time to shower and change before going next door to The Lamb for their evening meal and a drink or two.

The Lamb was a friendly place, mostly locals at this time of the year but also a few diners from round and about. They found that its reputation was well founded and the food was simple but all locally produced and tasty. The company was good too; Susan, the manager, a woman in her mid thirties, Alec judged, was a fount of local gossip and information. The next village having lost its pub in the latest round of rural closures, The Lamb served quite a broad local community – essentially anyone within walking or staggering distance home. By the second night, Naomi and Alec had been apprised of the effects down on the Somerset Levels of three bad summers, the lack of tourists adding to the loss of crops and grazing:

'Had to get the boat out and pull three sheep off the island. Lost another when the rhyne

29

spilled over.'
  'Rhyne?'
  'Dykes, big drainage ditches.'
  'Oh, those.'
Had been shocked to find that Susan had never even climbed the Tor:
  'What would I want to go scrabbling up some damned great hill for?'
Had been apprised of the merits of the vineyards in the area and the local microbreweries; had been informed of the best cider makers; and knew the debate from both sides regarding the sale of a now unused local church:
  'What damn fool would want to buy a place you can't even convert?'
  'Convert, that's a good one. Church, get it?'
  'Tied up with covenants. No electric, no water except that tapped-off spring. And whoever buys it has got to allow access for the graves.'
  'Graveyard still in use then?'
  'Up to a couple of year ago, yes.'
  'Why can't it be converted?' Alec asked.
  'Bishop of Bath and Wells says not, I suppose.'
  'A church should stay a church,' someone else said, putting in their tuppence worth, 'especially one that's got recent burials.'
  'But it's going to rack and ruin up there on the mount. There's not been a service there in years. Not even a burial in the last twenty years that I know of.'
  'Mount?'

30

'That bit of a blip, just before you have to turn left by the pink house at the crossroads. Half a mile before you get here. It was an island before the drainage. Site of an earlier church, some say, but it's a little brown Victorian jobbie up there now.'

'Right.' Alec could picture it now; he had noticed it but not taken any particular notice. He smiled at the last speaker, left the ongoing debate and took his beer back to the table, thinking how nice it was to be able to go out for a drink and not have to worry about either getting home or getting up for work the following morning.

'What kept you?' Naomi asked, though she had overheard the debate. 'And, no, Alec, we're not buying a disused church. That's going just a bit too far.'

'Well, from the sound of it, unless you're planning on starting a cult, it wouldn't be a lot of use anyway. What can you do with a disused church except use it as a church?'

And then there was 'Eddy' and his map, sitting in his accustomed corner night after night, nursing a pint for as long as he could make it last. Generally, Alec observed, one or other of the locals would buy him a second at some point in the evening and only then would the first glass be drained. He rarely seemed to join the conversation, though he listened with careful attention.

By the third night Alec felt comfortable

enough to contribute the second pint. He took it over, noting the scatter of books and what looked like maps that Eddy habitually laid out on the table and studied intently. No one else, Alec noted, ever seemed to ask him about them, so he figured this daily scrutiny, like the habitual nursing of the pint, must also have continued for some considerable time.

Alec set the beer down in the one tiny patch of unused space and Eddy looked up to see who his benefactor might be. He nodded his thanks and drained the dregs of the first glass, setting it carefully on the seat beside him. Alec glanced at the scatter of papers. 'Interested in history?' he asked.

'History is where we come from.'

'Um, yes. I suppose it is.'

Eddy jabbed at the map. Alec looked more closely. It appeared to show some sort of battle plan. Cavalry and cannons were marked in ranks and arrows showed the direction of attack. Sedgemore, he read. 'Oh, James the second? Monmouth's lot? Wasn't that—'

'The last pitched battle fought on English soil. It surely was.'

'Right,' Alec said. That wasn't going to have been his next comment, but it sounded more intelligent than what he'd had in mind so he accepted it gratefully. 'We're, er, thinking of walking the battlefield sometime while we're here,' he said. 'There's this leaflet I found at the B&B, tells you all about the trail.' He broke off.

Eddy had fixed him with a stern gaze and Alec suddenly felt oddly inadequate.

'Set up for the tourists,' Eddy said. 'You'll learn nothing about anything that way.'

'Right,' Alec muttered again, feeling thoroughly inadequate. 'Well, have a good evening.' He went back to the bar to collect their drinks, feeling like a child who'd been chastised for infringing some mysterious adult rule.

'Oh, don't mind Eddy,' Susan said fondly. 'Not quite right in the head, some ways, though in others he's sharp as a tack.'

'What's with all the maps and the history books?'

'Them's his treasure maps,' one of the locals laughed. 'Goes out with his metal detector and his papers. Looking, always looking. Got this idea in his head he'll strike it rich.' He turned away with a shrug. 'Good luck to the old nutcase, I say.'

'Treasure?'

Susan shrugged. 'Supposed to have been what some landowner buried to keep it from the crown,' she said. 'He backed the wrong side in the rebellion, knew he'd lose the lot, so, the story goes, he sent his daughter off with a servant and told them to get as far away as they possibly could, to avoid the repercussions, you know. The king sent that Judge Jeffries down here and he hanged folk just for talking to the rebels.'

'And did the daughter escape?'

33

Susan shrugged. 'Depends who tells the story. One tale is the servant killed her and ran away with the lot; another says they had to hide it to keep it from the army and that they never did get back to collect it. That's what Eddy believes. Been looking for it all the time I've known him and I've known him since I was a teenager. He used to come to the farm with his metal detector and such. Dad always gave him a meal and—'

'And so now you do,' Alec said.

'And why not? He's got no one to look after him, poor old bugger.'

'I think it's nice,' Alec said. 'I think Eddy is very lucky.'

'Not lucky enough to find what he's looking for,' Susan said ruefully. 'You ask me, the whole thing's just a story.'

Alec went thoughtfully back to their table and their meal arrived shortly after.

'We should do the battlefield walk,' Naomi said.

'Not tomorrow, though. Rain is forecast for the entire day, so I suggest we do something inside. I'd like to go back to Wells, if that's all right, and take some more pictures.'

'Fine by me. Then we can look round all those little shops that we didn't get time for last time.'

Alec laughed. 'More silver?' he asked. Lately, Naomi had started a collection of little silver boxes, loving the way the repoussé work felt beneath her fingers. That, and a collection of strange cutlery; it seemed to Alec that the Victorians had invented a spoon or a knife for every purpose known to mankind and that his wife was intent on owning an example of every single variation. Odd, he thought. Neither of them had taken a particular interest in antiques before, when Naomi could actually see what she was buying. Now it had become a major hobby and something they enjoyed together when so much else in their lives separated them. Work, for example.

'There's an evening concert too. I think it might even be tomorrow. We can check when we're there, have a meal in Wells. I bet the acoustics are amazing,' Alec said.

'Sounds good. Did you notice what it was?'

'Um, no. Something classical and choral. Sorry.'

Naomi laughed. 'Whatever it is will be lovely,' she said. 'It's ages since we heard any live music.'

'True.' It was hard to book advance tickets when work could be relied upon to interfere and, lately, it had done that a lot.

Alec leaned back in his chair and looked around. Through the hatch in the bar he could see their waitress coming out with their order. She smiled across at him.

'Penny for them,' Naomi said.

'Not worth it,' Alec told her. 'Not a thing on my mind worth paying for.'

35

FOUR

'I'm coming, I'm coming.' Eddy shuffled into his slippers and pulled his dressing gown on. The tapping on the front door wasn't loud but it was insistent. Who the hell would it be, that time of the night?

He put the landing light on and hesitated, shuffling his slippered feet on the frayed carpet at the top of the stairs as he gazed down at the front door and tried to make out, through the window of coloured and frosted glass, just who was knocking. Finally, he headed down.

'Oh, it's you,' he said. 'Bit late for a visit. You'd best come in.'

'You said to call round, collect those things. Sorry, I know it's late, I didn't think.'

'You never bloody do. Come on then, you'll be wanting a cup of tea, no doubt.'

'Be nice.'

'You know where to go.' Eddy pointed down the hallway towards the kitchen. 'I'll be with you in a tick.'

He made his way back up the stairs, grumbling as he went but secretly pleased to have the company, even if it was well after bedtime. Going into the spare room he picked up a backpack that had been left lying on the floor. A shirt and a pair of jeans lay folded on the bed. Eddy had washed them the day before. He stuffed those inside, and then oddments that had been placed on the bedside table, and then, just as he was about to leave the room, he turned back to the tall cupboard standing in the corner of the room. He thought for a moment and then, as though suddenly making up his mind, he opened the door and peered inside. Spare bed-linen occupied the top two shelves; the bottom one was occupied by old sheets and rags that Eddy kept to tear up as dusters. When he remembered. He slid his hand beneath the pile of old rags and pulled out a little bundle wrapped in the remains of a torn pillowcase. The fabric was faded now, but smiling at it, Eddy remembered the crisp blue linen trimmed with white lace that Martha had so triumphantly carried back from some big sale somewhere. She had loved her bargains, had Martha, loved the pretty things.

He closed his eyes and, just briefly, he pressed the little bundle to his chest before, utterly resolved now, he shoved it deep into the backpack and pulled the drawstring tight.

'Am I making a big pot?' the voice of his late guest floated up to him. 'Got any biscuits?'

'Yes to both,' Eddy called back. He sighed, already regretting his impulse, but feeling it was too late to backtrack now he made his way back downstairs and dumped the pack beside the kitchen door. 'All ready for you,' he said. 'I washed your shirt and jeans.'

'Oh, you shouldn't have bothered with that, but thanks anyway. Now, you reckon you've got biscuits, but I'm damned if I can find them anywhere.'

Eddy laughed. 'You should use your eyes,' he said, opening the cupboard door and retrieving a pack of custard creams, knowing his visitor was as big a kid as Eddy himself where favourite biscuits were concerned. None of this grown-up, digestive oaty muck.

'Good man. Now, sit and drink your tea and I'll show you what I found up in Bakers field this afternoon.'

FIVE

Dawn brought the promised rain, cold and steeply slanting as they dashed for the car that morning, but it had eased to simply drenching by the time they reached Wells.

Napoleon had accompanied them on all of their forays so far, but a day of browsing in small shops and admiring architecture seemed an unnecessary burden for the patient dog, and when Bethan suggested they leave him at the farm, Naomi agreed. There were two other dogs at the farm, both retired and given to mooching and sleeping. Napoleon would have a wonderfully restful day.

Theirs had been equally pleasant, she reflected as they sat in the choir of Wells Cathedral that evening. She had added to her collection of odd cutlery – a fish slice shaped like a fish, a sifting spoon with a trail of leaves on the handle and an odd-shaped and very small ladle made in Scandinavian silver.

'It's for toddies,' the shop owner had told her, and it was now Alec's mission to find out how to create the best possible recipe.

Lunch had seen the rain clear and a damp sun appear. Naomi had enjoyed the slight heat of it on her face while Alec had made full use of the digital SLR camera she had bought him for the previous Christmas and to which he had become very attached. She'd been told he had a good eye and she really wished she could confirm that for herself. He and a friend, another police officer, had tentatively discussed the possibility of putting on an exhibition somewhere and she was doing her best to encourage that thought.

It turned out the concert Alec had spotted was on another night, but there was an evensong, and so, at the end of a very satisfying day, here they were, seated in the choir along with the choristers and celebrants.

Most cathedral choirs were enclosed, but the one at Wells, Naomi thought, was almost like a walled garden, and, as walled gardens intensified the scent of the flowers, so this sheltered spot intensified and amplified the already powerful waves of sound. Voices shifted and built and drifted and enveloped her. She closed her eyes, as she would have done in her sighted days, seeking to drain every last drop of enjoyment from this performance dressed up in religious clothes. Neither she nor Alec went to church or had much interest in the spiritual in any form, but drowning in music, Naomi felt she came close to understanding what other people must gain from such an immersive, all encompassing religious experience.

'Beautiful service,' Alec commented as they

paused, after it was over, to speak to someone Naomi assumed must be an official something or other.

'Thank you,' a male voice said. 'We have a very proud tradition here and the acoustics are fabulous, and somehow the dark nights outside seem to make it all the more intense, don't you think?'

Alec agreed, but Naomi could hear in his voice that he was worried he was going to be dragged into a religious debate. Inner light, outer darkness, the dark winter of the soul. She gripped his hand sympathetically, but the male speaker had moved on to exchange platitudes with someone else and Alec was spared.

'It *was* a lovely service though,' she said. 'Do you think we're cheating a bit?'

'How do you mean?'

'Oh, just enjoying the bits we like. Not subscribing to the whole religious thing that goes with it?'

She was teasing, but Alec seemed oddly affronted. 'I love the way these places are built,' he said. 'I get a kick out of good music, wherever it comes from. You don't *need* the rest of the package. A place like this isn't just a religious building, it's a monument to everyone that ever carved a stone or sang a song here.'

'Sang a song?' Naomi giggled.

'Well, you know what I mean.'

They had reached the entrance now and Alec paused, peering out. 'More rain,' he announced.

41

'Low cloud. Miserable.'

And a cutting wind, Naomi thought as they hurried back to where they'd parked the car. The cold dragged her breath from her body and clamped her lungs tight. 'Lazy day tomorrow?' she asked.

'Lazy day it is. We'll get up for breakfast and then spend the day in bed watching the telly. I've always wondered what it was like to do that.'

She laughed. 'You'll be bored before eleven,' she predicted, reflecting that it was a very long time indeed since either of them had had time for that particular state.

Back at the farm Napoleon greeted them with tail beating enthusiasm and they sat up for a while with Bethan and Jim, eating sandwiches Jim had made and drinking tea.

'Good as gold, he's been,' Bethan told them. 'We've had another booking cancelled,' she added. 'I mean, I know it's late in the year, but we've usually got at least a trickle up until Christmas.'

'It wouldn't be so bad,' Jim agreed, 'but the past three summers have been a bit below par too. Still,' he sighed, 'what can you do? It's as cheap to take a package to Spain as it is to stay in Blighty and the weather's at least got a chance of being better. Bring on this here global warming, I say.'

'Well, anyway, the upshot is, plenty of room if you want to stay on for a few more days,'

Bethan added.

'Got a job to get back to,' Alec said regretfully. 'You never know, someone might be desperate for a bolt-hole and book in out of the blue, like we did.'

'Got to be optimistic,' Jim agreed.

But Naomi could not help but feel, as they made their way up to bed, that Jim and Bethan were anything but optimistic for their future, and this put a major dampener on what had been an erstwhile damn near perfect day.

Susan Rawlins locked up at The Lamb, bid goodnight to her chef and sat in her car, uncertain of what to do. Eddy hadn't appeared that night. That wasn't like Eddy. On odd occasions he might be late, but it was as much a part of his routine to come into The Lamb of an evening, as it was to get up in the morning. It was just what Eddy did – and, besides, it was the one way he could be sure of having a decent meal at the end of the day. He'd been doing it for so long that Susan almost saw him as a tax deductible expense.

She started the engine of her old Volkswagen, grateful that age had done little to inhibit the vehicle's reliability. Old faithful, it was, just like Eddy, and probably about the same vintage too. The car had belonged to Susan's father, much loved and much restored as a result. In her more rational moments she realized it was a bit like the proverbial shopkeeper's broom –

only five new heads and four new handles in twenty years – but she still thought of it as her father's car and loved it for all the memories its rather rattly, drafty body encompassed. 'Eddy's then,' she said aloud. 'Then, when we find out he's just fallen asleep in front of the telly, we'll get off home, shall we?'

Eddy's place was a scant mile down the road, set back down a short, rough track that he called a drive. It had been a farm worker's cottage long ago, had been near derelict when Eddy and his wife had taken it on; now, wife long gone and Eddy alone, it was falling back into its former state.

Susan hurried across the muddy frontage and hammered on the door with her fist. There was a knocker, in the shape of a Cornish pisky – she had asked why, but Eddy had professed not to recall – but it was rusted solid by long years of disuse. Quite a few people came to visit Eddy; of those, hardly any tried to use the knocker.

No reply.

'Eddy, it's me,' she shouted through the letter box. She didn't want to let herself in without a bit of warning, fearful of scaring the old man.

'Eddy?'

Still no reply. Susan bent lower and peered through the letter box. There were no lights on anywhere, so like as not he'd probably gone off to bed. Susan hesitated. Squinted harder, trying to make out the odd shape at the bottom of the stairs.

'Oh my God, Eddy!'

Large planters stood either side of the front door. Susan tilted one and retrieved the key she knew he kept there. She flung the door open and reached to turn on the light, but even as she stepped over the threshold, she knew it was too late and her fears had all been horribly confirmed.

'Oh Eddy,' Susan groaned. The old man was so obviously dead. His body still lay partly on the stairs, but his head rested against the tiled floor of the hall, neck bent at an unnatural angle so that his pale grey eyes seemed to be looking back at her. It was clear from the angle that his neck was broken.

Her mobile was in her bag and that was still in the car. Somehow, it felt wrong to go back out and fetch that. Instead she reached for the phone that stood by the door on a high, faux bamboo table that had, Susan remembered out of the blue, been home to a large planter full of bright geraniums when Eddy's wife had been alive. Fingers shaking, she managed to dial and ask for an ambulance.

'He's fallen down the stairs,' she said. It was only after she laid the receiver back on its cradle that she realized she had not told the operator Eddy was already dead.

SIX

Naomi and Alec got the news of Eddy's death the next morning at breakfast.

'He fell down the stairs. That's what the police reckon. Susan says she was forever warning him about that worn carpet.'

'That's very sad,' Alec said. 'He seemed like a nice old man.'

'Oh, he wasn't that old, not really,' Jim said. 'Late sixties, early seventies I suppose. That's no age these days, is it? No, but he'd had a lot of grief and I suppose that does add the years.'

'Grief?' Naomi asked.

'Lost his wife and then his daughter. She, the wife, died of cancer. I don't recall about the girl. Car accident, wasn't it?'

'Right,' Jim confirmed. 'Group of them out, one just passed their test. Wet roads and driving too fast, I suppose, and ... well. You can guess the rest.'

'There are some difficult roads round here,' Alec agreed.

'Oh, it wasn't nowhere here,' Jim told them. 'I don't recall where it was, but it was somewhere else. Visiting, she was. A relative, I suppose. The wife came from up north somewhere, I do believe.'

'Sad,' Bethan said. 'He never really got over any of it. Then someone gave him that metal detector thing and it seemed as though he spent all his time digging up the fields after that.'

'Susan said he had a bee in his bonnet about a treasure,' Naomi said.

'Oh, he's not the only one. There's rumours a plenty about landowners who buried their goods rather than let the crown get a hold of it or that Jeffries. An evil bastard, that one. Didn't care if you were innocent or not, so long as you could pay him off. Thousands of pounds people paid, just to avoid the gallows or worse.'

'I'm sorry?' Alec was at a loss.

'Judge Jeffries?' Naomi said.

'That'll be the one. People round here have long memories. Folk would be queuing up to dance on his grave if they could get near it. Hundreds he killed, and the king, such as he was, just let him have free rein.'

'And Eddy really took the stories seriously,' Alec mused. 'I saw him at The Lamb, all his maps and such. Did he actually find anything?'

'Oh, the usual stuff they find round here.' Jim was dismissive. 'Musket balls, harness fittings, the odd button. I don't know of anyone that found much more and they've been at it long enough, the detectorists and the archaeologists, and the fields round here are ploughed often enough you'd expect anything there was to find to have made its way to the surface by now.'

'Oh there's still copses and water meadows,' Bethan said. 'And wells and graveyards. That's what I'd choose. A graveyard. No one bothers much once a body's planted. I reckon there's some mileage in the stories, but I don't see the likes of poor Eddy getting lucky. Some people just don't find the luck, do they, and it strikes me Eddy was one of them.'

The Lamb was closed that night as a mark of respect and also because Susan had been up all night with ambulance and police and then neighbours who had come to investigate the sirens and lights. She had returned home late morning, called all her staff to explain and assured them they would still be paid, thinking – as she put the phone down on the last of them – that it was a promise she could ill afford. She had then gone to bed, not expecting to sleep, but had woken at six that evening, with no memory of falling asleep or of dreams that may have come.

She called the officer, who had attended Eddy's house the night before, on his mobile, knowing he would have gone off duty long since.

'Looks like a simple accident,' he said. 'I'm really sorry. I understand you were a good friend?'

'I'd known Eddy just about all my life. No,' she added in response to his enquiry. 'I don't know of any family. I have a vague idea his late wife had a brother. Yes, I'll take a look and let you know if I can trace anyone.'

She sat staring at the phone for several minutes after ringing off, reflecting that she had looked after Eddy in life and had always had this vague inkling that she'd be the one sorting out his affairs after death. She'd not expected it to be so soon, though, or so dramatic.

Susan glanced around the tiny flat that had been her home since the divorce and division of spoils a couple of years before. She'd chosen to sink everything into getting a place of her own and, though it was tiny and cramped, she had never regretted the decision. She wasn't even sure if Eddy actually owned his house. Didn't really know about other family of his, either; Eddy didn't like to talk about the past. Not the recent past, anyway; he was fine with anything a couple of hundred years or so distant, but more recent events were off the list so far as conversation went.

Sighing, she wandered through to the kitchen and made herself a cup of tea, dunking the bag in a mug and pouring boiling water on top. Eddy always used a proper pot. He had little ones for when he was alone and large ones for company, a whole array of them lined up on a shelf in the kitchen with a weird and wonderful assortment of mugs hanging on hooks beneath.

Susan splashed milk into her own rather plain mug and then leaned back against the counter, tea clasped between her hands for as long as she could bear the heat. She blew on the surface of the still-scalding liquid and took stock of her own little kitchen, deciding that whoever the next of kin turned out to be, she'd make a point of rehoming Eddy's teapots and mugs. She could visualize them all, each having its own place in the map of Eddy's world. There were china mugs that an elderly lady had given to him. A souvenir from Scarborough. One that was dark green and had a toad sitting at the bottom, ready to startle the unwary drinker. A large, pink striped vessel that Eddy awarded to anyone he wasn't really sure about. A sure sign that he had a stranger or a not yet proven friend sitting in his kitchen was that they were drinking from the pink striped mug. It had once served the same purpose, both functional and symbolic, in her mother's kitchen, and Susan found she could not recall the exact route of its migration to Eddy's.

Well, they would all be brought back to hers, have pride of place hanging beneath a shelf she didn't yet possess but which she would go out and buy first thing in the morning.

Abruptly, Susan set down her own as yet untouched tea, thumping the mug on to the counter hard enough that the contents slopped over the side. Suddenly she was crying. Hard, retching sobbing tears such as she could not remember shedding since her own parents had died, also far too early, far too abruptly five years before.

There was no justice, no fairness in life and certainly none in death.

When Eddy was a much younger man he'd had a brother. They had never been close, Guy being the flamboyant one who stole hearts and got the attention while Eddy waited for the fall-out to happen – and sometimes benefited when Guy's conquests rebounded.

By his mid thirties, though, Eddy had long since stopped waiting for bouncing lovers; he'd found one of his own and married her and they were desperately happy. One day Martha had confirmed that, at last, she was pregnant, and Eddy thought nothing could ruin the way he felt.

Guy, of course, had other ideas. It wasn't, Eddy thought at the time, that Guy deliberately upset even the best of moments deliberately. He was far too self-centred, and to assume that he meant to hurt people was actually overestimating his capacity to take account of feelings. When Amy Clark came to Eddy and confessed that she was pregnant and that Guy was probably the father, Eddy knew that the chances of his brother stepping up to take responsibility were so minimal as to be non-existent.

Worse, Amy was engaged, to a man she loved and who loved her. Guy was a mere fling born of sudden panic that this really was it, her days of being free and single were definitely numbered.

And, besides, Eddy knew how persuasive Guy could be. He saw no reason why decent people should suffer. Guy could never have been described as decent.

'What do you do?' Eddy said to her. 'Oh, that's simple, Amy. You get married a bit sooner than you planned. You tell Dan you've fallen pregnant and let him think it's his. For all you know it is. He'll love it and he'll put any doubts aside.'

'I can't lie to him.'

'You can, you must, you will. After a while the lie will become the truth.'

'But what about Guy?'

'Guy need never know. Guy won't bother you again, I promise you that.'

'You'll have to tell Martha, won't you?'

'I don't have to tell Martha, but I will do; she'd give you the same advice I am. Guy won't bother you, I promise.'

And Guy never did.

Seven months later a baby girl was born and Eddy's child with Martha arrived shortly after that. Amy and Dan named their baby Susan, and Martha and Eddy called their daughter Karen, and Eddy made it his business to always look out for his brother's child until the time came when their roles reversed and Susan became the one to take care of him.

SEVEN

One lazy day had been enough. In fact, they hadn't quite managed even that. Somehow the news of Eddy's death had darkened the mood. Naomi and Alec had returned to their room after breakfast and had, indeed, dozed for a while, watched the assortment of antique and house renovation based programmes on morning television and grown truly restless around lunchtime.

Napoleon in tow, they had driven to Somerton in search of lunch and more antique shops and spent the afternoon wandering the pretty little market town, snooping in galleries but without the impulse to buy, and then, for no better reason than that they had not yet stopped there, they decamped to Bridgewater for their evening meal, Bethan having warned them that The Lamb would be closed.

'This was where it all ended,' Alec said as they sat waiting for their meal in The Wharf.

'Where all what ended? Oh, you're in Eddy land.'

Alec laughed. 'I suppose I am.'

'So?' Naomi waited. She was aware that Eddy had been on Alec's mind all day.

'It took a bit of time for the King to get his act together and his army mobilized, but when he did they pushed Monmouth's troops back hard and they retreated here. I think it was July the third, or thereabouts, when Monmouth got here, expecting there'd be reinforcements waiting for him, but Churchill had attacked from the south and cut them off. So, Monmouth and his crew were alone and pretty much cornered.'

'What sort of numbers are we talking about here?'

'Between three and four thousand, I think.' He shook his head. 'Sorry, I just skim read the leaflets back at the cottage. You know, we should go and walk the battlefield tomorrow. The weather's supposed to be better and Napoleon could do with a good long hike.'

'Suits me.' She reached out cautiously for her wine glass.

'Left a bit,' Alec said.

'OK, so what's really getting to you? It's sad about the old guy, but he slipped and fell down the stairs, Alec. Nothing sinister, so switch the policeman head off. You hardly knew him, anyway.'

'True, but that's never stopped me, has it? Not stopped either of us really. We spent our professional lives getting involved in the problems of people we didn't know or had hardly met.'

'True, but—'

'Oh, you're right. I suppose I was just hoping that I could get a break from all the dark and

54

dismal, you know? But it seems to be following on behind like some—'

'Accident,' Naomi reinforced gently. 'It was an accident. They can happen anywhere. You are not attracting bad things. Alec, you've been really happy and relaxed these past few days. Don't let this spoil it. It's sad, but it's life.'

'Death in Eddy's case. No, I know. I'm sorry. You're right, I'm letting everything get to me lately.'

'It happens, we both know that.'

'Which one of you is the beef Wellington?' the waitress asked.

Alec confessed that it was him, the plates were set down, and the waitress was assured that there was nothing more they required and that they would, indeed, enjoy their meal.

Naomi felt for the cutlery. 'Careful,' she said. 'Plates are red hot. So, tomorrow we do the Battlefield Walk and we see if we can find out more about this uprising that Eddy was so stuck on. There's bound to be books for sale and stuff.' She grimaced. 'Doubt there'll be anything audio available so you'll have to do the reading. Now, eat and relax and after we've had the day out tomorrow you can have a talk to Susan, put your policeman head back on and see if there's anything more than a frayed carpet to investigate. Deal?'

She could hear the smile in his voice as he told her, 'Deal, then. God, it's not only the plates that are hot. Good though. I wonder if they do lunches here?'

Beneath the table Napoleon's tail thumped a contented beat, and Naomi tried to convince herself that for the rest of their holiday they could fall back into the pleasant rhythm of recent days, but in her heart of hearts she knew that opportunity had passed and gone.

Susan had been to Eddy's house many times at night, but always he had been there. The lights had been on, the fires lit, the atmosphere brightly melancholic, as Eddy himself had always been, his words cheerful but that sense of all-pervading sadness lurking just behind the eyes.

She let herself in; she had kept the key from the night before, then hesitated before switching on the light, almost afraid that she would see again the crumpled body of her friend at the foot of the stairs.

The hall light seemed harsh this evening, the bare bulb – Eddy was not a fan of shades on account of the fact they blocked out half the brightness – stark and ugly. Slowly, Susan made her way through the house, touching nothing, feeling oddly like an intruder. She'd come with the intention of starting the search for any family Eddy might have had. People to take over the funeral arrangements, to inherit, she supposed, to continue Eddy's story now that the old man was gone. Instead, she just wandered, room to room, recalling, as she looked out through the kitchen window, hot summer evenings sitting in the garden with a beer. Christmases when she had helped him deck out the tree with all the little ornaments he and his wife had bought and the paper angels his little girl had made so long ago that the glitter had flaked from their now crumpled wings. Long chats, sitting around the kitchen table, either just the two of them or, more often, with others from the metal detecting community. She'd never really thought about it before, but she realized now that Eddy had been at the heart of a large if disparate group, most of whom had converged on Eddy's cottage at some time or another. If they all came to the as yet unarranged funeral, she'd need to organize a sizeable buffet at The Lamb. Eddy might have lived alone, but he would certainly not go to his rest unmourned.

Somehow, that made her feel better, but it also increased the sense of puzzlement that had begun to coalesce. Eddy was liked; loved, even. He was known by so many people from so many different branches of local and not so local society and yet no one from his wider family had ever visited him, to Susan's knowledge. Not even when his wife had been alive and her family could have reasonably been expected to show up, even if Eddy's had not. Now that she thought about it, Susan remembered her parents commenting on that very fact. When Eddy's wife had died, the local church had been full to bursting, as had the crematorium. The wake had gone on for hours. When his child had been taken, the funeral party had been swelled by her friends from school, but at neither event could Susan recall there being family. It was as if Eddy and Martha and Karen, that little unit, had existed in glorious isolation.

More because of the feeling that now she was here she should be doing something, she went back into the hall and took the red-bound phone book from beneath the telephone. A quick flick told her that the book contained numbers for his detectorist friends, the local doctor and optician, that sort of thing, but no family. She tucked it into her bag anyway, thinking it would help her to contact friends who would want to be at the funeral, then she turned off all the lights and let herself out, feeling even more deflated and confused than when she had arrived.

From Roads to Ruin *by E Thame:*
News of Henry Kirkwood's arrest reached Catherine when she and Elmer stayed for the night at an inn just outside of Bristol. The disguise they had taken was that of a gentleman farmer and his wife, off to visit relatives. She rode pillion, respectably behind her husband, and a second saddle horse was used as a pack animal. Her maid, she told the innkeeper, had been taken ill, and they'd proceeded alone, the male servant who had attended her husband having returned with her to the farm.

58

It was not a good story and not very convincing cover, but they paid their money and were given a bedroom for the night. I think we must assume that keepers of seventeenth century inns were as used to the Mr and Mrs Smiths of the world then as they are now – a sorry state for the genuine Smiths who are destined, one suspects, always to be viewed with a suspicious eye.

Catherine's letters in the Lorenz collection tell us that she heard the news that night. They had been travelling for just less than two days.

'My hearte felt like lead,' she writes. 'Elmer tells me that the newes is bruited abroad that Henry Kirkwood and his household are now forfeited to the King for his parte in this treatchery. I wish to turn back but Elmer is a man of goode sense and I must be guided by him and by the wish of my father who sended me hence.'

Why they eventually did turn back towards home we can only speculate. Perhaps she wanted to be as close to her father as possible once he was sentenced; perhaps the King's lines were too tightly drawn for them to cross. We do know, from the Lorenz records, that by the end of July they were finally heading north after a long detour, which took them into Wiltshire and to the White Horse Vale. That they did head south and did hide the remainder of the Kirkwood hoard is not in question. Finds in Bakers Field point to the cache being in that area and it is significant that only items immediately identifiable as being from the Kirkwood estate or otherwise tied to the rebellion have been discovered. We have to assume that anything else of value went north with Catherine and Elmer.

EIGHT

The Lamb reopened the following night but the mood was subdued and quiet. No one sat in Eddy's seat, and Alec was somehow unsurprised when one of his usual suppliers of beverages bought an extra pint as usual and set it on the table, as though in silent salute.

'I heard,' he told Susan. 'We're really sorry.'

'Thanks,' she said. 'He's going to be missed.'

Alec nodded, was going to turn away, having done his condolence duty and painfully aware that he was only a visitor here, among people who actually knew the old man, when Susan called him back.

'Mind if I ask you something?'

'Sure, what's bothering you?'

'Well, it looks as though it's down to me to, you know, sort things out. I think I know who his solicitor is, or at least, who he went to to get his will drawn up, but as to next of kin ... I'm a bit lost, really. We all knew Eddy for a long time but I don't think anyone really knew about his family, not before they moved here.'

'Maybe the solicitor will know. If he made a will then that implies there was someone to leave his possessions to.'

Susan nodded. 'I suppose so, but I know, because he told me, that most of his stuff was left to friends who'd appreciate it. His books, his detecting gear, all of that, and I'm not sure if he owned the house or what. I never asked. It was just, you know, Eddy's house. It wasn't the sort of thing we talked about.'

Alec set his beer back down on the bar, feeling that this was going to take longer than he had first thought. 'What *did* you talk about?' he asked.

'Oh, what he'd found, the state of the world, art. He loved paintings. The books he'd found rummaging in the second-hand stores. His garden. Oh, we'd talk. Talk for hours. I know you only saw him here, sitting all quiet like, and he loved to listen, we all knew that. But get him on his own, on his own turf, and he'd talk.' She glanced around as if for confirmation, was supported by nods and mutterings that Eddy was a good talker once you'd set him off.

'But not about family?' Alec found he was now addressing the wider company.

The agreement was no, not about family. Not after Martha died, or even before, not really.

'So, I kind of wondered if ... if you'd got any advice. I don't know where to start, I really don't. I went to the cottage last night but it all feels so ... intrusive, you know? And you being a policeman, you must be used to dealing with stuff like this?'

Alec nodded. He was suddenly aware that he

was the focus of general expectation. 'OK,' he said. 'If there's anything I can do, I'd be glad to help out.'

He could almost see the weight of overwhelming responsibility lift from Susan's shoulders and he felt a sudden urge to move away from the bar before it changed direction and settled on his. By the time he returned to Naomi he had agreed to go with Susan to Eddy's little house, take a look around and see what they could find out about his wider family. He wondered how well that would go down with Naomi.

'I heard,' she pre-empted him. She sounded amused. 'Look, it's OK, I can amuse myself for a couple of hours. You'll be miserable as hell if you don't do your bit.'

Alec chuckled softly. 'You're right, as ever,' he said. 'I suppose I would be.'

Susan arrived back at her flat and pulled into her designated parking space. A familiar car was already occupying one of the visitors' spots and Susan sighed deeply as she noted who it was. That was all she needed.

Reluctantly, she got out of her car and the man in the visitors' spot left his, hesitating before coming over as though not sure he was welcome.

Good, she thought. Because he's not. Her ex didn't bother her very often, but even that was too much in Susan's view. He'd been a mistake, she'd realized that quickly enough; had spent the next five years trying not to believe it, before she'd finally left. The solicitors had dealt with the rest, not exactly amicably.

'Hi,' he said. 'I heard about Eddy. I just wanted to make sure you were all right.'

She hadn't expected that for an opening gambit. 'I'm fine. It was a shock, finding him like that, but I'm fine.'

'So, what happens now, funeral and that? You'll be organizing it?'

'I expect so, unless family turn up, which is unlikely.'

'He had much family, did he? I don't remember you mentioning any.'

'That's probably because you stopped listening to me once you had a ring on my finger.'

He looked away and in the yellow of the security light she could see the flash of anger as it skimmed his face. He was good looking, she'd give him that, and he was also aggressive and unpredictable and selfish and...

'Look, if there's nothing else, I've had a long day. If there is something else, say it quick or send a letter to my solicitor.'

He laughed harshly. 'You really are a piece of work, aren't you? I just came to offer my condolences, ask you if you maybe needed a friend. From what I remember, friends were kind of thin on the ground after we split.'

That, strictly, had been true. He had systematically removed her from any old friends or associations he had deemed unsuitable. What had been left had largely been *his* friends, *his* family, *his*...

'Thanks, but no thanks,' she said. 'Just go away, Brian. If I wanted a friend I'd call one up, and you wouldn't even be on the list.'

She turned away and keyed the code into the door lock, careful that he didn't see. She would not put it past him to try and follow her inside. He didn't move and she opened the door just enough to slip through, shoved it closed behind her, annoyed that he'd know, that he'd see just how much he still got to her.

Looking down from the window of her tiny flat she could see him in the car park, leaning against the bonnet of the car, and she was glad she hadn't switched the light on, knowing that was what he was waiting for. He'd never been inside her flat, never even been inside the block. He didn't actually know which window was hers and she was happier keeping it that way. She stepped back from the window, just in case he saw her shadow, and waited until she heard the car engine fire and her ex drive away. Only then, after another quick glance just to be sure, did she risk turning on the light.

Eddy had been against the marriage right from the get go. He'd said it was her decision but that Brian was a bad lot. He'd known people like him and they were good for no one.

Of course, she hadn't listened. Didn't women always think that they were the one? The catalyst by which such men changed their ways?

But she'd been wrong. She'd sunk her savings into the house they'd bought and had had the devil's own job getting anything out again. Eddy had advised her then; he'd directed her to his solicitor and she'd let them handle it. To her surprise, Brian had been forthcoming with her money and she'd been able to get a mortgage on this little flat.

One thing was for sure, he'd never set foot inside.

The following morning, Alec duly set off to meet Susan at Eddy's house, leaving Naomi alone for the first time since they had come on holiday. Despite what she had said to Alec, she felt oddly bereft and rather more isolated than she'd anticipated. She could now find her way around the B&B without too much trouble and had been outside into the farmyard alone. She had also accompanied Alec down to what Jim and Bethan called the cut, the place at the perimeter of the kitchen garden through which one of the many dykes flowed – not a major one, Bethan had told her then; rather, one of the many offshoots from the main rhynes. It was a pleasant place even in the depths of winter and Naomi, with Napoleon in his harness, followed the narrow stone path through the garden and down to the little jetty Jim had built so that their grandchildren could sit and fish for tiddlers in the summer.

The change of surface from stone to wood told Naomi they had arrived and she felt for the wooden railing she knew was there; finding it, she perched, Napoleon flopping down at her feet. The silence at first seemed profound but as her ears grew accustomed to the lack of ordinary noise – the occasional car, domestic noises from kitchen and farmyard – she began to hear what made up this new soundscape. The slow drip and slap of water beneath the jetty. The occasional plop of some small creature entering the dyke. Wind in the reeds and withies that Alec told her occupied the opposite bank. Every place had one, Naomi had discovered. Its own way of sounding – and, for that matter, smelling and feeling – and she wished she had paid more attention to those other senses when she'd still had her full quota. It had been a standing joke in Naomi's family that the first thing she put on in the morning and the last thing she took off at night had been her specs. Short-sighted from childhood, and basically nosy from birth, Naomi could not bear to miss anything. When she had been blinded, everyone had been terribly anxious that she wouldn't cope, even to the extent that the doctors had put off telling her that she wouldn't see again. But Naomi was also a pragmatist at heart; what you can't change you learn to make the best of, and she was actually very proud of the way she had adapted and fervently grateful to all the people who had helped her get there.

Footsteps on the stone path and the slow wag of Napoleon's tail told her that Bethan had come to join her. She moved over and Bethan leaned on the fence from the garden side.

'You all right out here?'

'Oh, I'm fine. Dog will make sure I don't fall in, won't you, Napoleon?'

'He's a marvellous animal,' Bethan agreed. 'Our two are too daft for anything useful.' She paused, clearly curious. 'Alec gone out for a bit then?'

Inwardly, Naomi laughed. 'We were in The Lamb last night. Susan asked him for a bit of advice, tracking down next of kin and such. She seems to have taken on the responsibility for Eddy's estate. Alec's gone out to see what he can do to help.'

'Oh, right. Poor love, she's known him since she was a little girl. We've all known him an age. He'll get a good send- off, that's for sure.' She sighed. 'Just goes to show, doesn't it? Life is so fragile.'

Naomi nodded and silence fell for a moment or so. Something large splashed into the water and she wondered if it could be a vole or if it was too late in the year to be hearing 'ratty'.

'I hope you don't mind me asking, but you've not always been blind then?'

'No. Car crash. One of those multi-vehicle things on the motorway. I was a police sergeant before that.'

'Oh, so is that...'

'How we met? Yes. I'm like Alec, never really wanted to do anything else until now, so it was all a major shock and something of a wrench.'

'I can imagine.'

Can you? Naomi wondered. She would certainly not have been able to; not until life changed and gave her no option.

'Wonderful, how you cope.'

Naomi laughed. 'People worse off than me and all that. Hey, when you have to do something, well, you just have to do it.' She looked for a change of subject, not comfortable with talking about herself to a relative stranger, however nice she was. 'You said you knew Eddy for a long time. Did you ever hear him mention family?'

Bethan thought about it. 'I vaguely think there was a brother or a brother-in-law,' she said. 'But he didn't come to either funeral. Not when Martha died nor when the girl was killed. You'd have thought...'

Naomi nodded. 'Families can become estranged, though,' she said. 'It doesn't always mean they don't care. Sometimes it's just that they don't know how to make contact again.'

'But you'd think something as big as a funeral would bring them back together, wouldn't you?'

'I suppose so. It depends how far apart they've drifted.'

'Doesn't seem right though, does it?'

'Does what?'

'Well, I know Eddy probably doesn't have much to leave, but it doesn't seem right that someone he hasn't seen in years should get it all, not when they couldn't be bothered to come and see him even when he must have needed them.'

Naomi didn't think there was a lot she could say to that. She shivered. She'd come out in a heavy sweater, but the day was damp and chill and the cold now beginning to permeate.

'Best come inside,' Bethan said. 'I'll make you a cuppa.'

Alec arrived at the house before Susan and wondered if he'd found the right place. Set back from the road and reached, as Susan had described, by a short but heavily rutted track, it was a pretty place ... or would be in summer, Alec guessed, when the now rather forlorn looking roses would be climbing around the porch and the – was that wisteria? – wisteria or whatever would be in flower. Alec liked gardens; he just had a rather vague notion of how they were made up. Naomi was the gardener in their house and she and her sister had managed to create a wonderfully lush, sweetly scented haven, despite Napoleon and Alec's efforts to help.

Closer inspection showed Alec that the window frames were in need of a coat of paint and the front door, though it had been daubed with red in the not too distant past, had been redecorated over previous layers of flaking paint. The knocker had rusted, and its face, which Alec presumed was some kind of pixie, was heavily pitted. 'A pixie with pox,' he said aloud.

The front room curtains were closed and he could see little through the letter box except for the bottom steps and an area of tiled floor. The scene of poor Eddy's death. He was about to go round the back and snoop some more when Susan's Volkswagen pulled up beside his own car.

She got out, looking flustered. 'Sorry I'm late. I seem to be having trouble getting the day started today.'

'No problem. You still want me here? I won't take offence.' She'd had the night to think on her impulse and Alec knew just how fast such impulses could seem wrong or foolish.

'Oh, do I want you here,' Susan said fervently. 'I've been driving here dreading the thought you might have changed your mind. I don't think I could face going in on my own again.' She shook her head. 'Which is silly. It was always a place I loved to visit.'

'It's hard after the person is gone though,' Alec said. 'My uncle died a while ago and left me his house. Going back there without him was really difficult. Right, what do we do now? Shall we go inside?'

Susan slipped the key into the lock and Alec followed her, then walked past as she came to a stop in the hall, staring at the place at the foot of the stairs.

'What's through here?' he asked. 'Ah, the living room.' He opened the curtains and let in the grey November light. 'Kitchen at the end of the hall? Yes?'

'Yes.' She finally braved the living room, glared at the empty fire grate.

'Maybe we should make one up,' Alec said. 'We may be here a little while and I'm guessing there's no central heating?'

'No, he didn't like the idea. He was a bit set in his ways. I don't know, it feels a bit ... intrusive, making up a fire.'

'Better that than freeze or let the damp take hold. You know, it would be a good idea to make up a fire every day or so, to keep the place dried out until all this is sorted. Houses like this, with solid walls, they're a devil to dry out once the damp gets in.' He knelt, sorting kindling and logs, and, after a moment more of hesitation, she fetched matches down from the mantelpiece.

'I think there are some firelighters somewhere. In the kitchen, maybe. I'm not that good with fires.' She laughed. 'I'm afraid I am a fan of central heating.'

'Firelighters would be good. I'm out of practice. Where would Eddy have kept his papers, do you think? Did you manage to sort out the solicitor's name?'

'Um, yes. Wright and Cole in Somerton. Apparently, they have the will. I've got to see

72

the doctor and get the death certificate to them and so on. They don't know about family either.'

'Right, so it looks like it's up to us, but I'll go and have a chat to the solicitors if you think it would be helpful.'

'Thank you,' she said. 'I really do appreciate this, you know.'

'You are very welcome. I know how hard it can be.'

She brought the firelighters and he lit one, tucking it beneath the kindling and trying to recall what else he should be doing. They had a wood burner back at home, but Naomi normally set it ready and he just did the manly thing of lighting one of the funny rolls of newspaper she placed beneath the kindling and which seemed to do the trick. It occurred to him suddenly, catching him off balance, that Naomi seemed to have made a point of taking over those tasks everyone assumed would be difficult for her to accomplish without sight. Gardening, setting the fire, cooking; she excelled at them all and, as he watched the fire reluctantly take hold, he realized too that this was probably her sister Sam's doing. Even before Naomi left hospital, and while the rest of them had been flapping round making sympathetic noises, Sam had been insisting Naomi learn to apply her own lipstick.

He sat back on his heels, other vague thoughts suddenly clarified. 'Do you have kids?' he asked.

Susan laughed nervously. 'Um, no. I've got an ex-husband, but thankfully we never got around to the having children part.'

'We're thinking of having some,' Alec said. 'I've been putting it off, I suppose. Work is so demanding and I always worried about coping.'

'You mean with Naomi? I mean, it must add an extra dimension, problem wise, not being able to see.'

'No, actually.' Alec smiled, more to himself than at Susan. 'I kept telling myself that was the problem, but, you know, I think I've just realized it was me. *I* was worried on the coping front. I want to do a good job, you know, and I've seen so many broken marriages in my job, especially once the kids start coming along. Sorry, you know how sometimes things just feel very clear very suddenly?'

Susan was laughing at him, her expression bemused. 'And kneeling on a frayed rug, in a stranger's home, trying to light a fire, it all became clear?'

Alec got to his feet, watching with satisfaction as the fire took hold. 'Put like that,' he admitted, 'I do sound like an idiot.' He glanced around the shabby little room – at the shelves, over-stacked with books; at worn chairs, their threadbare arms polished bare by years of hands. 'When did Eddy's wife die?' he asked.

'Twenty-odd years ago. His daughter two years after that. Karen was fifteen when her mother died. It was all very sudden and I don't think he ever recovered. The furniture wasn't new even back then and I can't think of anything he's bought since.'

'What did he do? Work wise, I mean.'

Susan moved through into the kitchen. 'We should light the fire in here too,' she said. 'He taught History, secondary school. When he lost his family, he lost his mind too for a while. Never worked again after that. I think there must have been a bit of a pension, but he was in and out of hospital, mental hospital, for several years. He had a lovely family, a lovely life, and when it all came crashing down I don't think he had the resources to cope, poor man. Hard to know how you'd react in a situation like that, isn't it? I think we just have to pray we never find out.'

Alec nodded agreement. The fire in the kitchen was already laid and Susan did the honours this time while Alec looked around. The kitchen was meticulously tidy. The table had been scrubbed so often that the grain had been raised, and the floor was spotless. He could see Eddy's wellingtons and walking boots in a little porch-style lean-to that extended from the back door, sweeping brush and mop and bucket strategically placed beside them. No stray pots on the draining board, no rubbish in the bin.

A meticulous man.

One small thing jarred against the rest. 'He

must have had a visitor,' Alec said.

'A visitor?' She looked to where Alec pointed. 'Oh, he used the big pot.'

'Two mugs.'

Susan nodded, taking in the fact that neither was pink striped; that particular cup still hung below the teapot shelf. Someone he knew well, then. A friend. She frowned. 'It must have been a late visit. He always made sure he washed up, put the rubbish out and set the fire for the morning before he went to bed. He liked his habits, did Eddy. Everything in its place.'

'As you say, it must have been late.'

'Odd, though. He'd usually have washed the cups and rinsed the teapot out before going up, however late it was. He hated mess.'

'Well, two mugs and a teapot. It's hardly mess. If he was tired...'

'To Eddy, that would have been mess.' She frowned, looking around for further evidence of Eddy's late night visitor. 'There's a biscuit wrapper in the bin. He always emptied the bins last thing.'

'Did he often have late night visitors?'

'I don't think so. Occasionally someone from the detectorist club would stay over. Some of them come a long way and a lot of them are doing it on a tight budget. He's got a spare room he leaves made up just in case.'

She led the way upstairs. Alec followed, noting the frayed stair carpet that was implicated in Eddy's death. It would have been very easy to have tripped and fallen.

At the top of the stairs was a long landing with four doors leading off. Susan opened the second, revealing a room with a single bed beneath the window, made up and ready for a guest. A wooden chair placed beside the bed served as both seat and bedside table. Closer to the door, a large cupboard that Alec thought might be a linen press occupied an inordinate amount of space. Curious, he opened the doors, finding nothing more interesting to his casual glance than piles of sheets and blankets.

'No sign of anyone up here,' Susan said. They returned to the landing.

'Do you mind?' Alec said, indicating the other doors.

'What? Oh, no, I suppose not. We're supposed to be looking for ... whatever ... after all.'

The furthest door was the bathroom. Alec guessed it must be directly above the kitchen and sharing the same feed from the water tank he assumed would be in the roof space above. It looked, to Alec, as though the bathroom occupied space divided off from one of the bedrooms, the house probably being too old to have had indoor plumbing when it had been first built. The bathroom was tiny. The bath squeezed into a corner and the toilet next to it. A washbasin so close to the door it prevented full opening. A quick look in the bathroom cabinet revealed a single toothbrush, paste, extra soap and a basic first aid kit with plasters and ointment.

The room next door was the guest room. Next was a large double room that had been Eddy's. A candlewick bedspread had been pulled back across the puffy pink quilt, but the sheets and blankets had been undisturbed. So, Eddy had come up to bed, but not actually gone to sleep before his visitor arrived. 'How was Eddy dressed the night he died?'

'Um, pyjamas, dressing gown, slippers. Why?'

'Just curious.'

'You think there was something ... that it wasn't an accident?'

Alec shook his head. 'That's a massive leap,' he said. 'Sorry, I just get my policeman's head on, you know.'

'The other room was Karen's.' Susan seemed reluctant, to Alec, to go in. He opened the door anyway and halted on the threshold, looked back at Susan, who shrugged.

Dust everywhere, layers of it. Stratified and heavy on bed and wardrobe and chest of drawers, even on the pink carpet. The curtains were open but they too were heavy with grime, and the net between had yellowed and was now falling into holes after years of exposure to the light.

Tattered posters had fallen from the walls. Some still clung grimly by their Blu-tacked corners, and once-loved soft toys, also covered in their veil of dust, stared at him from the end of the bed. The only disturbance to the archae-ology of dust was the arc created by the door as it disturbed the layers on the carpet.

'He shut the door the day of the funeral and never went in again,' Susan said. 'Funny, you'd have thought he'd have found it hard to sleep in the room he shared with Martha, but that seemed to just give him comfort. Karen's room was different. He never let anyone in here and never went in himself.'

'But you knew what to expect when I opened the door.'

Susan shrugged. 'Curiosity,' she said. 'I peeked in once, years ago. I think if he'd known he'd have been really upset, but I only opened the door a fraction.'

'Well,' Alec said. 'I doubt we'll find what we're looking for in there. Where should we start, do you think?'

'He had a desk in the other front room,' Susan said. 'I guess we should start there.'

With a last quick glance through the door, Alec began to close it and then something suddenly jarred and he took one last lingering look around the room. Dust covered everything, carpet included; it seemed impossible that any-one could have gone inside without disturbing it and leaving telltale footprints behind.

What was it he had noticed? The urge to look again had been in response to something so tiny as to be almost subliminal, and it was only Alec's experience, his habit of standing and just surveying a scene, that had caused it to register at all.

He withdrew his gaze to that portion of the room that could be reached from the door. On a chair close by, a nightdress and dressing gown had been tossed – probably, he thought, on that last morning before Karen left. Both were cob-webbed and flocked with the same soft layer, except for just one small area, which showed signs of fairly recent disturbance, the gentle strata not lying so thickly. He could see the pocket on the pink dressing gown, edged with something silky and embroidered with bright purple flowers. It was the satin binding that he had noticed – the sheen of it, against the almost powdery covering of every other thing in the room.

Alec could hear Susan's footsteps on the stairs. She had paused, as though puzzled he had not followed. Alec held on to the door frame and leaned in, fingers touching the satin edging on the pocket and then feeling inside.

At first he thought he might have been mistaken; there was nothing there. Then, 'Got you,' he whispered. He slipped what he had found in to his pocket – not sure why he didn't want to share the discovery with Susan, only aware that there was the possibility Eddy had hidden it there and that his secret should be kept for just a little longer. Then he followed Susan back down the stairs.

When Eddy had been a much younger man he had felt certain there was a solution to everything. Life had fallen into place for him. Good degree, good job, happy marriage, wonderful child, even though she'd been a little late coming on to the scene. From such a height of grace it seemed inevitable, in afterthought, that the fall should be so heavy and so far.

Cancer, the doctor said. Then, that it had metastasized. Then, that there were only months, and then weeks – and nothing that had fallen so neatly into place before could compensate for the chaos that those few words had brought.

Then, 'I'm sorry sir, but your daughter Karen. There was a car accident. I'm afraid...'

The fall from grace complete, and none of it of his making or in his power to change.

Eddy disintegrated. There was no other word complete enough to explain what happened to him. He dissolved into the morass that was grief and loss and emptiness, and when he finally climbed his painful way back out again, it was as though that man of certainty he had been was a mere shadow of a memory.

He wrote, 'I have lost all purpose. I am empty, a vessel that has been spilled out on to the ground.'

But he found something to fill that space. I'm not saying it was a good thing, just that this is what he did, and if I'd known all of it then I might have intervened. As it was, I knew Eddy now had something that was driving him, something that made it worth him getting up in the morning, and I told myself that it was his research. We joked about his treasure hunts and about what he'd do if he found his millions buried in some muddy field. If I'd known the truth, I think I would have acted.

'You think?'

'I don't know. That's just it. I really, really don't know.'

NINE

'So, what did you find?' Naomi asked Alec later that afternoon when Alec had returned from Eddy's house.

'Who says I found anything? You heard me tell Jim and Bethan we still hadn't tracked the long-lost relatives down.'

'I did, but I know you.'

'I should hope so by now.'

'So?'

Alec flopped down on the edge of the bed and Naomi joined him. 'I don't actually know,' he said. 'I only had a quick look before I put it in my pocket.'

'You didn't show Susan?'

'Err, no. And, before you ask, I don't know why. It was just in such an odd place and I almost missed it.'

He told her about Eddy's house. About the threadbare furniture and frayed carpet and the visitor who must have come very late to drink tea and eat biscuits. And about Karen's room, frozen in time beneath a layer of dust and cob-webs – 'like that woman in the Dickens novel.'

'Miss Haversham? Hardly, she'd been jilted.'

'But you know what I mean. Anyway, what I

found was this.'

She heard the rustle of paper. Something thin and then something else. He laid his finds between them on the bed and Naomi reached out to touch. 'A photograph,' she guessed, feeling the glossy front and more matt reverse. 'Small, one of those photo booth things? No, it feels too thick for that.'

'I think it's a Polaroid,' Alec said.

'Oh, right. Sam had one of those. Film cost a fortune and you only got eight shots. Fun though. A newspaper clipping?'

'Yes, Sherlock, it is indeed.'

'And a key. A little key.' She frowned. 'What is that? A suitcase key or briefcase or something?'

'Um, maybe, but what it reminds me of is that five-year diary you have from when you were a kid.'

'Ah, my *secret* diary.'

'That you kept for about a week.'

'Oh, it was longer than that.' She felt the key again. 'It might be,' she agreed. 'OK, so what does the clipping say and how exactly did you find it? I mean, I know in a dressing gown pocket, but...'

'I know what you mean. Folded together. Key and photo inside the newspaper clipping.'

'Karen might have put them there. I mean, you may well be right about the dressing gown being disturbed, but might Eddy have known about them?'

84

'Not likely. The clipping is about Karen's death and the photo is of her too.'

'Oh? Read it.'

'I'll summarize,' Alec said. 'Basically, there were four friends. One, a seventeen-year-old called Oliver Bates, had just passed his test. He'd driven them all to the cinema and they were coming home, didn't make it. The car was found wrapped round a tree and the report says that Oliver and the front seat passenger – Jill Wellesley, Oliver's girlfriend – died instantly. Those in the back were Karen and her friend, Sara Coles. Karen and Sara had been staying with Jill. Karen died at the scene before help arrived. Sara survived in hospital for three days before they turned off her life support.'

'Oh, God, that's horrible,' Naomi said quietly. They'd both attended similar incidents; both had had to tell parents that their kids would not be coming home. 'What caused it?'

'Well, no one seems to know. None of them had been drinking. There were skid marks on the road but the local police don't even know if they were linked. And there was nothing to suggest a collision. It was, apparently, a notorious accident black spot. He maybe tried to take the bend too fast and lost control. If another vehicle was involved, maybe something he had to swerve to avoid, then they didn't stick around and no one called for help. If they had, it's possible Karen and Sara could have survived. As it was, a taxi driver called the police, but they reckon that was maybe an hour after it all happened. There seems to have been some speculation about them being run off the road; an unnamed source alleged there'd been a drunk driver picked up on suspicion later on, but there's nothing very specific.'

'That makes it even worse,' Naomi said. 'And the picture?'

'Well, there's a picture in the paper of all four of them, then this little Polaroid of Karen and Sara. And this key.'

'But the key to what? And why did Eddy hide it in the dressing gown pocket?'

'Well, the only conclusion I could reach is that no one would have gone into that room. Anyone opening the door would have seen what we did, just a lot of dust and memories. I doubt one in a hundred people would have looked any further. The other question is, who visited Eddy on the night he died? If Susan's right, then he'd never have gone up to bed before washing up the mugs and rinsing the teapot out, but he did neither, which leads me to believe that he didn't get the chance. Either his visitor was there when he died, in which case, why not report it, call an ambulance? Or...'

'You think he may have been pushed down the stairs?'

'I've got nothing to support that theory except for two mugs and a teapot. But I might just have a word with the attending officer, you never know.'

86

'There'll have to be a post-mortem, won't there?'

'Well, in theory, yes. It's technically an unexplained death, and Eddy hadn't seen the doctor in years, Susan said. But most likely it'll be a fairly cursory exam. Cause of death is self evident. Eddy broke his neck in the fall. There's a patch of frayed carpet at the head of the stairs and the coroner will just bring a verdict of accidental death and that will be that.'

'Unless you stir things up.'

'Maybe, if I stir things up. Problem is, we're not going to be here for long and it isn't my jurisdiction and—'

'And this is bothering you more than you thought it would. Alec, phone work. Tell them you're taking your TOIL time and adding it to your holiday.'

'Oh, they'll just love that.'

'You're entitled. What are they going to do? Sack you?'

Alec laughed, thinking that his boss would have a good go at that. 'OK,' he agreed. 'We'll stay on for a bit longer, see what comes up, but it'll probably be a waste of time. I'm probably just looking for trouble where there isn't any.'

'Occupational hazard,' Naomi agreed. 'But anyway, we're still only on page two of your list. I haven't driven the tank yet. Or been to that abbey that brews its own mead, or what-ever it is.'

'Remind me not to let you do both on the

same day. Right, I'm going to make a couple of phone calls. Get ready to duck.'

'A couple?'

'Yes. One to tell work I'm not coming back when they thought I was and another to the attending officer. Susan had his card. Let's see if we can get a bit of professional courtesy extended.'

From Roads to Ruin *by E Thame*

We know from Catherine Kirkwood's account that Elmer managed to get into the trial of her father and witnessed the proceedings. That was a brave act. Had he been recognized he might have lost his own life, and I think we can allow ourselves to speculate here, just a little, as to his motivation. By this time, he and Catherine had been travelling together for about twelve days – they had fled north to Bristol, then turned east, but we can't be sure what circumstance finally brought them south again, to Dorchester, to see the infamous Judge Jeffries in session.

History rightly remembers these events as the Bloody Assizes.

Catherine must have been aware of what was going on and must have been in despair. Did Elmer obey her order when he entered the courtroom and stood with others in the public gallery, or did he obey something far more acute and ephemeral? From later material, the content of which leads us to speculate upon a

88

marriage between this high-born daughter and her father's manservant, we have to conclude that it was the latter that drove him to such a desperate measure. I hope they loved one another; the romantic that lurks in the heart of every historian must hold sway here and wish that happiness in some measure compensated for such desperate grief.

One thing we do know for certain is that Elmer had bad news to take back to Catherine. Her father had been sentenced to a traitor's death. To be flogged and then hung, drawn and quartered. Judge Jeffries had handed down twelve such judgements in that morning alone, and though five of those were then commuted to transportation to the colonies in the West Indies, and one man managed to pay for his freedom, Henry Kirkwood died a scant five days later. It is my hope that Elmer had taken Catherine north again by then and that she did not witness this final terrible scene, but her letters seem to hint that she was there, at least at the beginning.

She writes, 'I saw him on the cart, dressed only in a torn shirt of stayned linen. The hangman playced the halter about his neck and it was all I culd do not to cry out for mercy. His freyndes had failed him. I wrote letters and begged Lord Castleton and the Layde Claire if they culd but buy him and have him sent instead to work the plantations. Many such gifts having been made to those loyal to the king, their lives *were perhaps sayved, and I begged them to buy my father's bond that he might at least have a chance of life even if so far away I could not hope to see his face in my lifetime. But they did not reply. Elmer warned me that they wuld not, but even so theyre ill response all but drove me to despair. We left before we saw the rest, I half faint with heat and feare and sorrow, and Elmer carried me hence.'*

To the modern mind the idea of prisoners being sold off in lieu of execution is a strange one, but many had their lives gifted to loyal members of James's court. A man could be worth up to twelve pounds sterling if sold as slave labour in the colonies, though I have doubts that had Catherine really known what would have been in store for her father she would have wished so hard for it. Many died en route, crammed into ships like so much cargo. Those that survived the journey had to look forward to a life of hard labour, little food and regular beatings. The African slave trade has a well documented history; less so is the trade in prisoners from England and so-called indentured labourers: men and women without rights even over their own bodies, a practice that continued long after the official abolition of slavery and, indeed, did not end until well into the twentieth century.

Although The Lamb was to reopen that night, Naomi and Alec decided to eat, instead, at the pub they had discovered in Bridgewater, a decision largely made on the strength of Sergeant Dean agreeing to meet them that evening when he came off duty and Alec's feeling that they shouldn't really do that at The Lamb. Alec surmised that the promise of dinner probably swung the decision for Sergeant Dean. That, and inevitable curiosity.

Sergeant Andrew Dean was a short man, tending towards the rotund at first glance, but on closer inspection, Alec realized he was round in the barrel-chested way that some power lifters are round, not in a way that denoted lack of muscular development.

Massive hands enclosed Alec's as he shook them; Andrew Dean was a man who made use of what Alec thought of as a politician's handshake. One hand grasped, while the other patted, and Alec found himself checking that his watch was still there when he'd finally been released.

'My wife, Naomi,' Alec introduced. 'Good of you to come at such short notice.'

'Well, got to admit you've intrigued me,' Sergeant Dean said. 'What's your interest, then? Oh, beer, please, anything that's not lager. Can't stand the stuff.'

'Right,' Alec said and headed for the bar.

'We're actually here on holiday,' Naomi said. 'We got to know Eddy, slightly, and the friend that found him, Susan Rawlins, she asked Alec for advice. It sort of followed from there.'

Andrew Dean laughed loudly. 'Being a policeman is a bit like being a doctor,' he said. 'You're never off duty. Must be irritating for you though, love? Coming for a nice break and then getting dragged into this?'

'Oh, I'm used to it,' Naomi said. 'Alec and I joined the force at the same time. We spent years racing one another for promotion before I had my accident.'

'Ah,' Dean said and the sound was filled with meaning. Sympathy, curiosity.

'The force's inclusivity policies still don't quite come to keeping blind detective inspectors.'

'Oh, so you were both ... I see what you mean about racing for promotion.' He laughed as though the thought amused him.

Naomi didn't bother adding that she'd only actually got to acting inspector before her accident had intervened.

'My wife doesn't have any interest in the job,' Dean said. He seemed happy with that. 'She's got her own interests. Does a lot of gardening.'

'She's OK with you being late home tonight?'

'Oh, she's off on a coach trip with her sister. Inspecting the Lost Gardens of Heligan and such. They do it every year, one garden or another. Comes back full of it, she does. Me, I can't tell the difference between a dandelion and a daffodil, but it makes her happy, so that's all that matters, isn't it?'

The unexpected softness that crept into his

voice caused Naomi to slightly shift her opinion of him. External bluster, she thought; gooey-centred, probably. Alec arrived back with their drinks. And they consulted menus, settled down to exchange small talk and continue with their mutual summing up.

'Nothing to suggest it wasn't an accident,' Sergeant Dean said. 'We think he caught his foot in the carpet and fell. I had a quick look around, but everything seemed in order, and Mrs Rawlins, Susan, she said nothing seemed to have been disturbed. The doors were locked, back door bolted. I mean, yes, someone could have just let themselves out the front and the door would have latched behind them, but I saw nothing to worry about.'

'Post-mortem?'

'In a couple of days, I suppose. I can check, but he's not going to be a priority case so he'll just be on the normal list.'

'Can you have a word, ask them to take a look out for micro-bruising?'

'Micro-bruising? What is this? An episode of CSI?'

'It would have developed by now,' Alec pressed on, disregarding the tone. 'It's just possible—'

'You think he was pushed,' Dean said flatly.

'I don't actually think anything. I just promised Susan I'd check things out.'

'Because, of course, us local country bumpkins can't be trusted.'

'No one's saying anything of the sort,' Naomi intervened. 'Could someone hand me the pepper please? Thanks, Andrew. What Alec is saying is, no one would have thought anything of it, but Susan is convinced there was someone else there that night. It's bothering her and as she's the one coping with all of this single handed, trying to find family and taking on all the arrangements ... Well, a bit of reassurance wouldn't come amiss, you know.'

Andrew Dean was not entirely mollified. 'I can ask,' he said reluctantly. 'Anyway, what makes her think the old man had a visitor?'

'Oh, you must have noticed the teapot and mugs? Well, apparently Eddy was meticulous about tidying up. She's convinced he must have had someone visit and that Eddy didn't have time to clean up before he died. It worries her.'

'Oh, right.'

Naomi could feel him running back through his mental account of the night, trying to recall if he'd even noticed the mugs on the kitchen table. 'So, he had a visitor. That doesn't mean his visitor shoved him down the stairs.'

'No, of course it doesn't. Another drink?'

'Better make it a soft one. I've got to drive home. Look, I'll give Mrs Rawlins a call in the morning, tell her she's got nothing to be concerned about. Accidents like this happen all the time.'

'And will you give *me* a call when the PM has been done?' Alec said.

'You'll still be down here then?'

'Oh yes,' Naomi told him sweetly. 'Two more weeks, probably. We'll have to have dinner together again before we go. Maybe you could bring your wife next time.'

'So,' Naomi said as they drove back to the farm. 'What do you think?'

'I think our Sergeant Dean likes a quiet life and that's what he usually gets. I'm sure he did have a quick glance around downstairs, checked everything was locked up tight before he left and so on, but I doubt, until tonight, it even crossed his mind that what he saw wasn't necessarily the whole story. Susan would have told him about the frayed carpet, probably said how often she'd warned Eddy, and he'd have thought no more about it. Just a tragic accident.'

'Do you think he'll talk to the pathologist?'

'Yes,' Alec said, 'I think professional pride will force him to. Not that he'll mention being prompted, of course. By then it will have become all his own idea, but that doesn't matter so long as he asks – and so long as he then calls me, I'll be willing to forgive him his other sins of omission.'

'You think he *will* call you?'

'Ah, now that's another matter. I think he's just hoping we'll cut our holiday short and go home. That's probably what I'd be thinking in his place.'

Naomi laughed. 'What will you tell Susan?'

'I think, more to the point, will be what Susan will tell *me*. And that will be that she's now feeling foolish and hopes we didn't think she was being hysterical, and that while she's grateful for my help so far, she's fine to carry on without it.'

Naomi nodded. 'You could be right,' she said. 'It's bad enough losing a friend, but to think someone might have deliberately taken that life away is often so much more difficult to come to terms with. She'll want to back off from that. Want you to as well.'

'Which, of course, I can't now,' Alec said.

'Which, of course, you can't,' Naomi agreed.

TEN

A quiet few days followed. They ate at The Lamb in the evenings, toured the countryside during the day, asked politely after Susan's welfare in the evenings. They were told that she was coping, though there were two evenings when she left her undermanager in charge and when, he confided, she didn't even want to answer the phone, never mind face the customers.

Alec had been right in his assumption. She'd been polite and thankful for their involvement, but now wanted to get everything dealt with and put behind her. She was embarrassed by her own worries and hopeful that Alec would let things be. Alec duly backed off, but Naomi could tell he didn't like it and that his own feeling of unease was growing.

The phone call from Sergeant Andrew Dean came out of the blue. Alec had left him several messages, but had not had them returned.

'He wants to meet up,' Alec said. 'Lunchtime.'

'Then let's go. It must be nearly that. Did he say what for?'

'No, but he didn't sound happy.'

They met him in the same pub where they'd had dinner. Naomi and Alec, having further to go, arriving just after. Dean, who was now seated on the furthest side of the bar, was nursing a pint. Alec paused to get them all drinks before joining him. The barrel body seemed ill-suited to sitting on a bar stool, and when Alec suggested they adjourn to a table, he agreed. 'Didn't know if you'd be able to see me,' Sergeant Dean explained. 'It gets a bit busy in here come lunchtime.'

Busi*er*, Alec thought. Still not exactly crowded; though, he supposed, it depended what you were used to. 'So,' he asked as they seated themselves. 'What did you want to tell us?'

Dean took a long gulp of his beer and then wiped his mouth on the back of his hand. He was frowning. 'Well,' he said. 'It'll be common knowledge by evening, but I wanted you to have a heads-up and thought maybe you could be on hand for Mrs Rawlins too. She's going to be upset. I've arranged to meet her later on this afternoon.'

'Eddy was pushed,' Naomi guessed.

'Ah, no. He wasn't pushed. He was hit and then he fell. It wasn't obvious because when he hit his head on the tiled floor, it obscured the original wound. There was blood and bits all over the place so it wasn't possible to tell what was what. Then, when the doc cleaned him up and had a closer look, there it was. A long dent that transected the bash from where he'd smashed his head on the tiles.'

Naomi sipped her drink, trying to hide her smile. Sergeant Dean's mix of technical and vernacular language amused her, despite the seriousness of the news.

'So, someone hit him. Was that the cause of death?' Alec leaned forward across the table.

'No. COD was definitely the fall. He might have had a concussion from the first blow but it had hardly broken the skin. The doc reckons whoever hit him wasn't very good or very committed. Like, they didn't put any force behind it.'

'So, they weren't angry with Eddy. It wasn't a fight.'

'Don't look that way. More like they hit out but it wasn't something they really understood – not the violence, I mean. Like, they hesitated first. I mean, doc reckons it would still have laid him out for a second or two, but that's all. It wasn't enough to kill him.'

'But he fell anyway and he died.' Alec frowned. 'So he wasn't pushed.'

'Not down the stairs, no.'

Alec looked up sharply. 'But?'

'Well, if he'd been pushed down the stairs then that micro-bruising you told me to look for would have been here, on the shoulders, right?'

'Probably.'

'Well, there was bruising all right but it was all down here.' He indicated the length of his arm. 'And then here, on the temple. Where it was obscured by damage done when he landed. So, Doc and I thought about it and he did a bit of experimenting with his assistant and we think what happened was this. Eddy was at the top of the stairs. Someone shoves him into the wall, right on the corner. Shoves him hard and he bruises his arm, hits his head. He's stunned, he falls. He hits his head at the bottom and he dies. And we know he fell with a lot of momentum. No grazes anywhere, see, he didn't slide. He bounced off that wall and he fell outward. Crash.'

Alec was almost glad that Naomi could not see the arm-waving actions with which Sergeant Dean demonstrated such an action.

'Do you think he disturbed someone upstairs?' Naomi asked. 'Did you check the upstairs for signs of entry when you were there?'

For the first time that afternoon, Sergeant Dean seemed hesitant. 'Well,' he said. 'I didn't like to go trampling about upstairs. I checked the scene downstairs and made sure it was all secure, but the paramedics and then the ambulance was there and it all seemed very straightforward at the time, you know?'

'There were no open windows when I went there with Susan,' Alec said thoughtfully.

'Well, then. Maybe that visitor he had. The mugs were still on the table when I let SOCO in today. Did you touch them, either you or Susan?'

Alec thought. 'No,' he said. 'I'm almost sure

not.'

'Well, if you could drop in, we'll make sure we've got your prints for elimination.'

Alec nodded. 'So the cottage is a crime scene now.' He wondered if anyone would bother to go into Karen's room, or if they would, as he had done, just stand on the threshold. Would anyone notice the pocket of the dressing gown? Should he mention it?

'You said this would be common knowledge by evening?'

'Papers,' Dean said. 'It'll be in the evening news.'

Alec felt oddly deflated as they drove back to see the farm. They had promised to give Susan a ring after Sergeant Dean had spoken to her – he was planning on taking a female officer with him and had declined Alec's offer to be there with a slightly affronted tone.

'You wish you could get involved, don't you?'

'A bit of me does,' Alec admitted. 'A part of me feels annoyed that I was right. I'd have been happy enough to be told that Eddy died of a freak accident and the world isn't really full of people doing unpleasant things to other people. Sometimes it feels like you can't get away from it, however far you go.'

Naomi's burst of laughter seemed inappropriate but she couldn't help it.

'What?' he said.

'However far? Alec, we've driven a couple of hundred miles, not crossed continents.'

'You know what I mean.'

She choked back the laughter. 'Yes, I know what you mean. But it's not *our* investigation. It's a local matter and you can't get involved. Not unless Susan still wants your help tracking down relatives or something.'

'Oh, I doubt they'll need looking for, not when this makes the news. They'll be turning up in droves, wanting to know what the old man left and if they're entitled. When they find out they're not, they'll be looking for compensation for mental anguish or some such.'

'My, we are feeling jaundiced, aren't we?'

'Well, yes. One of us is anyway.'

She reached out and touched his arm. 'They might not hear about it,' she said. 'We can be pretty sure that Eddy and his wife and daughter travelled a long way from their family, in metaphorical terms at any rate. Who knows how far they came in real miles?'

Evening brought pictures on the local news of Eddy's cottage and a lone policeman standing outside. SOCO, it seemed, had been and gone, and just a pathetic band of white and blue tape now defined the scene. The lone officer had been left there to keep press and public at bay and to take the inevitable flowers from friends and strangers who, now they knew the cause of Eddy's death, needed to express their additional grief.

Alec had spoken to Susan on the telephone. She was deeply upset; understandably so. And guilty. What if she had encouraged Alec to get more involved? Would they have already known what had happened? Would they have already caught whoever did this to her friend?

Alec thought that unlikely. He'd had nothing to go on – nothing but a vague feeling based on the presence of an earlier guest, who may, or may not, have had something to do with Eddy's death.

She would not be reassured.

'Have you spoken to the solicitor at all?' he asked her, and her response helped him to understand this additional guilt.

'He'd made a will,' she said. 'Left a few bits and pieces to friends. He's left the house and everything else to me. Alec, I don't know what to do. I had no idea.'

'Look,' Alec said gently, 'you obviously meant a lot to him. He'd known you a long time and you'd always looked out for him. I suppose he felt he'd like to return the favour.'

'But I feel so bad. What if the family turn up and contest?'

'What did the solicitor say?'

'That the will was watertight. That Eddy made his feelings very clear and no one can contest it and have a hope of winning, but Alec—'

'Take it,' Alec said. 'You'd become his

family. Say a big thank you and honour what he wanted.'

She was silent for a moment but then, 'Thank you, Alec. That's what the solicitor said. I just wish it had all come about differently and I was finding this out in twenty years' time or so. It just doesn't seem fair.'

There wasn't a lot more he could say to that, so with a few more words of reassurance, he rang off.

'You think that will make her a suspect?' Naomi asked him.

'Not a serious one. Chances are, once they've established a time of death, she'll have a good alibi, most likely backed up by all the locals at The Lamb. Probably by us too.'

'So we're back with the mysterious visitor. Hopefully, there'll be fingerprints on the mugs.'

'And he'll have a record.'

'That too. So what do we do next?' Naomi asked.

Alec frowned. 'I don't know yet,' he said.

ELEVEN

Kevin Hargreaves had, of course, heard about Eddy's death, but it had not quite clicked that the night the older man had died was the night Kevin had visited late. In fact it wasn't until he was getting his pack ready for a weekend out with his detector that he remembered, and that was only because of the shirt and jeans Eddy had washed for him.

He stood, holding the clothes in his hands and trying to come to terms with the fact that he, a grown man who prided himself on being, well, just a bit of a macho type, was crying like a flipping baby.

'Whatever is the matter with you?' His mother stood aghast. 'Are you sick, boy?'

'No, I was just thinking. I seen Eddy, you know, just before he had that fall. I'd stayed there one night.'

'I remember you did, weekend before.'

'Right, well I left my stuff there, went straight to work from his place, didn't I? When I went back to pick it up, he'd done me bleeding washing for me, hadn't he? One of the last things he did, wash me mucky jeans.'

'Oh, stop it now. He was a nice old boy.' She

105

patted his arm. 'You got all the stuff you need in there?'

'I think so. Best check.' He wiped his eyes with the back of his hands and upended the pack, tipping the contents on to the bed. Compass, maps, various historic references he used to make sense of where he was and what he might find. Spare socks, thick and thin. Underwear. He always had more than he needed and some of it stayed in the pack from one week to the next, unused, just regularly checked and then returned to the depths of the bag. It was a habit he'd developed in childhood when he'd gone out with his dad on the weekends he'd spent with him after his parents divorced. It had been the one thing he and his dad really had in common, and by the time Kevin had grown up, there really wasn't even that any more. He and his dad drifted apart, but the hobby remained and the habits that went with it.

'What's that?' his mum said, pointing to a bundle she didn't recognize.

'Don't know,' Kevin said. He picked the bundle up, noting the blue linen and scruffy white lace. 'Looks like a pillowcase. Or a bit of one.' He unwrapped the bundle and laid the contents out on the bed.

'Where did it come from?'

'Eddy's place. It has to have. I've not been anywhere else.'

'But how did it get there?'

Kevin picked up the little book. It was pink

and floral and locked up tight with a brass catch and tiny padlock. The word 'Diary' was emblazoned across the front in curly letters.

She took it from him. 'Locked,' she said. 'Hang on a minute.'

She left the room and Kevin picked up the other documents. Two notebooks filled with close written script that he recognized as Eddy's handwriting. He recognized the books, too. Eddy kept logs of all his finds, buying batches of the same dull-red exercise books he had used when he was still teaching. Kevin scanned the pages, puzzled. He was sure he knew about most of what Eddy had found; the two of them regularly shared their successes and their failures over the odd pint or a cup of tea and 'kiddy biscuits' as Eddy called their mutual choice of creams and chocolate fingers.

Kevin was sure he didn't recognize most of these items.

He looked more closely, realized that not every entry recorded finds. Some appeared to be references to books or documents or parish registers – Kevin recognized the way Eddy annotated them. His mother returned and took the diary. She fiddled with something and then opened the little book and handed it to Kevin.

'There. I knew I had a hair grip somewhere. You can do it with a paper clip, too; any bit of tough wire really.'

'You got it open.'

'Of course I did. So what is all this stuff?'

Kevin sat down on the edge of the bed, flicking through the pages. Two hands had written these pages. The first was clearly young. The letters round and exuberant and, somehow Kevin felt, enthusiastic. The second was Eddy's familiar, tight lettering.

Kevin read a little of the first pages. He knew it to be intrusive and yet felt compelled, as though the voice of his old friend was telling him it was all right to look.

'I think this was Karen's,' he said. 'His daughter's diary.'

'She died, didn't she?'

Kevin nodded. 'Yeah. Eddy told me about her. He said she was seventeen and killed in a car crash. When I first met him he told me he'd had a kid; she died when she was my age, then. He hardly ever talked about her, like it hurt too much.'

'How long ago was it? When she died?'

Kevin shrugged. 'Dunno. I forget. Twenty years ago mebbe. But this is her book, must be.' He closed the book. 'What should we do with it, Mam? I mean, he must have put it in the bag. What did he want me to do with it?'

She took the diary from him and turned the pages slowly, pausing to read extracts. Kevin watched, seeing her lips move as she examined the words. 'Looks like she wrote this in the few months before she died,' she said. 'Look at the dates.'

She sat down beside him on the bed. 'Right,'

she said. 'Eddy trusted you with this, so you've got to figure out why. It was his girl's book, so it was precious to him someway.' She frowned. 'What night did you go back to pick up your bag?'

Kevin thought about it. 'Oh, must have been Tuesday,' he said. 'I went to show him what we'd found up at Bakers Field. Them coins, you know. Mam, what's wrong?'

His mother had turned very white.

'Don't you see,' she said. 'You were there the night he died. What if some damn fool of a policeman thinks you might have been involved?'

TWELVE

Somehow it had seemed more natural for Mrs Hargreaves to go to Susan for advice, rather than straight to the police, and it had seemed equally natural for Susan to go next door to the farm and fetch Alec back to the still-closed pub.

They sat around what had been Eddy's table – that, too, seeming natural – and Alec and Naomi listened to what Kevin and his mother had to say.

Explains the key, Naomi thought, reflecting that quite a bit of potential evidence seemed to have walked from the scene before anyone realized Eddy had been killed rather than just fallen.

Alec listened carefully to what Kevin and his mother had to say. Kevin, he learned, was twenty-two and had known Eddy well. Like Susan, Alec realized, Kevin had a real affection for the old man. His mother, a dark-haired woman who showed every one of her forty plus years – forehead lined, hair showing more grey than brown – was clearly anxious.

'They'll think he had something to do with it, won't they? Because he was there. The police will think he done it.'

'Aw, Mam. Everyone knows I wouldn't hurt Eddy.'

'The police don't know that, boy. How can they possibly know that?'

'What time did you leave?' Alec asked.

'Not sure. I got there at half ten, eleven, maybe. Eddy was in his dressing gown but he let me in and sent me through to the kitchen.'

'Late for a visit,' Naomi commented.

'That's what Eddy said. I told him I didn't think and he said I never did, but he weren't angry or anything. I often called round late. I'd been at Brian's. We'd been playing computer games and I had to come home past Eddy's so I thought I'd drop in. I'd found some coins when we were together at the weekend. Eddy couldn't find them in his books so I'd popped in to see Dr Matthews on the way to Brian's home. Mam, I told you I was going to do that.'

She nodded confirmation.

'Dr Matthews?'

'Local archaeologist,' Susan said. 'He helps run the portable antiquities scheme. You know, where people report what they've found and if it's valuable they get the money for it.'

'There's a bit more to it than that,' Kevin protested.

'Well, we'll come back to it,' Alec intervened. 'So you went to Brian's. At what time?'

'Be seven-ish. We ordered takeaway. I left maybe ten fifteen, ten thirty. News was on. I was passing Eddy's door so I stopped off to get my stuff and tell him what Dr Matthews had said about the coins.'

'How long does it take to get from Brian's to Eddy's?'

'Ten minutes, maybe. No more.'

'Not the way you drive.'

'Mam!'

'So,' Naomi said. 'If you left when the news was still on, that finishes at half ten. You couldn't have arrived at Eddy's any later than, say twenty to eleven. And you stayed, how long?'

Kevin had clearly been thinking about it. 'I went through and put the kettle on and he went upstairs. He was gone a few minutes. I'd made the tea by the time he got down. He'd said use the big pot, so I knew he wasn't annoyed about me coming late. If he'd wanted just a quick cuppa, to be polite, and then wanted to get to bed, he'd have said to use the blue pot. That only holds enough for a couple of mugs.'

Susan laughed. 'Eddy had a complete code wrapped up in his tea making,' she said.

'Like the pink stripy mug,' Kevin agreed.

'Stripy mug? Never mind, tell me all about it later. Let's get the timeline established, shall we?' Alec had slipped into work mode. 'So, you drank tea.'

'Ate biscuits.'

'Talked about the finds. How long would all that have taken?'

'Maybe an hour. I think it was no more than

that. Eddy liked his bed. I'd not have kept him up past midnight anyway.'

'You're sure of that?'

'Certain. I heard the kitchen clock strike eleven, but I'd left before it struck twelve. Certain.'

'That's the clock on the mantelpiece,' Susan chipped in. 'Eddy was fanatical about keeping that one wound.'

'And you saw no one. Heard nothing?'

Kevin shook his head. 'On that road at that time of night there's no traffic. I'd have noticed anything. I drove home, got in about half past twelve, I suppose. Stopped for petrol at the all night place at the supermarket.'

'Supermarket?'

'In Glastonbury.'

'Do you have the receipt?'

Kevin shrugged. 'Maybe. It'll be in the car.'

'He should be on their CCTV,' Naomi suggested.

'And when do they think Eddy died?' Susan asked.

All eyes turned on Alec and he could feel the pressure, their keenness that he let Kevin off the hook. 'Because the body wasn't found until the day after, probably a full day after, and because there were no suspicious circumstances at that point, no liver temperature was taken. And because the post-mortem wasn't carried out for several days it's all a bit approximate,' Alec said. 'Best estimate, and it is only an estimate, is anything between midnight and five in the morning. They may be able to narrow that.'

'So they'll still think it might be me.' Kevin was disconsolate.

Alec thought about it, wondering what words of comfort he could offer. Wondering, too, if this young man was a better actor than he appeared to be.

'The teapot and mugs, were they still on the table when you left?' Naomi asked.

'Yeah. I offered to wash up but Eddy said it would only take a minute. Then he was off to bed.'

'So you left and Eddy didn't get to tidy up. For some reason, he went upstairs and, if we're logical about it, that has to have been pretty much straight after Kevin left, but we know he wasn't going to bed because he'd not washed the mugs. So, did he hear something?'

'Maybe he just wanted to use the bathroom,' Susan suggested. 'There's a downstairs toilet, but it's outside, next to the old coal hole. He'd not have used the outdoor one, that time of night.'

'Whatever the reason, he went upstairs and someone killed him. It could have been acci-dental, of course. The indications are someone gave him a shove, he hit his head, and then he fell. It was smashing his head on the tiles in the hall that actually killed him, but...'

'But whoever they are, they were respon-sible.' Susan was adamant.

'But it wasn't Kevin,' his mother said.

'Of course not. We've just got to make sure the police know that.'

'Do we have to go to them?'

Alec could hear that Kevin was scared, out of his depth.

'I'll go with you,' he said. 'Better to get it over with. But, in the meantime, Susan, do you have a photocopier here?'

'Well, there's one of those all-in-one printer copier things in the office. Why?'

'I'd like to copy the diary and the exercise books before we hand them over to the police, that's all. I know it's not strictly my business but...'

'No, but it's certainly ours,' Mrs Hargreaves stated flatly. 'Eddy gave those things to Kevin for a reason. If you can help us work out why, then that's what Eddy would have wanted us to do.'

They spent the next hour copying the diary and the closely written text of the books. Naomi took the copies back to the farmhouse while Alec left with Kevin and his mother, having called ahead to make sure they would be met by Sergeant Dean. Susan had phoned the solicitor that handled Eddy's will – 'just in case', as she put it – and he was arranging for someone to meet them at the police station, should they feel the need for legal counsel. Naomi, saying goodbye to Alec, knew they'd be gone for a much longer time than Kevin or his mother expected.

Kevin was the first lead the police had in the case, and they would be glad to have something, anything, positive to report, even if that something turned out to be a false dawn. She and Alec had been in the same position enough times to know how they'd be thinking.

Had Kevin had anything to do with Eddy's death? Instinct screamed no, but instinct also told Naomi, and she knew it would be telling Alec the same thing, that Eddy had been expecting trouble. He had hidden the diary and the books and the key and the photographs for a reason. He might not have expected to be killed, but he knew something was wrong, that he was in trouble.

Why, then, had he not confided in anyone? Or had something happened on that day to make him realize that the situation was escalating? And, if so, had he seized the opportunity to hide those papers when Kevin had so unexpectedly turned up? He'd clearly been reluctant to involve his friend before, so what had happened on that day that had caused him to change his mind and use Kevin?

The other conclusion she had reached was this. Whoever had killed Eddy, accident or not, had not discovered where Eddy had hidden those papers. If they had, then Kevin or his mother would have been targeted, Naomi was sure of that.

Had they searched the house after Eddy had died? If so, then it had been a tidy search, but had anything else been taken? Susan had mentioned nothing, but then, when she'd gone there with Alec, they had been focussed on looking for evidence of relatives, not on finding something they hadn't even known existed.

Susan should go back, see if she noticed anything out of place or no longer there.

Was the house still a crime scene or had the officer left?

Making up her mind, Naomi turned around and let a puzzled Napoleon lead her back to The Lamb.

'We need to go back to Eddy's house,' she said.

'Why? Won't the police still be there?'

Naomi shook her head. 'I doubt it. They won't waste resources like that. The house will be made secure and that's that.'

'But go back, why?'

'Just a feeling,' Naomi said. 'Susan, you weren't looking for anything that might be missing last time. You and Alec were focussed on one thing, not on the bigger picture. If Eddy felt he had to hide those documents, then they must have been important to him. If whoever killed him came looking, then they might have searched the place before you and Alec did and there's just the possibility they might have removed other things.'

'I'm not happy about going back there.'

'Napoleon and I will come.'

'You think it's important?'

'Yes, I do.'

'OK, then. We'll do it, but I'm sure we didn't miss anything. OK, let me take your arm and we'll get my car. Napoleon can go in the back.'

'You've still got your key?'

'I've still got the key,' Susan confirmed. 'And I've just sort of realized. Once everything's gone through it's not going to be Eddy's house any more, is it? It's going to be mine.'

THIRTEEN

'Careful of the mud,' Susan said. 'Now, there's a shallow step. Just let me get the door undone.'

In the end she had decided to leave Napoleon behind. At The Lamb, this time, the lunchtime staff having started to arrive just as they were leaving. Harness off, so he knew he was off duty, Napoleon had been enjoying the adulation of the chef and the bar staff as Naomi departed.

'So, describe the place to me,' she said, standing in the hall and aware of the smooth surface beneath her feet and the chill of a house that had not been heated for several days.

'OK, right, where to start. Stairs ahead of you to the left, the hall carries on into the kitchen. On the right there's a door to the living room, and to the left there's what was the dining room when Eddy could be bothered, but mostly he used it as a study cum storage cum junk room.

'There's a little table just near the front door with the telephone on it and the door is wood and has glass in the top part with a sort of coloured glass fleur-de-lis thing in the middle. Black and red and white tiles on the floor. Edwardian or Victorian, I suppose. There's a mat near the door, but no rug. He didn't like putting rugs down, said people slipped on them, but I think when the old one wore out he just didn't bother replacing it. And just now, there's black and grey powdery stuff everywhere. You'd think he never cleaned.'

'That'll be the fingerprint powder,' Naomi said. 'Try not to touch any of it. It's a swine to get out of your clothes.'

'You think we should be here?'

Probably not, Naomi thought. She had the strongest feeling, now, that the CSI would have to come back, but she couldn't say why, not yet. It was just a feeling. She wanted to ask Susan if the house felt 'right'. If it felt as it had done last time she was there, if it still felt like Eddy's house, but she knew that would sound foolish. Though she knew too, beyond doubt, that the answer would be 'no'.

'OK.' Naomi focussed on her mental picture. 'Which rooms did you know the best?'

'Living room and kitchen, I suppose. I only went into the study occasionally. It was the one messy room in the house.'

'Messy?'

'No, that's not fair, really. Eddy used to pin stuff to the walls, have stacks of his research notes laid out, that sort of thing. *He* knew what it was all about, but it made no sense to anyone just glancing in. Looked just like a big mess.'

'I think we'll keep that for last. Did you go in there when you'd got Alec with you?'

'Well, briefly. To be honest I wasn't happy

about even being there. That was Eddy's private room and it didn't seem right. I had a quick look for any address books or letters he might have kept there, but didn't find anything, so we left it. I think we'd both had enough by then.'

'So, if we do the kitchen first?'

'OK.'

Susan led her forward, taking her hand as the hall narrowed. Naomi let her free hand trail against the wall. Wooden panels clad the space beneath the stairs and she felt the latch of a door. 'Cupboard under the stairs.'

'Hoover, ironing board, laundry basket. That sort of thing. OK, come into the kitchen. Right, we've got the quarry tiled floor, table right in front of you. Not much in the way of worktop, so Eddy used it for preparation too. The stove is to your left, in a sort of alcove. On the right there's a fireplace. It has its own chimney. The one in the living room links up with the old, closed off ones in the bedrooms. I know that because I had to find him a chimney sweep a couple of years ago. Sink under the window so he could see out into the garden.' She paused. 'What else do you want to know?'

'Anything that might be different? Take a look in the drawers and cupboards too.'

She stood still, listening to Susan opening doors and drawers.

'No,' she said. 'It's just as I remember it. I mean, not that I went through the drawers or anything. The clock's stopped,' she added sadly. 'Eddy used to be so careful about winding it.'

Naomi heard her cross the room towards the fireplace. 'What kind of a clock is it?'

'Oh, nineteen thirties. One of those wooden things with the round face. Nothing special, but he liked it, and it kept good time, considering. Maybe I should take it with me, keep it wound. What do you think?'

'I don't see why not. What else is on the mantelshelf?'

'Right. Well, it's a high wooden shelf and the fire has a tiled surround. On the shelf there's, well, the clock, and the brass pot where he kept the key. I think it's made of an old shell casing he got somewhere. There's a couple of candle-sticks: one brass, the other pewter. He kept them handy. They're a bit prone to winter power cuts out here. A photo of his wife and—Oh.'

'What?'

'There *should* be a picture of his wife. It was in a pretty silver frame, and one of Karen too. One each side of the mantelpiece.'

'Would he have moved them?'

'I don't see why. They stood up there all the years I knew Eddy. Why move them now?'

'Anything else missing?'

'Not that I can see.' Susan sounded tense now, anxious.

'Where did he keep other family photos?'

'In the living room. He had an album and a

couple of pictures on the shelf.'

Together they went through to the living room and Naomi listened as Susan rummaged in the sideboard, which was where she was certain Eddy kept the albums.

'I don't understand it,' she said at last.

'Tell me?'

'Well, I'm sure they were all together in here. There was a wedding album, which I never saw inside. Then some books just full of Karen and Martha when Karen was young. School photos, holidays, birthdays. Just ordinary stuff. Well, *they* seem to be gone, *and* one of the more recent ones. Eddy had this little digital camera, just a cheap thing, but he took it everywhere and he documented all the finds with it. Took pictures of everyone when they were out together, you know?'

'Yes, I know.'

'Well, *I* know that there were four albums filled with that stuff. Finds and detectorists and well, you know, men getting drunk and playing the idiot. Three of them are still there, but the most recent one is gone. What do you make of that?'

She was trying hard to sound calm, but Naomi could hear how shaky she really was.

'I don't know. Could he have taken them into the office?'

'We should look.'

Again, they went together. Susan's hand was shaking as she drew Naomi's through her arm.

'Oh my God.'

'What is it?'

'Well, it's the office. It's like someone came in and chucked stuff everywhere. I mean, I said it was untidy, but it wasn't like this.'

'Not when you were here with Alec?'

'No. No way.'

'OK.' Naomi took a deep breath. 'So we're not the only ones looking for something. The big question is, what?'

FOURTEEN

Kevin was understandably nervous, and Alec did most of the talking, aware that his position as a serving officer both gave him kudos but also meant that he was treated with understandable suspicion. This was not his patch; he couldn't just come along and butt in to local affairs.

Sergeant Dean arrived shortly after, and Alec and Kevin were handed over to him. He led them into an interview room and then excused himself, saying he'd try and rustle up some tea or something. Clearly, Alec thought, he'd been caught off guard by their sudden arrival, and he was probably also taking a moment to search his memories and check for anything indiscreet he may have let slip when he'd met Alec so informally in the Bridgewater pub.

'What happens now?' Kevin, seated nervously at the table, glanced around the small room as though looking for a means of escape.

'Well, you'll make your statement, tell Sergeant Dean and the other officer he'll bring in with him what you told us. We'll hand over the diary and exercise books and then I'll run you home.' Hopefully. If they held Kevin for further questioning, it could take considerably longer and get far more complicated than that.

'They'll think I did it, won't they?' The young man was pale and already flustered. Alec was glad of Susan's foresight in phoning the solicitor. Hopefully he'd have sent someone over soon. Kevin was anxious already; he wasn't going to be his own best witness.

'Just give them the facts,' Alec said. 'I'm not going anywhere, Kevin. I might not be able to sit in on the interview, but Susan's sorted that out and you'll have legal counsel with you, so don't worry. Just tell the officers what you know and don't let them push you into speculating about anything else.'

Kevin stared, alarmed. 'Like what?' he asked.

I'm not doing a good job of this, Alec thought. His attempts at reassurance seemed to be having the opposite effect. He wasn't used to sitting on this side of the table. 'It will all be fine,' he said with as much certainty as he could muster. He noted that Kevin did not look convinced.

Alec took stock of the little room Sergeant Dean had left them in. Small, windowless, more of a broom cupboard than a proper interview room. The table, he noted absently, appeared to be one half of a table tennis table, and the chairs were that ubiquitous metal framed, orange plastic variety the British police force must have acquired as a job lot way back in the sixties.

A grey Linoleum tiled floor and dark-green walls added to the general sense of make do and mend and long overdue redecorating that Alec was also familiar with. He had spent large chunks of his adult life in rooms like this, but he couldn't recall them looking so bleak and dismal before.

It was that 'wrong side of the table' feeling again.

The door opened and Sergeant Dean entered with another officer. Dean was carrying a tray of mugs and he set it down on the table before introducing: 'Inspector Blezzard. Help yourselves, there's sugar in the bowl.'

Blezzard took a seat opposite Kevin and looked expectantly at Alec. 'So what's your involvement, Inspector Friedman?'

'Nothing official. I'm here on holiday and right now I'm just moral support.'

Blezzard considered that, nodded briefly as Dean put two sugars in a mug and set it down at his elbow. 'So?' he said. 'Fill in the background for me.'

So far so friendly, Alec thought as he began, noting that Blezzard's focus was entirely on him, and Kevin all but ignored. It was Dean, fussing with the tea and finally taking the other chair, who quietly studied the young man, watching for his reaction to Alec's words. Alec recognized the technique, had used it himself on occasion; knew that information, informally gathered in this pre-interview chat, though it had no legal use in and of itself, was often what provided the wedge driven into the statement when the formal interview began.

'We're staying at the B&B next to The Lamb,' he said. 'Eddy, Edward Thame, he was a regular there and the manager was a good friend. She, Susan Rawlins, was the one that discovered his body. She knew that I was a police officer and she asked for my advice in tracing next of kin. Susan felt she had to take that on, that and organizing Eddy's funeral. This was, of course, before anyone realized his death may not have been accidental.'

'But you had your doubts?'

Alec frowned. Had that been true? 'I think,' he said, 'that I was trying very hard not to have doubts. I'd come down here on holiday, after being involved in a very difficult case. I really didn't want ... I didn't really want the darker side of life intruding, I suppose, but...'

'But?'

Alec sighed, suddenly feeling that he and not Kevin was being interviewed here. He described how he and Susan had gone to the house to look for names of potential kin. How they had found nothing, but had noted the teapot and mugs that Susan had considered strange because Eddy was so meticulously tidy.

'We didn't find anything useful that day,' he explained, 'but Susan seemed uneasy and she gave me Sergeant Dean's phone number. He was good enough to extend the professional courtesy of agreeing to meet and I explained Susan's concerns.' He noted that Dean relaxed as Alec stressed the word professional.

'So he told me,' Blezzard said. He waited as though Alec might find more to say, his gaze fixed on Alec's face. Alec looked back, noting that the man must be close to retirement age. Either that or he'd aged badly. Blezzard was creased and worn, with a face like old, tanned leather and calloused, solid hands that should have belonged to a manual labourer. Alec wondered what he liked to do in his off duty hours. Blezzard's eyes were the palest grey, flecked with green, and his deep crows' feet hinted that either he laughed a lot or spent his days squinting at the light.

'Then we had the news that Eddy's death was suspicious,' Alec continued quietly when it was plain that Blezzard had no plans to break the silence.

'And then you discovered that our young friend here was with him on the night he died.'

Alec nodded. 'Kevin hadn't made the connection until today.'

Kevin cleared his throat, 'Mam said we ought to tell someone so we went to The Lamb and we told Susan and she went next door and fetched Alec, here.'

'And it didn't occur to you that your first call ought to have been to the police?' Blezzard asked.

Kevin thought about that. 'No, not really,' he

said.

Alec hid a smile, had the strangest feeling that Blezzard did the same.

'Right,' Blezzard said. 'We're going to need a statement from you, Kevin, and I'm going to need to record a formal interview. No doubt Alec has told you this?'

Kevin nodded, the panicked look back on his face.

A soft knock on the door interrupted proceedings and a female officer opened it, smiling at no one in particular as she informed them that 'Mr Hargreaves' solicitor' had arrived.

Blezzard looked to Alec for explanation.

'Susan was worried, and so was Kevin's mother, so Susan called Eddy's solicitor. He said he'd have someone come over and make sure Kevin was all right.'

'Any reason why he wouldn't be?' Blezzard asked innocently.

Alec had played that game too. 'Yes, actually,' he said. 'Kevin's never been in trouble, only ever seen the inside of a police station on a school visit. He's bound to be anxious. I told Susan that I thought it was a good idea, as I didn't think you'd let me sit in on the interview.'

He let that inferred question hang on the air. Saw Blezzard consider it, then shake his head.

'I think one accompanying adult should suffice,' he said.

A second knock at the door brought the message that Alec was wanted on the phone. His hand automatically went to his pocket and then he remembered he'd switched off his mobile when they'd arrived. His second thought was that only Naomi, Susan and Kevin's mother knew they were here. What was wrong?

He excused himself, passing in the corridor a man in a sharp grey suit that spoke of legal counsel arriving, and followed the female officer to the front desk.

He listened as Naomi told him about their visit to the house, turned as he heard Dean and Blezzard coming through from the interview room, having left the solicitor and his client to consult.

'You'll want to hear about this,' he said. 'My wife has just called. She and Susan Rawlins went back to Eddy's house.' He noted the raised eyebrow and quizzical look. Decided that, as he didn't know why either, he wouldn't rise to the bait. 'Someone's been in there since I went over with Susan. They've searched the place, ransacked Eddy's office and taken several photographs. Susan doesn't know what else.'

'Photographs?' The quizzical look developed further but was no longer directed at Alec. 'Why would anyone take photographs?'

Why indeed, Alec thought, guiltily recalling that he had done exactly that. Evidence seemed to be leaking from this particular scene with the regularity of a dripping tap. But why indeed?

'Are they still there?'

'No, they got worried and left. They're back at The Lamb.'

'Good.' Blezzard continued to nod, as though listening to some internal debate with which he thoroughly agreed. 'Sergeant Dean will go over and have a chat and I'll get a uniformed presence back at the house. Sounds like the CSI will be back there too.'

He looked at Alec. 'No doubt you'll want to go and see that your wife is all right,' he said, and Alec felt this was more of an imperative than the mild suggestion it appeared to be. 'Your friend, Kevin, is in good hands. He won't notice your absence for the next hour or so. At least that, I'd think.'

'Right,' Alec said, knowing he'd been dismissed but also reassured that there was nothing he could profitably do by hanging around the police station reception. 'I'll be back later. You will keep me informed, of course?'

'I'm sure Mr Hargreaves' solicitor will be in touch,' Blezzard said. 'Nice to have met you, Inspector Friedman.'

Alec shook hands, trying to think of something sensible to say.

He only recognized one of the two women who'd been at the cottage. He knew her as Susan Rawlins and knew that she had been a friend of Edward Thame's. That alone made her the enemy. The blind woman was new to him and he could think of nothing in the albums he had taken, or the notes his father had, which might refer to her.

So, she was new on the scene then. Trouble? Incidental? Did she need dealing with?

The slow burning anger that had been ignited on the day he had found the cards and letters his father had not destroyed had been fuelled by the knowledge that this woman, this Susan, would inherit so much and he had been left with nothing. Somehow the knowledge that this Edward Thame had money and a house to leave to anyone seemed utterly unfair. All his father had left to *him* was a house mortgaged up to the hilt, a pile of debts – which he had no intention of dealing with – and a stack of pathetic birthday cards written out to a girl he had never heard of. It was only when he'd had time to examine the papers more closely, had read the letters and the news clippings and had talked to people who actually remembered the incident – his mother being one – that he understood what his father had been hiding for all these years. The persecution he had suffered.

'The police cleared him,' Gavin's mother had said. 'No evidence to take it to court.' But he had been able to tell by the tone that she'd not believed in her husband's innocence, only that he'd managed to wriggle off the hook somehow. Obviously this Eddy Thame had found him guilty, even though the courts hadn't, and this same Edward Thame had hounded Gavin's father until he'd finally topped himself by getting drunk and driving his car into a frikking wall.

Gavin could remember the father he'd had before Edward Thame had stuck the knife in. Yes, he got drunk and maybe drove when he shouldn't have done. People did, back then. It wasn't such a big deal, was it? But he also remembered a funny, happy man who'd spoilt him rotten and taken him to the football, not just one who had started beating up on Gavin's mother. That had only begun after this Karen kid had been killed and *her* father had started persecuting his.

Gavin felt he was owed. Had Edward Thame given one moment's thought to the family he was destroying? Gavin's dad had kept the whole thing secret all this time. His mum reckoned it was because if the truth had come out about the persecution and the blackmail – not that Gavin was absolutely sure there had been any blackmail, but it stood to reason, didn't it? – that the police would have had to look again, and the longer he kept quiet about it the more guilty he looked. Just like his dad, Gavin thought. He handled everything wrong, though it hadn't always been like that. Gavin could remember a time when his father got things right. Dead right, spot-on right.

But this Eddy person, would he listen to reason? No. Did he want to hear that Gavin's father had been cleared? No. Did he want to hear how Gavin's dad had killed himself, was he interested in that? No, like hell he was.

Gavin took a deep breath. He'd been about to go back to the cottage when he'd seen the car pull up and the women get out, and so he'd moved a bit further up the road and walked back, watched them as they'd got out and gone inside. They'd not even looked his way.

Everyone he spoke to reckoned this old man had money. That he'd found something valuable when he went out with his detector. But then there'd been all the rumours about the old man leaving money and the house and that he had no family. This Susan woman would be the beneficiary.

The rest had been a no-brainer. Find the late Eddy Thame some family. Nephew was good, trying to mend a family rift. Gavin didn't know if he'd be able to challenge any kind of will, but he did know women, especially women like this Susan Rawlins; women could be guilted out of anything if you knew how to strike their conscience. And Gavin knew how to do that. A lifetime of living with a manipulative mother and a weakened father had taught him a lot about human nature. He'd get something back of what he was owed, and Edward Thame owed him a childhood, a youth, a life without all the baggage his father had packed for him and all the resentment a disappointed mother had added to the burden.

He watched the house for a while longer. Satisfied now that the women would be some time inside he drove away, intending to return later. And then again and again. As often as it took until he had everything he needed to enable him to pull off the transformation into Gavin Thame, long-lost nephew looking for belated reconciliation.

'What did you think you were playing at?' Alec demanded when he and Sergeant Dean arrived at The Lamb.

'We weren't "playing at" anything. I wondered what else might be missing, that's all. It's pretty obvious Eddy was trying to hide something. Big question is what, and from who, so get off your high horse and listen.'

Alec exchanged a frustrated look with Sergeant Dean, or he tried to. Dean just looked amused.

They had gathered in the small office Susan used for dealing with the paperwork at The Lamb. Sounds from the kitchen and the post-lunchtime customers drifted through to them. Susan had provided tea and coffee and one of the bar staff had just brought in a fresh pot and set it on the heat pad in the corner.

Susan and Naomi both looked pale, Alec thought. Both upset, as though the experience at Eddy's house had in some way frightened the two women rather than just puzzling them. He knew that Naomi wasn't easily scared, and he didn't think Susan was either, and that bothered him most of all.

'So, these photographs,' Dean said. 'Can you describe them?'

Susan shrugged. 'There was one of his wife and one of his daughter, Karen, both in the kitchen on the overmantel. They were in little silver frames; an art deco style one, and Karen's in a frame embossed with little flowers.'

'Valuable?' Dean said hopefully.

Susan's look was withering. 'The most valuable thing Eddy owned was his metal detector. You can pick up frames like that for bugger all.'

'OK, and the others?'

'A group photo on the living-room bookcase. Eddy, his wife and Karen. Karen must have been about thirteen because it was before Martha took ill. She died when Karen was fifteen. Cancer,' she added, saving Dean the bother of asking. 'I don't know who the woman in the other picture was; Eddy never said and I didn't ask. He said once it was just some relative and he kept it out because he liked the frame. I asked why he didn't just take the picture out and reuse the frame, but he just shrugged. All I know is that it was an elderly lady with a lot of very white hair. It was a pretty frame, though. Lacquer work, do they call it? Black and shiny with little gold flowers and butterflies. Now that one, I'd say, would have cost a bit,' she said, looking at Sergeant Dean.

'Random thieves don't just take photographs,' Naomi said. 'No matter how attractive the frame might be. They take televisions and electrical equipment.'

'Eddy didn't have a lot of that kind of stuff,' Susan mused. 'Even his computer was one someone had given him 'cos their kids reckoned it was useless.'

'What did he use his computer for?' Alec wanted to know.

'Recording his finds, doing his research, I think.'

'But the computer wasn't touched?'

'Well, it wasn't taken,' Susan confirmed.

'Which is not quite the same thing,' Alec agreed. 'Susan, is Eddy likely to have password protected the computer?'

She laughed. 'I wouldn't have thought so. Where was the need?'

'And the photo albums you think are missing?' Sergeant Dean's tone revealed that he was less than interested. Or convinced. 'Are you sure he couldn't have just lent them to someone?'

'Why would he, and what about the other pictures? The albums were just family photos and friends. Nothing important.' She sighed. 'I don't know about the wedding album, I never looked through that one. I think Eddy found it painful. He really loved his wife and child. It broke him into little pieces when he lost first one and then the other in the space of a couple of years.'

'I can imagine.' Sergeant Dean got up and prepared to leave. Naomi could hear in his voice that he thought they were all just creating problems for the sake of it.

'You think this is all cut and dried, don't you?' she said.

'I'm sorry?'

'You think Kevin and Eddy argued over something, that Kevin gave him a shove and Eddy fell and all the rest is just an attempt to get Kevin off the hook by making it sound more sinister. You think we're making this up.'

'Making it up? No. But I think you might all be mistaken, and as to me thinking it's all cut and dried, as you say, isn't that what you're thinking too, only from the other direction? Kevin *can't* be guilty of anything because you've all decided he's not, so you're all looking for reasons to blame someone else. Some mysterious someone that goes around stealing photographs!' He laughed. 'Look,' he continued as Susan began to protest, 'I don't for one minute think the lad meant to do any harm, but yes, I think they argued. Maybe they found something they didn't want to share or hand over to the authorities.'

He laughed harshly. 'For all I know, Eddy found his treasure. But yes, I think the lad pushed him. I'm *more* than prepared to think he didn't mean to do the old man harm, but these things happen and the best thing you can do is accept it, deal with it, move on. Sorry if that sounds harsh, but there it is.'

'You knew Eddy well, didn't you?' Naomi

139

guessed. Sergeant Dean's tone was not the one an officer would normally have adopted. The usual response to her question would have been a soft pedalled, 'No, of course I don't think anything of the sort'. Naomi herself had responded to such accusations many times from distraught family members. His response had been vehement and felt very personal.

'Yes, I knew Eddy, knew them both as it happens. They were older than us by a good bit and they'd had Karen late on in the marriage, but our kids were friends with Karen, one was in the same year, and we all got along well. I saw what he went through when Karen was killed and I thanked God my Gracie had been poorly and hadn't gone with her that weekend because it could have been her funeral we had to go to as well as Karen's. Eddy was a good man, a strong, determined man, and we watched as he all but died from the sheer grief of it all.'

'Your daughter should have been in the car?'

Sergeant Dean sat back down and Susan murmured something about fetching more coffee. Naomi heard her cross the room and bring back the coffee pot.

'Karen, Gracie, Sara Coles and Jill Wellesley had been good friends all the way through school. Jill's dad got a job that meant they had to move away and the girls were all heartbroken, talking on the phone most nights and seeing one another every chance they could.

That weekend, they were all going out together and were staying at Jill's house for the week-end. Then Gracie took ill and couldn't go. Next we know, they're all gone. Karen and Jill and Oliver and Sara. And Oliver's mum and dad going through it the worst because all the other parents blamed him. He was driving that night.'

'And the cause of the accident is unknown, isn't it?'

'The coroner said it was most likely some-thing ran out into the road. A fox or a deer. That Oliver tried to avoid it and he rolled the car and hit the tree.'

'The car rolled? So, how fast was he going?'

She sensed Dean shaking his head. 'No skid marks from Oliver's car. He didn't try to brake, so they figure maybe he swerved hard, hit mud. The road was in a state; rain and muck left from the local farms. We know the car rolled, and one theory is that he had a blowout, tried to correct his line but didn't have the skill. It's a brute of a bend. The truth is no one knows. We just know that four kids were dead by the end of the night. And it could have been five.'

By the time Sergeant Dean had left, Naomi felt drained and yet stretched taut from too much caffeine. She didn't know if she wanted to go to sleep or go for a long walk. Somewhere along the line they opted for the latter and they drove out to the coast to a little village they had found earlier in the week. Kilve was famed for its fossil beach, but today they walked the cliff path, oddly grateful that the exertion of the slow climb and the breath-taking cold and wet wind blowing off the estuary saved them from the need to talk. The drive there had been almost in silence, Alec and Naomi both sinking into their own thoughts and, though they had walked hand in hand for the first part of the cliff path, Naomi wasn't sad when Alec left her to Napoleon's guidance and strode on ahead. She felt oddly proud that he was able to trust her – and the big black dog, of course – even in such a potentially risky spot.

Finally, the breath buffeted out of her lungs and her ears burning from the November cold, Naomi halted and turned her face towards the sea and fully into the wind, hoping that the chill gale would somehow blow the angry thoughts away. At her feet, Napoleon sat and then snuffled unhappily. He was very much an all-weather dog, but he wasn't at all keen on the strong, salt-laden wind.

'Hey,' Alec said. He took her hand.

'Hey. Do *you* think Kevin pushed him?'

'No, not really. Dean sowed the seeds of doubt though, just for a while.'

'But if Kevin didn't do it, then who? Alec, is it possible someone else was there that night? There already, I mean, when Kevin arrived, and that Eddy didn't want them to meet for some reason?'

'Anything's possible. It's the timing that's so

difficult; that, and Eddy's habits. Kevin left, something happened, and Eddy died before he had time to wash the mugs and put everything away. How long does it take to clear up two mugs and a teapot? And yet, from what Susan told us, from what we saw of Eddy, he'd have done that straight away.'

'So, we assume he intended to, that he only went up to use the bathroom. That he was on his way back down when...'

'When someone pushed him down the stairs. Someone who was either in the house when Kevin arrived or who had arrived in between Kevin entering and Kevin leaving. So why did neither of them hear anything?' He paused. 'Right. Come on.'

'Come on where?'

'Well, first to Eddy's house, and then back to see how Kevin's getting along in Blezzard's tender care.'

'But won't the CSI be at Eddy's place? Besides, we don't have a key.'

'I don't need a key, just to see from the outside.' He took her arm and Napoleon huffed to his feet, grateful to be moving again, though he was still obviously grumbling at the fact they'd brought him up to this wet and windy spot in the first place.

'It's getting dark already,' Alec said.

'Can you see OK or are we both relying on Napoleon?'

'It's not quite that dark yet. Naomi, you know

what we've been talking about?'

'You leaving the force, us settling down and having kids and a market garden.'

'I don't remember the market garden. Did I miss something? Well, yes, that.'

'Yes.'

'Well, let's just do it. I'll write my resignation letter tonight and then we don't even have to go back, except to put the house on the market and say goodbye to people and—'

'And you're moving too fast. You promised, remember. *After* the holiday, not in the middle of it, and, besides, if you're intent on getting away from the nasty things people do to one another, just have a think, Alec Friedman. This isn't something that happened at work, it's a thing that happened when you were trying to run away from work, so writing your resignation letter isn't going to insulate you from the fact that you're like that woman in that *Murder She Wrote* thing.'

'You mean, wherever we go I'm going to be tripping over corpses? Nice thought. Thank you for that.'

Naomi gripped his hand. 'What else do you want to do with your life, Alec?'

'Oh, I thought you'd decided on it all. House, kids, market garden. Sounds good to me.'

'Does it? Alec, do you actually have any idea what you'd want to do if you gave up being a policeman? You know, it's not good to just be running *away*. You need to be running *to*.'

'Oh, words of wisdom. OK, we're at the stile, let Dog go and I'll help you over. Bit higher with the left foot. Actually, I do know what I want to do but you'll probably laugh.'

'I will not. Is Napoleon through?'

'Oh, he went under the fence. The wind's dropped a bit. That probably means we're in for more rain. No, what I really want to do is go back to school. University, I mean. Though don't ask me what I want to do. I've got a short-list of five options so far.'

'Seriously?'

'Seriously. To be honest, it's something that's been on my mind for a while, and there's the money to do it now and to move if we sell the Pinsent house as well and—'

'So, do it. You know I'll back you, whatever.' The ground seemed firmer here and she guessed they were now in the car park. She giggled. 'My husband, the mature student.'

'I knew you'd laugh,' Alec said, but she could hear how relieved he sounded and wondered just how long this idea had been festering really, nagging at the back of his brain.

'Do it,' she said again. 'Fresh start, new direction.' And she, too, felt a sense of profound relief. One thing she had realized these past days – and that was that she really wasn't ready to become a parent. A doting aunt, yes, maybe even later on a besotted mother, but not right now. Somehow, she felt that Alec 'going back to school' was a way she, too, could be let off the hook without hurting his feelings. She took a deep breath. 'So we put the kids on hold,' she said.

'You want to?'

'I want to.' She laughed then. 'I wouldn't mind the market garden though.'

FIFTEEN

Back at the car, Alec phoned Kevin's newly appointed solicitor. They'd taken the required break but now the interview was about to continue.

'I've told him to keep his statements short and simple,' Ben Tolliver told Alec. 'He's very upset but that's no bad thing. Blezzard seems to like that.'

'Tell him I'm heading back. What are the chances of getting him home tonight?'

'Good, I think, but I'm guessing Blezzard will keep the pressure on for a bit longer.'

'Um, I don't mean to be indelicate,' Alec said. 'But I'm guessing your fees won't be paid by legal aid, so...?'

'Mrs Susan Rawlins will be covering the costs, I believe. I'm prepared to wait until Mr Edward Thame's estate has gone through probate.'

'So,' Alec mused when he got off the phone. 'Susan's picking up the tab.'

'And that bothers you, why?'

'I didn't say it did.'

Alec started the engine and switched on the headlights. Rain beat down upon the roof of the car and the windscreen wipers were hard pressed to clear the screen even for seconds. It was going to be a careful drive back. 'Forget Eddy's tonight,' he said. 'We won't be able to see a damn thing. We'll go and find out what's happening to Kevin, shall we?'

'I thought you had just found out?'

'Well, yes, but ... You don't mind, do you?'

'No, I don't mind, but remember we neither of us had lunch and Napoleon will want feeding too, so...'

'Right, well, we'll go and see if I can get a word with Blezzard, see if we can liberate Kevin. If not, then back to The Lamb, fill Susan in on what's going on and feed Dog, then take it from there.'

Naomi felt the car jerk over the two speed bumps at the bottom of the hill that led back up into the village. Alec was taking it slow; the road was narrow, single track for the most part, and unpleasant in the dark and the rain. She could feel his impatience though, and it didn't seem just connected to half a mile of slightly awkward track. 'What's bothering you now?' she asked.

'I don't know,' he admitted. 'I want to get back and look at those copies we made,' he said at last. 'I can't help feeling that we've just been wasting time this afternoon when I should have been reading what Eddy left with Kevin.'

'You felt all right about it earlier. Besides, we both needed a break. It helps with the thought processes. Besides, again, you've finally let me in on your plans – and, might I say, it's about time. I'm only your wife, after all.'

'Sorry,' he said. 'I really don't think it had crystallized properly before. No, it just suddenly washed over me. Not the wanting to go back to uni; just the feeling that I was getting left behind, that we should be chasing harder. I don't know, you know that feeling you get sometimes, when things start to fall into place at the back of your mind and you know there's something there but you can't quite pull it into focus.'

'I remember that,' Naomi said. 'OK, so we go and see if Kevin's fine, we see to Dog – and Susan – and then we see what Eddy felt was so important he had to hide it from everyone. You know what's a bit odd though? The way he hid the key, like it was going to stop anyone who found the diary from looking inside.'

'Well, it might have stopped the casual snooper.'

'But he, presumably, didn't keep it where the casual snooper would have seen it. No, what I mean is, you can open those little locks with anything. Kevin's mother used a hair pin but anything would do. The lock was there because it made the diary feel a bit special but I don't think anyone really took the secret bit seriously. No, it's almost like it was symbolic. The key with the article and the photo.'

'Unless we're completely wrong and the key

was for something else? Your first thought was a suitcase or a briefcase. Maybe we got it wrong.'

'Well, Blezzard has the diary now. We can hardly go and ask him if the key fits, can we? Not being as you've failed to mention taking possible evidence from the house. Incidentally, why haven't you told anyone about the key and clipping and photo?'

'I told you.'

'*I* don't count. *I'm* now an accessory. But seriously, why?'

Alec sighed. 'Seriously? I don't know. I don't know why I didn't mention it to Susan on the day or why I've stayed quiet about it since. Just something, instinct maybe, telling me it's important, but I don't know why. Look, maybe I'm losing it here. I'm so used to seeing deceit and conspiracy and evil intent that I can't believe a sad and lonely old man might not have had his own agenda. Maybe she always kept that key in her dressing gown pocket, and maybe the photo was the newest one he had of her, and so maybe it seemed appropriate for him to wrap all three items into a little bundle and hide them in his daughter's room.'

'OK, well as long as we've got that clear in our heads. Actually, what keeps bothering me is that Eddy and his wife broke all contact with their families. Why would that be? What was he running away from?'

'Oh, now who's overreaching?' Alec said.

'Lots of people lose touch with family. I quite like mine, but I don't see them much. If I didn't like them and I'd moved away, I probably wouldn't bother.'

'Not even when your wife and child died? Wouldn't you even think that they might have a right to know about it? The right to mourn?'

'I don't know. If they hadn't got involved when my wife and child were still alive. If they'd maybe not approved of my choices, then I guess not. I might decide they'd forfeited that. Anyway, we're assuming it was Eddy that made that choice. Martha was ill for two years; if she'd wanted to get in touch with her family and make her peace there was plenty of time for her to do that. Wouldn't that have been the natural thing to do?'

'Maybe she did,' Naomi objected. 'Maybe they rejected her.'

'Well, unless someone turns up claiming to be a long-lost distant cousin, we may never know. The way I see it, Susan looked after him so she deserves what Eddy left to her. But that's not what you meant, is it?'

Naomi shook her head. The car had stopped now, Alec waiting to check for traffic before making the sharp turn out of the narrow lane and back on to the main road. 'What I meant, I suppose, is: what if someone from Eddy's past finally caught up with him?'

'Surely they'd have found him long before now. When Karen died it made the television news, apparently, and the papers. Four teens dead in a mysterious car accident? That would have been quite a splash. Which actually begs another question. Why did Eddy choose to keep that clipping and not others? What was it about that particular report? Anyway, surely if anyone was looking for him they'd have found him then. Edward Thame isn't exactly a common name. Karen Thame would have made people wonder.'

'Unless he changed his name.'

'No. People trying to disappear call themselves Smith or Jones or Pritchard, not Thame.'

'Pritchard? Why Pritchard?'

'I don't know; it just came to mind. Look, maybe we're getting too complicated here. Back to bare facts as we know them. Eddy let Kevin into the house at about half past ten. He left just over an hour later, called to get petrol, so there'll be a record of that. He was home by twelve thirty. In all likelihood, *if* we take notice of the unwashed mugs and teapot, Eddy was killed just after Kevin left, which seems to imply that the killer was either in the house or very close by. Either way, he would probably have been aware of Kevin and maybe even delayed his approach because Kevin was there. I mean, Eddy wouldn't have stood much chance against an attacker, not being on his own, but with Eddy and Kevin together, things could have been very different.'

'I thought we were tracing facts, not speculating,' Naomi reminded him.

'True. OK, so, it's likely that Eddy died just after midnight. Next day, when he fails to occupy his usual seat at The Lamb, Susan gets worried and goes to check on him. She says that was about eleven forty-five, after The Lamb closed for the night. She finds him dead, calls the police. Rigor mortis was already well established, according to Sergeant Dean, and the time of death, according to the preliminary report, is anything between midnight and five, largely based on how advanced the rigor was and the absence of any body temperature data. No doubt they'll be able to hone that a bit, but it still leaves plenty of time for Kevin to have gone back or even for Susan to have visited and hit him over the head.'

'Why would she?' Naomi said. 'Oh, if she knew what was in the will, I suppose. So, we're back to those damned mugs. Look, maybe he got tired, thought sod it, I'm leaving things tonight, went off to bed.'

'He still had his dressing gown on; his bed hadn't been slept in,' Alec said.

'True, which supports the idea that he was killed just after Kevin left.'

'Which leaves us with a mysterious stranger either knocking at the door or breaking in and surprising him.'

'What if he thought Kevin had come back for something?' Naomi suggested. 'He closes the door, goes upstairs, someone knocks on the door again, he thinks Kevin forgot something and he opens the door to his killer.'

'Who then has to go upstairs, with Eddy, in order to push him against the wall and then have him fall?'

He had a point. Naomi thought about it. 'OK, so the visitor asked to use the toilet. Logical.'

'Which implies it was someone Eddy was happy to let into the house. Yes, that would work, except, why would Eddy go up with him? The other option, which we will check out once it's light, is that the killer got in through an upstairs window and Eddy heard them moving about.'

'Or that Kevin did go back. Straight back,' Naomi said.

'I don't believe that.'

'Neither do I, but other people will. Other people would have no difficulty with that.'

'People like Blezzard and Sergeant Dean.'

The reception at the police station was blindingly light after the dirty, sodden darkness outside. Alec had run in, splashing through the puddles that had collected in the dips and hollows of the car park. He had left Naomi in the car, listening to the radio. Napoleon was snoring gently on the back seat. Alec had promised to go back for them if it looked as though he'd be a long time.

Alec blinked, willing his eyes to adjust. The stark light from the fluorescent tubes threw sharp shadows across the grey tiled floor, illuminating the scuffs from years of feet and the mud everyone that day had trailed in with them. The rubber-backed mat just inside the door was sodden and no longer even attempting to do its job.

The desk sergeant recognized him. 'Inspector Blezzard came through a few minutes ago,' he said. 'Shall I let him know you're here?'

Alec thanked him and stood impatiently in the centre of the reception area as the desk sergeant stuck his head around a half glazed door behind him and spoke at some length to someone.

'He'll not be long,' he said finally and dropped his gaze back to his paperwork.

Alec studied the posters on the long pinboard hanging on the wall of the reception area. Official directives rubbed shoulders with adverts for lost cats and Christmas fairs, tourist brochures and even a bus timetable. Here, it seemed, the police station was certainly the hub of the local community. Assorted chairs stood in regimented lines against the walls, and a small table had been piled high with magazines and the odd newspaper. Alec was put in mind of a rather downmarket dentist's waiting room.

Idly, he picked up a newspaper from the top of a pile and flicked through it, noting that the same people seemed to be killing one another as they had when he had left Pinsent twelve days before. He had lost the daily habit of newspaper reading since being down here and not really missed it. He dropped the paper back, noting that the one below was of local news. He'd seen it at the B&B. He flicked through that as well, growing steadily more impatient with the length of time Blezzard was requiring him to wait.

An item on the seventh page caused him to pause and look more closely.

'Murder of a gentle man', the headline said, and it seemed to Alec that the header itself was unusual. A picture of Eddy, holding a pole while some children, standing on boxes, peered into or at a theodolite, told him who this gentle man was.

Eddy, it seemed, was well known in the local area for visiting schools and showing his finds. For spinning great yarns that captivated the local kids. Tales of the Pitchfork Rebellion, led by the Duke of Monmouth and defeated by the king's men. Of buried treasure and the little finds that kept seekers like Eddy going year after year. One of the teachers called him inspiring. A Dr Matthews – the history guy, Alec reminded himself – noted him as a major influence in local groups. The picture, it seemed, showed Eddy helping out a group of archaeologists who had invited fifty schoolchildren to a dig site and were explaining everything from initial surveying techniques to washing the mud encrusted finds. The children in the picture were laughing, clearly excited, and Eddy was smiling. A very different Eddy to the one Alec had seen in The Lamb.

'He talks,' Susan had told him. Once you started him off, he talked for England. Only in The Lamb did he prefer to just listen to the company, to be the quiet man sitting alone with his treasure maps and endless speculations.

Alec glanced at the byline. The tone of the article suggested that the writer, Adam Hart, knew the old man well. He folded the paper and tucked it into his coat pocket just as the door to the inner sanctum opened and Blezzard came back through.

'You can give him a lift home, should you want to. I imagine his brief will be heading back to Bristol. He's costing someone enough already without him charging for being a taxi service.'

'You're letting Kevin go?'

'For now. For what it's worth, we've seen the CCTV footage from the petrol station. If he'd just killed someone then he's a damn good actor or he's so cool he's a bloody psycho. He chats for a good five minutes to the cashier; seems they were at school together. Then he leaves and turns his car like he's going home and we pick him up again when he passes the bank in High Street. He could have gone back, of course.'

'But you no longer think so?'

'I'm keeping an open mind. Take him home to his mother. If I want him back, I'll know where to find him.'

157

Kevin was brought through by his solicitor a few minutes later. He looked pale and tired and shaky and touchingly glad to see Alec, a man he'd not even known before that day but who now seemed to be regarded as his agent of salvation.

The solicitor nodded to Blezzard, shook hands with Alec and patted Kevin on the arm. Then glanced at his watch and was gone.

'I wanted a word with him,' Alec said.

'Can't we just go too?'

'Of course. Naomi's in the front with me, so you'll have to share the back seat with Napoleon. Hope that's OK.'

'You could have a full sled team in there and I'd happily squeeze in. I just want to be home.'

Alec nodded his farewells and led Kevin back to the car, moving the big black dog over and seating Kevin inside. It was still pouring with rain.

'Was the solicitor helpful?' he asked as they drove away.

'Mr Tolliver seemed to be doing a good job for me, but I wouldn't know a bad job. I've got nothing to compare it to. Hope I never have anything else to compare it to, neither.'

'Blezzard says he's keeping an open mind, but you're off the hook so far as he's concerned, I'm sure of it.'

'I hope so. I'm not cut out for this. He kept going through stuff in the diary, like I knew what he was talking about. Reading bits out and such. That and the notebooks. I mean, I knew some of the stuff that was in the notebooks, so he made a big thing about if Eddy found something and I wanted it, but I told him, if we found anything good, any of us, we'd be knocking on Dr Matthews' door like a flash.'

'So, how does this work, this small finds thing?' Naomi asked, joining the conversation.

'Portable Antiquities Scheme,' Kevin said proudly. 'Well, it's like this. You're meant to catalogue all finds. Most of us photograph them, and Eddy and me and a lot of the others, we use GPS as well, so anyone will know where and when we've found anything. It's got to have a context, you see. It's no good just picking up a musket ball or a bit of harness and not knowing where it comes from, cos then you won't know how it might have got there or who it belonged to. The real value is in the context, that's what Eddy taught me.'

'And most of what you find, you get to keep, yes?'

'Sure, we record and report and make it available for research, but Eddy had a collection and so do I. It's good, cos then you can compare, you know? Then you know if what you're finding is more of the same or something more exciting. I go field walking too, with a local group. Eddy came along some of the time.'

'So, that's a sort of surveying, right?'

'Yeah. We do it in winter or when there's nothing growing in the fields. Just after ploughing is good. The machinery turns up new finds every year.'

'And these entries in the books, you said you didn't recognize them?' Naomi enquired.

'Not all of them, no. And the way he'd annotated them? It wasn't like he usually does. It wasn't using the GPS, but he knew he could always borrow it if I weren't there. Instead, he did it the old-fashioned way, taking a compass bearing off what he could see round him, like trees and church spires.'

'So, he didn't borrow the GPS and he didn't tell you he was going out,'

'No, that's right.'

'So, back to this, what did you call it, Portable Antiquities Scheme.'

'Right. If we found gold or silver, precious metals, we'd report it, and if there was any value to the find then it gets sold and the proceeds split between finder and landowner. It means, if any of us find something that might be worth money, we'd go to Dr Matthews.'

'And you don't think Eddy would keep anything like that secret.'

'No. Not from me, any road.'

'But he didn't talk to you about the books,' Naomi pointed out.

'But he would have done, if he'd found anything. I know he would. Eddy were like that, honest as the day, and he knew *I'd* have told him. Straight away. That's why I went to see him that night, tell him what I found in Bakers

Field. We'd been up there together and when I went back I struck out.'

'What did you find?'

'Coins. Well, not really coins, more like medallions that's been struck to commemorate something. Two – one silver and one gold – and I reckon there'll be more. Dr Matthews thinks so too.'

'Commemorate what?' Naomi asked.

Kevin laughed. The first time that day he had shown any emotion other than despair or fear. 'That's the thing, you see. They commemorate something what never happened. Dr Matthews reckons as how the Duke of Monmouth had them made to celebrate his victory, but of course he never had a victory. The king won, everyone was hanged or worse, and that was that.'

Alec frowned, recalling something he had read in the pamphlets on the battle of Sedgemoor. 'I thought Monmouth's lot were short of money,' he said. 'That they couldn't afford to pay their army or provision it properly.'

'Yeah, that's the odd thing. Why spend money getting medals struck when you could be paying for more troops? Eddy and me, we talked about it and we reckon it was a sympathizer round here that had them made ready. When it started going badly, maybe he sent the medallions to the Duke so he could fund the invasion. Gold is still gold and silver is silver. He could melt it down, do what he liked with it, but it never got to him. Either that or Eddy reckoned they might have hidden it after the battle, when they knew Monmouth had lost. It's not the kind of thing you want to be found with.'

'Eddy's treasure?' Naomi asked.

Kevin laughed again, sadly this time. 'No, it weren't the hoard he were looking for,' he said. 'That was part of a different story, but I think he'd have settled for this 'un. It would have been a nice end to his story, wouldn't it, even if it wasn't the one he'd been looking for? Better than he got at any rate. Much better than he got.'

SIXTEEN

It was three or so hours later by the time Alec managed to get on to looking at Eddy's notes. They had dropped Kevin off, had had to explain to his mother what was going on, then had briefed Susan and fed a huffy Napoleon before getting an evening meal for themselves. Speculation in The Lamb had been rife, and Alec and Naomi had listened as Eddy was discussed and his life and death dissected. They had gratefully escaped, only to be waylaid by Bethan and Jim, understandably anxious and curious.

Only after reassuring them had Naomi and Alec finally managed to escape to their room, taking a tray of tea with them.

'Right,' Alec said. 'So where do we start?'

'Earliest entries,' Naomi said. 'So, with the diary.'

'Right you are. OK, so she must have had the diary for Christmas, but she didn't actually start to write in it until her birthday, February the twenty-sixth. She says, *"Now I am seventeen, only a year to go until I'm officially an adult so I'm going to record this last year of being a kid, just so I always know what I felt like back here and now so that when I have kids of my own I'll remember and I won't be so hard on them just because they've not grown up yet."'*

'Interesting. Do you think she thought her dad was hard on her?'

'I think we all do. It's part of being seventeen.'

'She goes on, *"So I'm writing in my diary. My dad gave it to me for Christmas as a sort of joke. When I was a little girl I wanted a secret book and he brought me a bright pink fluffy book with a funny little lock on it and I was always losing the key. Then I lost the book. I don't think I ever wrote much in it, I don't really remember. But I took it to the park one day and lost it and I remember how much I cried. At Christmas he brought me this one and he tucked it into the pocket of my new dressing gown because that's what I used to do with the pink fluffy one and he said this was the last 'little girl' present he would ever get me because I was almost grown up now. And then we cried because it was another Christmas without mum and we always cry when we open our presents and see where hers should have been underneath the tree."'*

'Sounds to me as if they were really close,' Naomi said.

'It does, doesn't it? She finishes there, but the next day she talks about a boy she fancies at school who has a girlfriend with spots, and then about a teacher who is *"a complete bitch"*, though she doesn't say why, and she's got the results of her mocks and is heading for high grades in her exams. Presumably her A-levels.'

'Anything there that might—'

'Have to do with Eddy's death? No. She's seventeen; most of the time she seems to be happy. On the eighth of March she says that they are breaking up for the Easter holidays in just over a week and: "*We're all going to stay at Jill's house for the first weekend. It'll be sooo good. Proper time together. Oliver will be there, I suppose, but he's OK. Not what I'd have thought she'd have gone out with. He's got a hell of a nose! But Jill says he's really good fun. Anyway, he's just passed his test! So we can all go out without having to bother the parents all the time.*

"*I wish Jill didn't have to move away. It's all so wrong. She's like my sister not just a friend. I wish I had a sister, but if I had then I suppose there'd be one more person to miss mum and I guess it's bad enough me and dad missing her. You'd think it would kind of get less painful, but it hurts me just as much and I know he hurts such a lot too. Why do people have to die? If I could have one wish I'd bring her back. I'd never have let her go away.*"'

'Sad,' Naomi said. 'And she was dead just over a week later. That's just tragic, isn't it?'

'Very,' Alec agreed. 'There are a couple of other small entries. One seems to be a home-work reminder. It says, "*Hand in project!!!*", and there's a phone number with the name

Steve written under it, but that's all.'

'When does Eddy start to write in it?'

Alec flicked pages. 'July,' he said. 'The year after. The first entry reads, *"I took flowers to both graves today and when I came back I thought I'd just sit in Karen's room for a while. The need to be close to her was terrible. It feels like my heart has been breaking into smaller and smaller pieces every day since she died and for some reason it was so much worse today.*

"I drove past the school last night and saw the kids all going into the Leavers Dance. All of them dressed up and laughing and so alive. The young have no comprehension of how beautiful they are or how fragile. My Karen was so beautiful and oh so fragile in the end.

"She would have taken her exams by now, soon she'd have been off to University, and tonight she'd have got herself all dressed up and I'd have driven her off to meet her friends and I'd have teased her about coming to pick her up at ten, like I always did.

"When Martha died, I thought what I felt then was agony, but I know now that what I felt only scraped the surface of suffering. When the doctors told us what we were facing, we knew we could do it together. I don't think I believed it, not until the day we buried her, but I'd had two years of, not getting used to the idea, but of losing, slowly and gradually, not just such sudden loss. In the end, I was glad Martha had gone. Poor love she was in pain and couldn't

166

stand more of it. Karen and I, we clung to one another and we were neither of us afraid to cry or to talk about what happened to her mum. We shared that and I'm so glad we did.

"But Karen. One minute there and the next minute gone and no rhyme and reason to it. We don't even know what happened, just that Oliver crashed and all four of them died and my Karen didn't get to go to the Leavers Dance and that's just the first of all the things I didn't get to see her do.

"So I came in here and sat on her bed for the first time since the funeral and I saw the diary sticking out of the pocket of her dressing gown and I read what she had written there. My Karen, celebrating her last year of childhood. I'll raise a glass to you tonight, my sweet girl. To you and your mother, and as you can't write in your book now, I'll try and do it for you, try and celebrate it for you, but I won't come into your room again. I'll close the door and let the dust fall and that will be that. Take care, my darling, and I hope you are with your mother now."'

Naomi blinked back tears. 'Poor Eddy,' she said softly. She bit her lip, recalling the losses she had experienced in her own life. Then took a deep breath. 'What else does he write? And why would he give something so personal to Kevin?'

She could hear Alec turning the pages. 'He writes nothing else for a couple of weeks and

167

then there are a few rather restrained pieces. It's as though he's trying to find his way through his own feelings. He talks about seeing friends and going shopping and then in August, on the anniversary of Martha's death, he tells Karen that he can't find the words to do this any more. Everything stops until about eighteen months ago.'

'And what happens then?'

'He finds a ring, apparently. Here, I'll read it to you. "*Gold, with a seal.*" I assume he means a seal as in sealing wax and not sea creature. "*It has been dinted by the plough and the shank is broken, but from the weight and size it was a man's ring and a valuable piece. I took it to show to Matthews and he confirmed that the date is right, though, of course, he doesn't believe it could be part of a larger hoard, the field had been ploughed so many times since 1685, but he agrees with me that the seal is a cedar tree, just as described in the Florenz document. Is it too fanciful to believe that the last wearer of this ring was Henry Kirkwood? And if this much is true what else could be?*"'

'Kirkwood?'

'No idea. Eddy's treasure? The daughter sent away to save the treasure from the king? But the interesting thing is that at the top of the page he writes the words "Bakers Field". Isn't that where Kevin found the coins – medallions or whatever they were?'

'It is. So, did Kevin know about the ring? Did

he make that same connection?'

'Well, I'll phone and ask him, but there seems to be more. Eddy found a couple of coins and fragments of what he thinks are bindings from books. I suppose he means those corners and locking bits you sometimes get on Bibles.'

'Does he say what this Lorenz document is?'

'No, but he mentions it again. A lot of this is going to need an interpreter and a linguist.'

'Aren't they the same thing?'

'Not in this case. My Latin is very rusty. It never was that good, but there's quite a bit of it, like he copied it from somewhere. There seems to be some kind of family tree and something that I think is an entry from a will, but, like I say ... And the interpretation is for all the map location stuff. I'm guessing Kevin can do that bit but a visit to this Dr Matthews seems in order.'

He dropped the diary pages on to the bed and skimmed through those photocopied from the notebooks. 'More of the same,' he said. 'He ran out of pages in the diary and moved on to the notebooks. Kevin was right, Eddy *didn't* intend to hide anything from him, that's why he dropped the books into Kevin's pack, but what made him decide that now was the right time?' Alec sighed. 'This is so densely written it could take weeks to get through.' He fell silent for a moment, then Naomi heard him reach for the discarded copies from the diary.

'Find something?'

'Not sure. He starts talking about some letters, something he received that upset him.'

'What does he say?'

'Well, halfway through the first notebook he says: "*Another of those damned letters arrived. I wish I'd never approached that bastard. And the phone calls. I've changed the number but he's threatening a visit. I hoped I'd made it plain years ago that I wanted nothing more from any of them. My fault, I suppose, but I thought if I made the approach through the solicitor then I'd be protected somehow. If I could have found out another way, then I would have done.*"'

'Strange,' Naomi said. 'But it doesn't have to be about the finds. It could be something else. Family, maybe?'

'Could be. I'll have a talk to the solicitor.'

'Who probably won't tell you. He might tell Susan, though. What's the earliest mention?'

'Hoped you wouldn't ask. God knows! There is so much here.' He flopped back on to the bed. 'No offence, love, but this is going to take more than one pair of eyes and one person reading to you.'

'Then tomorrow we co-opt volunteers. Susan and Kevin and maybe this Dr Matthews. People who can actually understand what Eddy was on about. Any more tea in that pot?'

'Probably stewed. I'll go and get more, shall I? I left my coat downstairs, anyway.'

Naomi heard him pick up the tray and the door swing to as he left. She began to gather the pages he had left scattered on the bed, hoping she wasn't getting them too much out of order. Alec's comment about more than one pair of eyes hadn't hurt, but it had put her slightly out of sorts and made her feel impatient with herself. There were so many things she could still do. Several she could now do that she hadn't been able to before the accident. She was still very patchy when it came to using Braille, but voice activated software enabled her to write and email. She'd taken up swimming again, something she'd left behind long before she even left school. Could apply her own make-up. Could even read ordinary texts, with some really snazzy equipment that scanned pages and read them out loud.

But sometimes the frustration over what she *couldn't* do was overwhelming.

Alec came back up a few minutes later with more tea and his coat. 'I picked up a newspaper at the police station. I'd forgotten. It had an article about Eddy. The journalist obviously knew him well; it's just possible he may be helpful.'

'Read it,' she said.

'"*Murder of a Gentle Man*",' Alec started.

Naomi listened as Alec read the article out and explained about the picture of the children helping with the survey. 'He was well liked and well loved,' she commented. 'Whoever was spiteful enough to take his life, even accidentally, was utterly out of kilter with the rest.'

171

SEVENTEEN

Although it rained all night the dawn brought a glimmer of hazy sunlight and a bitter wind blowing across the levels. Alec took Napoleon out first thing and returned shivering despite his thick coat. Even the dog seemed put out and underwhelmed. He looked reproachfully at Alec, who shrugged. 'I know, I know. The North Sea coast is meant to be the chilly one. Frankly, this one has my vote. Bloody bitter, it is.'

'We get very cold winters down here,' Bethan confirmed. 'The wind seems to pick up all the wet from the land and freeze it through. Sometimes it feels like you're breathing ice.'

'At least the sun is shining and the rain has stopped. I did wonder if we should buy a boat.'

'And herd the animals in two by two? Give it a week or so and it'll all be falling as snow.'

Alec wasn't sure if she thought that was a good thing or not.

Breakfast over, Alec sat down upstairs and began the phone calls. Twenty minutes later he had arranged to meet Susan and Kevin at The Lamb that lunchtime and had appointments with Dr Matthews and the journalist Adam Hart arranged for that morning. He thanked the curiosity of both men for their promptness in agreeing to the meetings.

'So,' Naomi said. 'Where first?'

'To see Adam Hart. He works for a magazine called *History Time*, but also does the occasional feature for the *Bridgewater Gazette* and a couple of other local rags, or so the editor says.'

'I bet he didn't call them rags.'

'No, maybe not. Anyway, it seems Eddy's name opens doors. Mr Hart is expecting us in half an hour. We're meeting him at Westonzoyland Church.'

'Um, why?'

'Because that's where he said he'd be.'

Adam Hart was a tall man. He walked towards them with his hand extended, ready to shake. His loosely jointed knees swung far too far as he strode over, his balding head thrust slightly forward. He reminded Alec of a heron just about to spear a fish.

His smile, though quizzical, seemed genuine, and the hazel eyes were alive with interest.

Alec introduced himself and Naomi. Adam Hart's handshake was firm. He had, Alec noted, massive hands.

'I've borrowed keys for the church tower,' Adam said. 'It's a bit of a climb. I hope you don't mind heights?'

'Not now I can't see them,' Naomi told him.

'Really? Now, isn't that interesting. They

bothered you before?'

It was an unusual start to a conversation, Naomi thought, but the man's interest was so obviously genuine. 'Hated heights,' she said. 'I even avoided ladders, and the high diving board was completely off limits. Now, no problem.'

'Seriously? You dive? Doesn't it bother you that there might be someone below?' He laughed. 'I'm just working out the logistics of that.'

'I go with my sister and her kids. Actually, I'm lying, I don't do the high board, I'm not that good, but I'll dive off the side now. It's embarrassing when your five-year-old nephew can do something you can't so...'

Adam Hart laughed again. 'I can imagine. We're on to grandchildren now. Boy, do they give us the run around. Now, the stairs are narrow and steep. Best leave your dog down here, if that's all right?'

'He'll be fine,' Naomi reassured him. 'So will I. Who is the church dedicated to?'

'Oh, Mary, in her virgin state. It has the most beautiful tower, and they've been doing restoration on the windows. Made a lovely job of it. Not over restored, if you get my meaning. Right, through here. Did you know they kept four hundred prisoners here after the battle? Executed twenty-two of them the following day on the grass outside. No trial, no questions, just a length of rope. Then the King charged the villagers the cost of it all later on. Eddy was fascinated by it, was trying to put some flesh on the bones in that book of his.' They were inside the tower now, climbing the stairs, and his voice echoed loudly.

'Book?' Alec asked from up ahead, his voice somewhat muffled and breathless.

'Oh, didn't you know? He was writing a book. He'd already published a number of articles. Quite the scholar was Eddy Thame.'

Unlike Alec, Adam had plenty of breath for both walking and bellowing, Naomi thought. She concentrated on the worn and slippery stairs and on grasping the rope that served as a handrail.

'Don't worry,' Adam boomed. 'I'll catch you if you fall. I'm too bony for a soft landing though, I'm afraid.'

'Right, so I'll try not to land on you.' How high was this flipping tower? The sound of a door opening and a cold draft on her face told her that Alec must have found the top.

'Wow, what a view. I can see for miles. Is that Bridgewater over there?'

'It is indeed. Take care now, Naomi. If you reach out your hand you'll feel the parapet. That's it. Not a lot of room, I'm afraid.'

Naomi touched the rough stone. She could feel the lichens clinging to the surface and the pitting from centuries of long winters. 'What can you see?' The wind was stronger up here; she had to shout for Alec to hear her across even the tiny space atop the tower. Perhaps this was why Adam was so loud.

Adam touched her shoulder. 'Across to your left you can see Bridgewater. We're high enough you can glimpse the sea on a clear day, which today is not. Now, down there was an airfield. In World War Two, it was home to the 101 Airborne. They ferried spies across to France, or so I'm told. We're on a series of islands here, really. Or would have been before the land was drained. When Monmouth and his ragged little army came here, there were already drains, or rhynes, keeping the villages and the farmland above the water. That, of course, proved to be his undoing.'

'Are those the drainage ditches?' Alec asked. 'I can't make out if that's water or road.'

'Which? Oh, that's the King's Sedgemoor Drain. Not here in Monmouth's time, of course. No, you can glimpse the line of the old drainage ditches. See that border of sedge over there? Many of the old dykes are dry almost year round now, but when the battle occurred they were a major obstacle.'

'Someone failed to find the crossing point,' Alec said. 'I remember reading about it.'

'That's right.' Adam Hart's enthusiasm was evident. 'Imagine, it's a summer night, dark and misty and about two in the morning. Monmouth and the rebels have crept out of Bridgewater and followed the drovers' roads five miles across the moor. They've greased the wagon wheels and muffled the horses' hooves with rags, but even so, every sound must have seemed super loud. One cannon had a noisy wheel, so they abandoned that and also had to leave the ammunition wagon two miles from where the final battle took place. That must have been a major blow. The troops were poorly armed and badly trained and were about to face an army of regular soldiers who were *well* trained and supplied and disciplined. To make matters worse, by the fifth of July, many of those who had originally joined Monmouth's cause had already deserted – taken up the offer of the King's amnesty and quietly gone back to their homes.'

'It wasn't totally hopeless, though, was it?' Alec argued. 'If they'd managed to sneak up on the King's army, they would have been at a massive advantage.'

'True, but bad planning and bad luck scuppered them. The King's army, apart from the cavalry which had billeted itself on the surrounding villages, was drawn up behind the Bussex and the Langmoor Rhynes, two of the older drainage ditches. They'd made their camp on higher ground, and most had gone to bed for the night; all except the Scots. Their commander was convinced that Monmouth would make a night attack, and he was right, of course.

'Anyway, Monmouth and his men, some three or four thousand of them, made their way across the moor. They had one or two near misses, but they almost achieved their goal. What was left now was to cross the rhyne and take the fighting to the King's men while they were still encamped. You can imagine the carnage, had that succeeded.'

Naomi, shivering, wished she could be imagining the carnage back down in the church, or even better in the local pub if it had opened yet.

Too early, probably, she thought ruefully.

'But they didn't manage to find the crossing points,' Alec said.

'Right.' Adam sounded triumphant. 'When the troop came to the first of the rhynes, the Langmoor, the local guide failed to find the crossing point. Was he a spy? Did he plan to lead them into an ambush? Or was it just too hard to spot in the mist and dark? I suppose we'll never know, but the outcome was as bad as if he had deliberately misled them. Movement was spotted, a shot rang out into the night, and scouts ran pell-mell back to the King's men camped at Chedzoy, crying out to "beat your drums, for God's sake, beat your drums". You can imagine the scene, can't you? The dark, the frightened and untrained men and their skittish horses, and the King's men scrambling from their beds.'

Naomi shivered again. It wasn't that she was unimpressed by Adam's presentation, but couldn't they hear the rest somewhere warm?

Alec, however, was entering into the spirit of the account. 'Didn't Lord Grey manage to lose the other one?'

'Oh, yes. Now he and his cavalry had been sent to find the crossing point over the Bussex Rhyne. You've got to remember, you're looking for a shallow ford in the dark, in unfamiliar terrain. The crossing, the lower plungeon as they called it, was a point where the drovers' road cut across the ditch, but in the dark, looking for an area of water that was less deep than the water a few feet either side of it? Grey was completely at a loss and, according to some accounts, he'd been too impatient to wait for the local guide. Some of the cavalry did make it across though, under the command of one Captain Jones, who had fought with Cromwell's Ironsides and, it seems, actually knew what he was doing. He led his men against the one hundred and fifty of the King's men who met his advance across the Rhyne. Jones survived the battle and it is significant, in a campaign that was marked by the vengeful nature of the aftermath, that his life was spared, largely because the King's own men spoke of the great courage he had shown.

'But, the truth is, three hours later Monmouth's men had all been defeated and he'd fled the field. As I say, four hundred of them, many wounded and dying, were packed into this church overnight. The records say it was such a mess in the morning that the villagers were forced to scrub it clean and then fumigate, so you can only imagine the kind of mess they were sorting out.'

'And Eddy was writing about this?' Naomi asked, trying to keep her teeth from chattering. 'Do you mind if we go down? I'm frozen.'

'Oh, I am so sorry, my dear. I rarely feel the cold. My wife says it's because I never keep still.' He laughed. 'Let's go down then and I'll tell you about Eddy's book. Pity The Sedgemoor Inn isn't open yet, we could adjourn there, but it's about an hour too early for the time of year. No tourists to speak of in November.'

He led the way downstairs and Naomi concentrated on keeping her footing. The steps were worn shallow in the centre and rubbed smooth after centuries of use. To make matters worse, her feet were now wet. She clung to the rope handrail, aware that Alec's hand was ready to catch hold of her if she fell and that Adam Hart had already bounded ahead. Not even a bony man to fall on, she thought wryly. She could hear his voice booming out, echoing in the church nave as he told Napoleon what a wonderful dog he was to be waiting so patiently.

'Are you OK?' Alec asked as they cleared the last steps.

'Fine, just frozen through. I thought I was good with cold but today is just freezing.'

'Bright and sunny though,' Alec said. 'That really blue sky you get sometimes in the winter, but the wind is too strong to feel the sun and the ground is so sodden. I think Bethan's right; the wind does pick up all the wet and it does chill the air.'

She took his arm and could feel that he, too, was shivering. 'What's the church like?'

'Rather grand. Big wooden pews and nice windows with pointed tops. What style would that be?'

'Norman? Ask Adam, he'll know. Where's he got to, anyway?'

'Um, he's up in the pulpit,' Alec said. 'I think we're meant to be his congregation.'

Taking Napoleon's harness in her free hand and keeping her other on Alec's arm, Naomi walked slowly down the aisle, listening to the particular soundscape of the building. The echo of their feet on the stone floor, Napoleon huffing and yawning, a blackbird singing despite the winter cold. She turned her head. 'There's a clerestory?'

'That line of high windows? Yes.'

She nodded, satisfied. 'I can hear a bird high up outside.'

'Take a pew,' Adam called out to them. 'Sit yourselves down.'

She heard him descend the pulpit steps and Alec's muttered relief. Instead, as they seated themselves in the front pew, Adam took up a position on the altar steps. He *felt* quieter now, Naomi thought, more thoughtful, and his voice was soft when he spoke again.

'Eddy and I were friends for more than thirty years,' he said. 'When I first met him I was nineteen and Karen was ten. My younger sister used to babysit for her and I got to know Eddy and Martha through her. Karen was a lovely kid. Happy and open and very bright. She and Tina, my sister, they used to hire soppy films and watch videos far too late, but Eddy and Martha didn't mind. They'd come home and all have supper together, then Tina would often stay over and Eddy would run her home the next day. Martha was in her thirties when Karen was born and that was more unusual then. Eddy would have been seventy-two next month, had he lived. It seems so wrong that he's gone.'

'You say you became friends. So, more than just brother to the babysitter?'

'Yes. I wanted to study history or archaeology, I couldn't make up my mind what, and you know Eddy taught History?'

'Yes. Did he teach you?'

'No, my parents sent me to a private school. Eddy taught at the local comp, but he talked to me, helped me sort out in my own mind what I wanted to do, and so I ended up doing a combined honours course, then switched to history in my final year, but he was right. It gave me the perfect grounding for what I ended up doing, which is mainly document based research. I went on to do an MA in Museum Studies and specialized in conservation, but we corresponded all the way through university, and the more I learnt, the more equal we became, until, eventually, I helped Eddy get some of his work published and opened doors for him he couldn't open for himself.'

'And this book?' Naomi asked. 'Is it finished?'

'Pretty much, or the first draft is. I'd taken over some of the editorial aspects. Eddy was wonderful when it came to collecting and collating material and bringing episodes alive; he was less interested in the indexing and the final preparation. I was writing a foreword too.'

'And it had a publisher?'

'Yes, yes indeed. In Dublin. They're shocked by Eddy's death but have agreed, since so much is already in place, that I can complete the process.'

'And what, exactly, was the book about?'

'Weeeell. Eddy has already published a series of articles on the so-called Pitchfork rebellion, but from the perspective of the little people involved. A Victorian antiquary, in particular, by the name of Alfred Lorenz.'

'Lorenz? He mentions him in the notebooks,' Alec said.

'Well, he wrote a rather controversial account in the eighteen sixties, apparently based on a box of papers he claimed to have discovered in a Bristol bookshop. Well, wherever he found them, the papers then disappeared for over a century. They finally turned up again in the collection of Frederick Lowe, a local historian and mutual friend of ours. I don't even think he realized what he'd got. It wasn't his period – he was an Anglo-Saxonist at heart – but he bought up anything that looked interesting and his wife thinks he acquired the papers in a house sale somewhere. Eddy and I were allowed to take our pick from his library after he died and between us I think we must have taken fifty or so volumes and a dozen boxes. The rest was donated to the reference library in Shepton. Anyway, the Lorenz papers came into Eddy's possession and he started to research for the book.'

'So, what did they consist of?'

'Well, it's an odd assortment. Maps – some contemporaneous with the rebellion. Letters, notebooks and a family bible from the Kirkwood family, who were quite prominent landowners at the time.'

'He found a ring. A seal ring with a cedar tree. He thought that belonged to the Kirkwoods.'

'Did he? I didn't know about that. But the various accounts intrigued him and he started the book by writing about Catherine Kirkwood. She and a servant were supposed to have been sent off with the family jewels, trying to keep them from the King.'

'The Kirkwoods backed the wrong side. I heard about that. The locals at The Lamb joked that Eddy was looking for the Kirkwood treasure.'

'Did they?' Adam laughed. 'I suppose it may have seemed like that sometimes. Eddy could be a little obtuse. Treasure, to him, was information. I don't think he literally expected to strike gold.'

'Did he ever talk about family?' Naomi asked.

'No. He and Karen and Martha were all that I ever knew about. We never discussed anything like that. I don't think Tina ever did either. It wasn't that he told us not to, just that he never did.'

Susan was leaving for work and just about to get into her car when she saw him. She swore softly. 'Brian, what do you want?'

'I thought I might have another go at talking to you. I don't think I got through the other night.'

'Oh, I heard you all right. I just didn't want to listen. I've heard enough, Brian.'

'Really? You see, I don't think you have. Susan, just hear me out for a minute. Please.'

She sighed. 'You've got thirty seconds.'

'Oh, come on.'

'Twenty seconds.'

'OK, OK, look. It seems to me that we were good for one another, that it was outsiders who pushed us apart.'

'Like Eddy?'

'Well, he didn't help. He was against me from the start. Against us.'

'With good reason. He said you were a liar and a user and you proved to be both. You cheated on me from the first month after we married. You lied about your job, your income, your family, your women. So I think Eddy was right, don't you?'

'And I admit that and I'm sorry. For all of it. Susan, please, let's give it another try. Please. We deserve another go.'

She scrutinized him carefully. 'You've heard about the will, haven't you?'

He shrugged. 'It's no secret that Eddy left you his house, but that's not it. I just want—'

'Money. Nothing changes, does it? Goodbye, Brian. You've had more than your thirty seconds.'

'Susan, please. A loan, then.'

'You make me sick.' She got into her Beetle and drove away, leaving him standing, not noticing the dark-haired man in the red hatchback who'd been watching it all.

Gavin got out of his car and wandered over to where Brian stood. 'Excuse me,' he said, 'but I couldn't help overhearing.'

'Oh, is that right? Well, what's it got to do with—'

'I'm Eddy Thame's nephew. I'm going to contest the will. I just thought that might interest you.'

'Why should it? How does that help me?'

Gavin smiled; the words said one thing, the look in Brian's eyes quite another. Human nature, he thought. Self interest was the one thing you could rely upon. 'Let me buy you a drink,' he said. 'And we can see.'

186

Late morning found Naomi and Alec knocking on Dr Matthews' door in a quiet road in the village of Walton, just behind the village church. The entire village seemed to be constructed of the same grey stone, and in the unexpectedly bright winter sun, blue shadows softened the marl, which Alec knew could be so stark and drab on dull days.

'Mr Friedman, Mrs Friedman, please come in, come along through.' He led them into a small living room at the front of the cottage. Lined with bookshelves and crammed with overstuffed furnishings, the room felt claustrophobic and, to Naomi, muffled and deadened. She sat down beside Alec on a two-seater sofa. Behind her neck a faint draft and a definite chill told her they were sitting with their backs to the front window.

'Good of you to agree to see us,' Alec said.

'Oh, that's no problem. Edward was a friend and a frequent visitor. A knowledgeable one too.'

'Something of a scholar, we've been told,' Alec said.

A slight hesitation. 'Oh, yes, I suppose that's true. He published a short article or so, I believe.'

'You didn't read any of them?'

'Not, um, not my area. Eddy was a seventeenth-century man; my interests are mostly medieval.' He laughed, briefly. 'I'm afraid it takes me all my time to keep up with that.'

'I suppose it must,' Alec said. To Naomi's ear he sounded puzzled.

'So you didn't know about the book he was writing?'

'He was writing a book? Oh, good for Eddy. Oh, but I suppose it's a bit late to say that.'

They fell silent, each with their own thoughts. Naomi, confused now by the different Eddy Thame that Dr Matthews and Adam Hart seemed to have been intimate with.

'But he brought his finds to show you?' Alec said, evidently feeling he was on firmer ground with this.

'Well, yes. Anything he thought might be important. Eddy was excellent at recording what he found and he was very good at encouraging others to be as meticulous. Young Kevin, for instance.'

'In his notes he mentions a seal ring, with a cedar tree. He associates it with the Kirkwood family?'

Matthews laughed fondly. 'Ah, yes. Eddy's treasure hunt. I'm afraid he became a little obsessed. It's right for the period and could well have belonged to the Kirkwoods. Who knows?'

'Kevin found coins at the same site,' Alec said.

'Ah, yes.' Matthews leaned forward. 'Now, they are interesting. They shed light on just how fanatical and how *convinced* of victory Monmouth's followers were. The notion that you could go ahead and strike commemorative medals under such circumstances, well, that speaks of certainty, unreasoning certainty.'

'You believe they are genuine.' Naomi was intrigued by the change of tone.

'Yes. Yes, I do. There's no reason to suppose fakery, and because of that they are intriguing, but in the scheme of things they are a mere footnote. A rather special footnote, but nothing more than that.' He paused, and laughed. 'It's an amusing and somewhat sobering thing, though, to see medals with the head of King James III and it be the son of Charles II, and not the son of James II, as is usually the case.'

'I'm not sure I follow,' Alec said.

'Ah, right. Well James, Duke of Monmouth, was the illegitimate son of Charles II. James II was the brother of Charles and he was the king at the time of the rebellion. He was a Catholic and the general public had become very suspicious of members of the Roman church, but anyway he was generally unpopular. His son, who would have become James III, never actually came to the throne, because only a couple of years after the rebellion, James II was deposed in an almost bloodless coup when we went and asked the Dutch if we could borrow a couple of their spare royals. Hence we ended up with the Protestant William and Mary of Orange.

'Anyway, the medallions Kevin brought to me were inscribed King James III and the date is 1685. He is also described as being defender of the faith: i.e. the Church of England.'

'Right.' Alec still sounded doubtful. 'So you don't think Eddy was on to anything more than that? Just interesting but random finds.'

Matthews' tone changed, almost imperceptibly, but Naomi noticed it and knew Alec did too. He tensed.

'Look, I can understand the draw of the treasure hunt, but those incidents make the news precisely because they are so unusual. I'm not sure that Eddy believed it; I hope not, but *I* certainly never did. The Kirkwood treasure is a lovely story, but that's all it is.'

There was little more to be said after that and they left a short time later.

'Well,' Alec said. 'Lunch, I think. Back to The Lamb. What do you make of Matthews?'

'I don't know. I'm disposed to dislike him because he put Eddy down, but I'm probably being picky. Kevin seems to rate him and Eddy did too, apparently. Adam Hart is easy to like, which automatically gets my spider sense tingling.'

'Oh, you were a copper for far too long. Funny though, the thing that really strikes me is that Eddy was careful, tidy, odd in what he told people. No one seems to have the full picture. It's like he fulfilled whatever their expectations were, even with people he is supposed to have liked and been close to.'

'Don't we all do that to a certain extent? I

mean, Sam knows things about me even you don't. Not because I'm hiding anything; just because they're sister things, girl stuff, you know?'

'Sure, I suppose so. Maybe that's all it is.'

'But you're not sure that's all it is.'

'No, I'm not so sure.'

EIGHTEEN

Lunch was an oddly sober affair. Susan was distracted by the mundane weekly task of ordering and resupply for the pub; Kevin, oddly quiet, had taken up residence in Eddy's corner, if not yet in his chair. A few locals drifted in, but they were a largely evening, post-work phenomenon and at lunchtime were thin on the ground. Trade at lunchtime was steady and, Naomi noted, generally older people, Susan having a discount policy twice a week for those of pensionable age.

'I've got great staff,' Susan said when Naomi tentatively asked if she could make a profit overall. 'Regular lunch customers who come back week after week, a couple of walking groups who have monthly bookings for thirty or more, and in the summer there are several B&Bs who put custom my way, so we all get by. I'm in this for a steady living for me and my staff, and that means building loyalty, so we do OK.'

She didn't know Eddy had been writing a book and neither did Kevin.

Post lunch, Alec intended to drive out to Eddy's

house, so he sought Susan out in her office in order to borrow her key, leaving Kevin and Naomi ensconced by the fire and examining Eddy's notebooks. Kevin had brought with him a digital recorder so Naomi could listen back later to their discussion. It was a thoughtful move and much appreciated. Alec was now kicking himself for not having thought of it.

'What do you hope to find at Eddy's place?' Susan asked, handing the key over.

'I don't know. He talks about some interesting papers that he used for researching his book. I'm probably barking up the wrong tree but...' He shrugged. 'Have you heard anything from the police?'

She shook her head. 'No, but the solicitor phoned this morning, said he'd been looking over Eddy's estate and there's more to it than just the house.'

'Oh?'

'Yeah. We always assumed Eddy had some kind of pension he was living on, but it looks like he had money apart from that, some kind of trust fund that came from his wife. It should have passed directly to Karen when she was twenty-one, but of course she died, so it came back to him.'

'I see. Do you know how much?'

Susan shook her head again. 'No, Mr Cole says he's still collating all the details. Apparently Eddy made several investments with the interest and there's stocks and shares and such.'

'Sounds as though it's a large sum, then.'

'When I asked if there'd be enough to hire a solicitor to look after Kevin, and he said yes, I thought he meant that we'd settle up after I sold the house or whatever, but it seems like this is what he meant. That there is actual money. I know it sounds silly, but I'm a bit daunted, Alec.'

'I think that's understandable. It's all happening rather quickly.'

She nodded and turned back to her desk to continue with the day to day concerns of running The Lamb, but Alec was pensive. More mystery, he thought.

Alec drove along the winding road to Eddy's house deep in thought. It had not escaped his attention that all they'd done so far was uncover random facts about Eddy's life; nothing that actually gave them a lead on who had killed him.

More and more, Alec was drawn to the notion that Eddy had quarrelled with a friend and the death had been accidental. Why on earth would anyone want to hurt a man whose main interests in life were events that had happened centuries before?

Susan would have been a possible suspect had she known about the will, but as she'd got a pretty solid alibi and, as even Eddy's solicitor seemed to have been vague about his estate until now, that really didn't seem likely.

'What about Kevin, then?' Alec spoke his thoughts out loud, trying them on for size. 'He had opportunity; did he have motive? Did Eddy find something that Kevin wanted? Did they argue about it? Did Eddy fall and Kevin was too scared to call for help?' Alec frowned at the road ahead. 'I don't see it,' he said. 'I'm missing something.'

He pulled into the short drive that led to Eddy's house, switched off the engine and sat, mulling everything over in his mind. What had Eddy really been like? It seemed he had been trying to be all things to all people – at least some of the time. But was Naomi right and Eddy had merely been magnifying that habit everyone had of showing the most acceptable face in any given situation?

He got out of the car, fishing Susan's key from his trouser pocket and then, remembering how cold Eddy's house would be, taking his heavy winter coat off the back seat and shrugging it on. It was unbelievably quiet out here, he thought. Just the sound of the wind and a few extra hardy birds.

Before going inside, Alec wandered round to the back of the house, through a little wooden gate and into the rear garden. He halted in surprise. He knew that rural gardens could be large but he had expected nothing like this. The garden meandered, there was no other word for it. The boundary line on his right was roughly straight, marked out by a hedge of hawthorn and ash and other plants Alec couldn't name. To his left the garden arced around, first to the right then sharply left. It then curved and snaked out into the middle of a neighbouring field before bounding back to join the hedge line. But it was vast. Long and wide, once it left the environs of the cottage and the paved area of old bricks that formed a sort of patio immediately behind.

Alec moved to stand by the back door, just outside the little porch he had noticed when he stood in the kitchen with Susan. A brick path led down to a plashed hedge, its structure clear now the winter had denuded it of leaves. An arch led through to what Alec discovered was an extensive vegetable plot and beyond that a small orchard with perhaps a dozen trees. He wasn't good at estimating acreage, but he reckoned there was a small field's worth of land here and, from the look of the still-stocked vegetable patch, kale and onions and winter cabbage ready to crop and the neat beds up towards the house, it was all well loved.

He could see now the reason for the odd shape. A little stream wound its burbling way down the side of the garden and across the ploughed fields beyond. There was no other boundary here, and quick examination showed that the stream was shallow, easily forded, and the line of a footpath could be discerned a hundred or so yards distant where the road looped to touch the farmland. It would have been a muddy journey from footpath to stream and thence into garden, but it would not have been a difficult one.

He turned to look back at the house. The lean-to porch didn't look sturdy enough for anyone to use that as an access point to the upper floor – and, besides, Kevin and Eddy had sat talking in the kitchen, so they'd have heard anyone climbing it. Conversely, a person coming up the garden path could clearly have seen them both in the kitchen, though with the lights on inside, neither Kevin nor Eddy would have been able to see *them*.

Carefully, Alec walked back up the path, looking for signs that the CSI had been out here and examined the scene. He found none. Evidently their search had been focussed inside the house.

He walked round the other side of the cottage. A rain butt had been set below the downpipe from the roof. He had noted several, set around the cottage. This, like the others, had a wooden lid. All the rain of the past few days had washed it clean and filled the butt to overflowing. Beside the butt, a couple of ageing wine crates had been upended and stacked one on the other. It was a precarious balance, but would have been enough to assist anyone trying to gain the top of the water butt. Alec examined them, saw no sign of shoe prints. He tested them for sturdiness and, with one hand on the downpipe, managed to balance and then step on to the wooden lid of the water butt. Alec looked up. A small window, which he figured must give on to the landing, could just about be reached by someone climbing the downpipe. Plumbing from the bathroom overflow protruded through the wall and Alec reached for it. It broke as he touched it, the pipe coming away clean in his hand. He tucked it into his pocket and looked more closely at the wall. Scuff marks, as though a foot had slipped from the pipe and scraped down the wall, could just be discerned, and he figured that someone lighter and more limber than himself could just about have reached that upper window.

He jumped down from the water butt and took the short length of plastic pipe from his pocket. Of course, he couldn't be certain, but the break looked new and a tiny scrape of mud still clung to what had been the upper side. Feeling in his pocket he found a couple of ziplock bags, thanking his long career which meant he almost always had evidence bags somewhere about his person. The pipe was too big to fit into one and he slid a second over to cover the top, knowing that he was probably wasting his time with this; any forensics would have been compromised by his interference and the fact that he could not establish a proper chain of evidence. Still, it might add to what could be classified as circumstantial; it might pique someone's interest.

Returning to the front of the house, he let himself in. Without the slight benefit of the hazy sunlight, the house was as chill and damp as he had expected. It didn't take long, he thought, for a home to feel just like another neglected space. He went upstairs, noting here and there the evidence of the CSI return but also the absence of any crime scene tape on the front door, just a sad streamer of blue and white tied to the foot-scraper outside, left when the rest had been removed.

The window at the end of the landing was closed and Alec noted the fresh traces of fingerprint powder on the sill. Gingerly, he lifted the latch, noting traces of grey here also.

'Right, so there's where you came in.'

Looking down he could see the top of the water butt. The downpipe passed the window before continuing to the roof. Could you lift the latch from the outside? The windowsill was narrow on the outside, not much room for perching while you tried to open the latch, but what might be a footprint, smudged and muddy, marked the cracked paint. Alec photographed it with his mobile phone and made the assumption that the CSI would have done the same. He pulled the window closed, then opened it again. Tool marks on the wood, scraping marks, showed that something had been slid between latch and badly fitting frame and the latch had, in all probability, been lifted from its place.

Would you have heard that had you been sitting in the kitchen? Alec wondered. This was, after all, the external kitchen wall. Would you not have heard someone landing on the floor upstairs if you sat below?

The latch was an odd one: a little curl of wrought iron, with holes drilled along the length which fitted on to a small metal peg. There had once been a second catch, further up on the frame, but that was broken off and, Alec thought, had been long gone.

He dropped the catch back against the frame. It fell with a dull, metal on wood thunk and a little click where metal hit metal. Would you hear that in the kitchen? Maybe not that, but the getting through the window without making a noise would be far harder. Would you hear it in the hall?

He thought about it, wishing he had someone with him so he could try it out. Probably, he decided. Was that why Eddy had come up-stairs?

Turning, Alec made his way back down the corridor, opening doors as he went, checking rooms for signs that someone else had been there.

Everywhere were the signs of the CSI presence, but Alec was certain that they hadn't been the only ones to search this house. It was just a feeling, but it wouldn't go away. He open-ed drawers and cupboard doors in the guest room, feeling beneath the stacks of towels and sheets in the big cupboard, searching beneath the mattress and under the bed. Then Eddy's room, noting that although the clothes were folded they were not stacked in the drawers but crammed inside as though someone had grabbed them out in handfuls and then crammed them back to establish the semblance of order. Nothing beneath the bed, not even much in the way of fluff. The wardrobe contained a couple of suits and three jackets. Shirts on hangers, jumpers in neat piles on the shelf above, and shoes in rows on the cupboard floor. Nothing had been moved here, Alec was sure of that. So, why look in the drawers but not bother with the wardrobe? Had they found what they were looking for?

Alec stood on the bright red rug in the middle of Eddy's room and looked around. Whoever had searched this room had been looking for something small. Something that could be fitted into a drawer, hidden beneath clothing. He thought about the diary and notebooks that Kevin had discovered in his pack. Had that been what they searched for? If so, why did he have this sense that they had stopped looking? Had they realized that whatever they wanted had already gone?

He crossed to Karen's room and slowly opened the door but nothing had changed. The room still nestled beneath the strata of dust and the soft toys still glared at him from the end of the bed. He closed the door again and returned to the foot of the stairs. Glancing at his watch he noted that he had been at the house for a little over an hour. It felt longer. A swift check of the kitchen confirmed that nothing seemed to have been disturbed there, and the living room looked the same, so far as he could recollect, as when he had examined it with Susan. A little bored now, and somewhat frustrated, he went back into the hall and into Eddy's office.

The mess was still there: boxes opened, papers scattered, files taken from the cabinet and emptied on to the floor. The computer was missing and Alec remembered that Sergeant Dean told him the police had taken it. He wondered if they had found anything. If Eddy had kept back-up files. A search of the desk drawers revealed nothing but pencils and printer paper.

What would the key fit? The desk drawer had the wrong kind of lock. The filing cabinet?

Feeling in his pocket for the key, he crossed the room and tried it in the lock but the lock was too large and the wrong shape. No, Naomi was right, this was more like the cheap keys issued with suitcases. Made of flat, stamped out metal, it was too thin and too flimsy to be for anything that required force or a strong mechanism.

Did the key even mean anything?

A small sofa occupied a corner of the room and Alec sat down, trying to see the office from Eddy's perspective. Eddy must have sat here, with his cup of tea and his notes or his research. A rickety little table had been placed at the end of the sofa. The surface was worn and covered in marks from hot mugs having been set there.

'So, he sat this end of the sofa, and he read or thought or ... looked at his maps.'

Where *were* Eddy's maps? And what about this Lorenz cache that had provided so much information for his book?

Alec sat back and tried to think. The last time he had seen him in the pub, Eddy's maps had been on the table in front of him. At the end of the evening, what had he done with them? Alec visualized the scene: Eddy at the end of the evening, draining his glass, picking up his maps and books and assorted bits and putting them into a document case. Not a proper briefcase, just a slim red folder. He opened his eyes, surveyed the room once more, stood up so he could see. Knowing what to look for now, Alec scoured the room, lifting stacks of paper and spilt filing and rummaging behind the cabinets that stood wonkily against one wall.

'Got you.' On impulse he had tipped the furthest cabinet slightly to the side. It was heavy, but not impossibly so, and in the hollow beneath the plinth he glimpsed a red folder. Clinging to the cabinet, he kicked at the folder, dislodged it from its place, and then drew it out from beneath the cabinet with the toe of his shoe. Sitting atop the folder was a small tin box fastened with a tiny padlock. Alec laughed aloud.

A small sound attracted his attention and, frowning, he lowered the cabinet again, picked up the folder and box and peered out into the hall. Nothing, and yet he was sure that the sound had not been merely from the old house settling. It was unfamiliar, a difference in what Naomi would have called the natural soundscape of the place.

Not really understanding the impulse, but acting on it anyway, he shoved the box and folder out of sight beneath the sofa, then went out into the hall once more. 'Who's there?'

He could see through the living-room door that the room appeared to be empty. The kitchen? A few steps down the hall and a quick glance through the door told him that this room had no occupant.

Upstairs?

Alec set a foot on the lowest step, looked up at the spot Eddy had fallen from and that was as far as he got. Pain, hard and heavy and acute, filled up and overwhelmed his senses and then the world went black.

NINETEEN

'What time is it?' Naomi asked.

'Just after four. Shouldn't Alec have got back by now?'

'Depends what he found, but I'd have thought so. Is my bag over there?'

Kevin passed her the shoulder bag and went to get them both more tea. The Lamb was very quiet at this time in the afternoon, the lull between the lunchtime crowd and those in search of an evening meal. The chef went off home at two, picked his kids up from school an hour after and came back for the evening rush. His wife worked too and the flexible hours, though a bit frenetic, fitted them both. Evening staff started to arrive at five and for much of the afternoon Susan was alone with maybe just one other member of staff. She said she liked it that way. Naomi got the impression that she was trying to employ as many people as she could. even if that was only part-time.

She rummaged in the bag for her phone and then listened to the beep of the keystrokes as she found Alec's number. She was used to this phone now and knew what keys got her where. Alec had bought her a voice activated smartphone but she couldn't get along with it at all.

No reply. Voicemail cut in and she left a message. 'Alec, is everything OK? Get back to me when you get this.' Frowning, she set the phone on the table.

Kevin returned with tea. 'Problem?'

'He's not answering. I left a message.'

'Maybe he's busy, maybe he's driving.'

'He's got a hands-free. He'd at least answer.'

'Busy, then.'

Naomi shook her head. 'Something's wrong.'

'Try him again in a minute or two. You want me to drive you out to Eddy's place?'

'I don't know. I'll try him again. It's possible he's gone somewhere else and we'd miss him. It must be getting dark?'

'Um, yeah, pretty much, I think. Try him again.'

He watched as Naomi picked her way through menus and again received no response.

'Isn't that hard? Why don't you have one of those you can talk to?'

'I've got one. For some reason it doesn't understand me. I use voice activated input on the computer, but I've found it easier to just memorize how to do things on this phone. Where on earth has Alec got to? Why isn't he picking up?'

'I sometimes ignore my phone,' Kevin said tentatively.

'Most people do, but not Alec. It's like a habit you get into in the police: you take messages and you answer the phone. It gets to be a habit.' An annoying habit at times, but why wasn't he doing that now?

'Look, give him fifteen more minutes and then we'll go out there. Oh, I wonder if Eddy's phone is still connected? You know, it's just possible he can't get a signal.'

Of course, why hadn't she thought of that? They'd noticed in their travels round the county, when they were still playing at being tourists, that Alec's phone tended to lose service more often than hers did.

'I'll try phoning Eddy's place. If he's there he'll probably pick up.'

Naomi waited, listening hard as Kevin made the call. 'It's ringing,' he said. They waited. Nothing happened. 'Maybe he's already left. Give it a few minutes. He might be on his way.'

Naomi nodded, seeing the sense in that but not liking the nag at the back of her brain that told her something was definitely wrong.

Alec roused; he was hearing a phone ring. Stiff and cold and with a head that threatened to explode, he lifted himself gingerly from the cold tiles. A cautious exploration of the back of his head revealed the main source of pain: a lump the size of half an egg. When he looked at his hand it was black and he realized the sticky substance must be blood.

It was almost dark, faint light filtered in through the half glazed front door. He was lying pretty much where Eddy had been found, a sobering thought. What had happened? Muzzy headed and in considerable pain, he couldn't quite put it together. The floor was threatening to turn into the ceiling and Alec collapsed back on to the bottom step, listening for any sound that might announce his assailant's return. He'd suffered concussion before and was in no doubt that the next hours would be interesting ones. Already the nausea was almost overwhelming and he felt chilled to the bone from lying for however long it had been on the hard, cold floor. He blessed the fact that he was still wearing his winter coat. Hypothermia could well have been adding to his problems by now.

How long had he been out?

He tried to focus on his watch but the hands kept moving and finally he gave up, groped instead for his phone and wondered if he should call an ambulance or try and drive back to the farm. He attempted to get up. Nausea and dizziness intervened again and he sat back down, trying to control both. He must have passed out again because when he woke the phone was ringing once more and the hall was even darker. This time he made it to standing position, hauling himself up and clinging to the newel post. The ringing stopped.

Naomi would be worried. He had to try and call her.

Alec staggered over to the wall attempting to locate the light switch. He managed to find the one by the office door and the sudden brightness blinded him. Don't be sick, he told himself, not at a crime scene. That was a rookie's job, not that of an experienced policeman. Experienced! He laughed, then stopped. It hurt too much. What had he been doing when he was hit? That's right, about to go upstairs because he'd heard something, except, whoever it was, they hadn't been upstairs.

What had he been doing before that? He really did need to call Naomi.

He had found a box and that red file, that was it. Floor became ceiling again and he sank to what he hoped was ground, leaning against the door frame. The sound of a car engine caused panic. What if they, whoever they were, had come back? And then he heard Kevin's voice and a crash against the door and the frame splintering as he burst through.

'He's here. I think he's hurt.'

Too right, Alec thought.

'Alec, can you hear me?'

'Under the sofa. A folder and a box, under the sofa.'

'What?'

Oh God, he thinks I'm losing it, Alec thought. 'See if they're still there. Please.'

Kevin left his side and his space was replaced by a large black dog with a curious nose and a tongue that licked his eyes. Napoleon's attempt at sympathy.

Naomi knelt beside him. 'What happened?'

'Someone hit me on the head.' He felt her fingers exploring the wound, protested that it hurt.

'Is this what you wanted?' Kevin asked.

Peering at him through a haze, his eyes still refusing to focus properly, Alec saw Kevin holding a red folder and a little box, the padlock still in place. Despite the hurt, he smiled. 'Found what the key fits,' he said and then it all went black again.

From Roads to Ruin *by E Thame*

The next solid evidence we have about Catherine Kirkwood is from the winter of that terrible year. She is in Dunfermline, visiting with a relative and preparing for her marriage. She writes that she is happy, or: 'As happy as a woman can be when all that she ever knew is now lost. I consider myself grateful for the small mercys God has shown to me and that Elmer is with me. So I will be Catherine Grove, though it has been decided that, since there is no male heir to carry the name, my husband will take my family name for his own in honour of my dead kinsmen. What is left of the Kirkwood wealth is no more than we had the fortune to carry away and I do not hope to return at this time for that greter treasure which we were forced to hide.'

So, as far as we can ascertain, the Kirkwood hoard is still there for the finding.

TWENTY

Late afternoon, the day after Alec had been attacked, he was resting in their bedroom at the B&B, having been released from the hospital only an hour or so before. Kevin had called the police – Blezzard, ironically – and the ambulance, and Alec had been taken to the local A&E but he didn't recall any of it.

Vaguely he remembered Blezzard talking to him in hospital and the fact that the DI was not amused. Then he'd slept, and he had eventually persuaded the doctors to let him leave that following afternoon. They had been of the opinion that this was a bad idea, and the way he felt now he was inclined to agree.

The bedroom door opened. 'You have a visitor,' Naomi said. She came in and sat down on the edge of the bed. Adam Hart followed, carrying a large box with a selection of folders balancing on top.

'I've just heard what happened,' he said. 'If I'd known I'd have delayed coming over. Sure you're all right?'

He was, Alec realized, making a great effort not to 'boom', but he still sounded incredibly loud. Alec tried to smile and made an effort to

211

sit up. Adam dumped the boxes and tried to help, plumping pillows and fussing. Alec, eventually arranged, smiled his thanks. 'What have you got there?'

'Oh, boxes. Eddy's things. I've brought over the Lorenz papers – I thought you'd like a look – and a copy of Eddy's manuscript.'

'You had the Lorenz papers?'

'Well, yes. Eddy left them with me so I could fact check. Didn't I say?'

Alec laughed, then regretted it profoundly. 'No. That was one of the things I'd gone looking for.'

'Oh, I'm sorry. Maybe I could have saved you a bash on the head. I've brought you something else as well, but I'm not sure ... Look, when Eddy lost Karen in the car crash it so happened I'd got friends in various places that I thought could be useful. Well, to cut a long story down, I got a copy of the accident report. Eddy read it, of course, but somehow or other it ended up filed at my place along with a lot of other stuff.'

'Somehow or other?'

'Well, Eddy stored a lot of his papers in my spare room. Much of it is his research into what happened to Karen.'

'Research?'

'Investigation, I suppose you'd call it. Eddy called everything research and he was as meticulous about this as he was about everything else. I just thought, you know, seeing as you're interested.'

212

'Thank you,' Alec said. 'Did he find anything?'

'No, I don't believe so, not then, though recently he asked me to dig it out again, which is how I knew where to lay hands on it now. I had the feeling he'd found something new, but...'

'He didn't say what?'

'No.' Adam sounded uncomfortable. 'To be honest, we argued a little about this. Oh, not enough to spoil the friendship, but we did reach the point of not discussing it any more. Not Karen's death. That fell off the list, if you like. I thought he should be leaving things alone after all this time. What good could it do reopening old wounds? But Eddy seemed decided that something more could be done now.'

'You don't know what?'

'Not really. He wanted to look at something in the file about a man arrested for drink driving on the same road. They checked out his car and there was nothing to connect him to the scene, but Eddy seemed to have found something else about him. I really don't know more than that, I'm afraid.'

'You didn't ask him?' Naomi asked. 'I'd have thought that would have been the natural thing.'

'Oh, no doubt you're right.' Adam sounded miserable. 'Look, Eddy was the most delightful companion, but the thing with Eddy was he'd get these sudden enthusiasms, sudden interests. They'd absorb him, utterly, and if you didn't share them, then ... I won't say he shut you out, but he just didn't share that part of his life with you any more. When Karen died I did everything I could to help him come to terms with it and reading the accident report for himself really did seem to help. When he started this all over again I didn't feel ... It didn't feel appropriate and I told him so. After that he ceased to mention it, and when I asked him he just shrugged and moved the conversation on. Eddy was an odd man in some ways. A good friend, but not someone you ever knew completely, if you see what I mean. I don't think anyone ever knew the complete Eddy Thame, not after Martha died.'

After Adam left, Alec tried to read through the accident report but his eyes still wouldn't focus and his head began to pound once more. Naomi firmly took it away from him. 'You are meant to be resting.'

'Yes, boss.' He closed his eyes, mind racing, but not in any particularly conclusive direction. 'How did you get on with Kevin? What was in the notebooks?'

'Well, as we already knew, there was a list of finds, including the cedar tree seal ring and various others. Some of which Kevin knew about. Eddy had recorded compass positions for each find and Kevin reckons he would have plotted them on a map, apparently that's what he usually did, but he doesn't remember seeing one. He assumed Eddy just had random finds out of that field, not the quantity he actually turned up. I think he was a little put out; he'd shared everything with Eddy.'

'Picking and choosing on the information front seems to have been typical behaviour for Eddy though. Any clue as to why he'd been so secretive?'

'No, not really. Kevin reckons Eddy must have been putting everything together first and then planning on surprising him with it. I mean, after all, he gave the notebooks and diary to Kevin, didn't he?'

'Gave them secretly. Which brings us back to the notion that he was worried about something, that he wanted to hide them or at least keep them safe. What was in the box?'

'Ah, the box. Actually, we didn't get to look. I just shoved that and the folder into my bag, and Kevin and I followed the ambulance. He's getting a friend to take him out so he can bring our car back when he gets back from work.'

'Ah, of course, it's a Monday for the rest of the world. A workday. I'm losing track. Get the box. The key's in—'

'My purse. Don't worry. Right.' She rummaged, came back with the folder and the tin box. 'You want to do the honours? Incidentally, I think you're going to have to talk to Blezzard about all this. You were rambling about boxes of buried treasure when he came to the hospital last night.'

'Oh, God, really?' He took the box from her

and looked more closely. About the size and shape of a pack of after dinner mints, it was made of green tin, textured with a mock leather paint job. The latch was closed with a shiny new padlock but had probably simply fastened with a hasp in its earlier existence. He fitted the key into the padlock, momentarily afraid that it wouldn't fit, and then opened the lid.

'Bloody hell!'

'What? What's in there? You're not telling me he really found treasure, are you?'

'I'm not sure I'd go that far, but...' He placed an object in Naomi's outstretched hand. 'That, I'm guessing, is the seal ring. You can feel the intaglio. Definitely a tree of some kind. More of the coins that Kevin found. Seven, eight of them, all the same. And a locket; that's gold, too, by the look of it.' He placed that also in Naomi's palm.

'Heavy,' she said. She ran her fingers over the surface. 'Engraved?'

'That Cedar tree again on one side. Some sort of starry design on the other.'

'Oh, yes. There was a stone set at the centre, I think. It feels like a gallery of some kind.'

'I think you could be right. Let me see if I can get it open. Did he mention anything like this in the notebooks?'

'Not a locket, no. We found references to more James coins, so we assumed he must have found more of these medal things. But we didn't read through everything. Does it open?'

'It's tight, it got a bit warped, but yes, it opens. Empty.' He sounded disappointed. 'So we can assume all this stuff belonged to the Kirkwoods and was part of the hoard the daughter and the servant were sent to hide. What happened to them, I wonder.'

'Probably in Eddy's book,' Naomi said. 'It looks as though there was some truth to the stories after all. Alec, you don't think he was killed for this, do you?'

'People have been murdered for less, but no, it's hard to figure that was the reason. Unless, of course, someone suspected there was more and that Eddy had found it?'

Later, after the application of large quantities of painkillers and tea, Alec read about Catherine Kirkwood:

The night Catherine Kirkwood left her father's home, she knew, despite his assurances, that she'd never see him again. The last battle had been fought and the Kirkwoods had chosen the losing side.

Catherine's brother, Thomas, had ridden out ten days before to join the forces of the Duke of Monmouth as he headed north. He had taken with him a dozen men from the estate and, more importantly, gold, especially struck for the occasion. More of the same – little medallions in silver and gold commemorating a victory they had been so certain of – remained at Kirkwood Hall.

TWENTY-ONE

Wright and Cole, solicitors, occupied a mews-style office reached through an arch and across a courtyard. Susan had told them it had once been part of a coach house. The building, here in Somerton, was of more golden tone than the one a few miles away in Matthews' village of Walton, and Alec decided he preferred it.

'If we bought a house down here,' he told Naomi, 'I'd want it to be of this stuff rather than the grey.'

Mr Cole was expecting them. A short, rounded man, slightly balding, he was wearing small rounded glasses that framed even smaller rounded eyes. He had a blob of a nose and a beam of a smile. He welcomed them into his office and bid them sit down.

'Mrs Rawlins, Susan, has authorized me to give you every cooperation,' he said. 'So what can I do for you?' He smiled at Alec. 'I had a meeting with Inspector Blezzard yesterday,' he said. 'He seems to regard you as something of an interfering nuisance.'

'That sounds about right,' Alec confirmed. 'I do seem to be getting in the way – of someone, anyway.'

218

'Yes, he mentioned you'd been hit over the head. I did rather get the impression he thought it should have been a bit harder.'

Alec laughed, then regretted it. His head still wasn't up to laughter. 'I think he feels I'm poking my nose into his business,' he agreed. 'I imagine I'd feel the same, but there you go.'

'Anyway, about Mrs Rawlins. Edward left just about everything to her. There are some small gifts to friends, his books, his finds, small bequests to charities. The largest is a sum of five thousand pounds which goes to Kevin Hargreaves, with the proviso that he uses at least a part of it to pursue his education. The balance from the house, the trust fund and a variety of investments goes to Susan.'

'No mention of family?'

'No, none at all, and the will is very specific. My colleague, Mr Wright, actually drew it up. He's now deceased, but he was very careful, in accordance with Mr Thame's request. He even arranged for a medical assessment to be done so that no one could oppose the will on those grounds.'

'Which implies someone might.'

'Indeed.' Mr Cole regarded him with his small, round, bright blue eyes. 'And it seems he was right.'

'Oh?'

Mr Cole sighed. 'In my experience death tends to bring relatives you didn't know existed out of the woodwork. Of course, many just feel bad about not having been in touch and want to make up for the oversight by, how shall we say, celebrating with the proceeds of bereavement.'

'And have such relations appeared in this case? Susan didn't mention anything.'

'No, I thought I'd wait until today, until I'd spoken to you both. Susan seems to value your advice. The person in question, claiming to be a nephew, arrived in my office last evening, just as we were about to close. He had various letters and family documents that he said proved who he was. I told him, frankly, it didn't matter who he was, Edward Thames's will was very forthright and very straightforward, but he didn't seem equipped, shall we say, to accept my word for that. He gave me the name of his solicitor and I called my opposite number this morning and read the will to him. He agrees with me that the idea of challenging it is unwise, to say the least. Particularly as there has been no contact between Edward Thame and his family in the past thirty or more years.'

'And this nephew, what claim does he think he has?'

'Common justice, he calls it. The fact that he's a blood relative. But he doesn't have a leg to stand on.'

'What would happen,' Naomi asked, 'if anything should happen to Susan?'

'Ah, there speaks the suspicious mind of an ex-police officer. I am right in that assumption?'

'You are.'

'So, should Susan die before she formally inherits, then everything, apart from the smaller bequests, will be sold off or liquidated and the beneficiaries will be the various charities already mentioned in the will. The family, the nephew, still have no entitlement.'

'This trust fund...?'

'Was set up by Edward's wife, Martha, née Martha Whitehead. Her family owned a chemical company that created dyes and pigments. Martha's parents died when she was young, and the company was wound up and the proceeds put in trust for her. When she married I believe she used a portion of it to buy the house they lived in. It was in a bad state when they bought it; they renovated it and occasionally seem to have drawn small amounts from the interest. When Karen was born, Martha and Edward both made wills and the arrangement was that a portion of the trust should come to Karen on the occasion of her mother's death or her twenty-first birthday, whichever came first. Of course, poor Martha Thame died and then Karen died shortly after. As Martha had left everything to Edward, should Karen not be able to benefit, then of course it reverted to him. The wills themselves are very straightforward. Essentially, Edward left everything to Martha and Martha did the same.'

'But he worked. They didn't live on the trust

fund?'

'That's right. There was a sum paid into their account every month, which constituted part of the interest, but Edward Thame saw teaching as a vocation as much as a job of work, I believe. When Martha became ill they used money from the trust to pay for various alternative treatments, but the bulk is still intact. Eddy had additional interest paid into his bank account every month after he was no longer able to work, but he lived frugally, the house was paid for.'

'How much are we talking about?' Alec asked.

'Something in the range of two million, I think. That's a conservative estimate.'

'What?'

'Does Susan know?' Naomi asked.

'Not the full amount, no. Frankly, I didn't have a very full picture until yesterday and Mrs Rawlins seems to be having some trouble coming to terms with the fact that Edward left her anything at all. I am a little concerned about her reaction. And now this nephew has turned up I'm even more concerned that he may bring unwanted pressure to bear.'

'Can't you do anything?'

'In theory, yes. In practice, if Mrs Rawlins felt guilty and wanted to share the wealth, as it were, it would be hers to share.'

'I see,' Alec said. 'This nephew, does he know who she is?'

'He seems to have a good idea. How, I can't tell you, but Eddy didn't have a wide social circle. I imagine a few questions in the right places...'

They absorbed this in silence for a few moments. 'Did Eddy ever talk about family, do you know?'

Mr Cole shook his head. 'As I told you, my colleague, Mr Wright, dealt with this. I don't know what they talked about informally, only what is on record in our files. But it is significant that no family members are mentioned at any point in the will and that the will was very carefully prepared. One can only surmise that there was a rift.'

'Mr Cole, did Eddy ever talk to you about his daughter's death?' Naomi asked. 'We think he may have tried to look into it himself.'

Cole hesitated. 'I think you may be right,' he said. 'But I don't really have the details. Eddy asked me to write two letters for him and I did. He then regretted the decision quite profoundly, I believe.'

'Letters?'

'About two years ago, he came to me and asked me to draft two letters. One was to Oliver Bates' parents, asking questions about the night the young people died; something about a newspaper report, if I remember rightly. I think something about the possibility of another vehicle being involved. The parents assumed that Eddy must have uncovered some new evidence about the accident. They wrote to him, they phoned him, they wrote to me and called the office. Edward became very distressed and asked me to get a restraining order. He changed his phone number, returned their letters. The second was to DI Bradford, who'd been the investigating officer. I understand that he went to see DI Bradford, but I can't tell you what passed between them.'

'And did you get the restraining order on Oliver's parents?'

'No, that seemed just too harsh. I called Oliver's family and explained that Edward's mental health was still very fragile and that I worried about the effects they were having on him.'

'His mental health?'

'Edward had a serious breakdown after Karen died. He was hospitalized for a while.'

'And could that be used by the nephew? Him not being of sound mind or anything?'

'Oh, no, not at all. I mean, had the circumstances surrounding the writing of the will been in any doubt that way, of course, but Edward Thame was in perfect health when the will was written. It's been updated from time to time, to take account of changes in his investments, and the bequest to Kevin Hargreaves is a relatively recent addition, but otherwise it stands as it did when he and Martha created them.'

'Hang on,' Alec interrupted. 'You're saying that this bequest to Susan was made before he lost Martha or Karen?'

'Well, yes. Susan Rawlins, née Evans, was born in the same year as his daughter Karen. Edward, with Martha's full knowledge and consent, made the will then.'

TWENTY-TWO

It was all rather disturbing and surprising. Arriving back at The Lamb, Naomi and Alec found Susan in a state of shock, the solicitor having called her shortly after they left. He had also warned her about Edward's nephew, Mr Gavin Thame, and she was in a twitter about the possibility of him showing up.

'You don't have to have anything to do with him,' Naomi told her. 'The money is yours, not his. He has absolutely no claim.'

What the solicitor didn't appear to have mentioned, and what they refrained from saying, was the fact that Eddy had left his estate to Susan long before she was even conscious of knowing him.

It was, Naomi thought, inevitable that the nephew should turn up at The Lamb, and equally inevitable that he should arrive at the same time as they were having dinner and were actually chatting about something other than Eddy Thame.

Susan, seeking moral support, brought the man who introduced himself as Gavin Thame over to their table. She sounded nervous,

Naomi thought. Not a good sign, especially when this Gavin Thame sounded so in control.

'I understand you've been helping Mrs Rawlins sort out my uncle's affairs.'

'In a small way,' Alec said. 'Her solicitors have been dealing with it all, really. I've just been the moral support.'

'Well, thank you, I suppose, but I just wanted to say that I think we should perhaps do without too many external influences. It would be better if Mrs Rawlins and I were allowed to sort this out amicably. Alone.'

'As I understand it,' Alec said, 'there's nothing to sort out. Edward Thame's wishes were very clear, very precise and not in the least open to interpretation. Apart from a few small bequests, he left the bulk of his estate to Susan Rawlins. I think it might be best if you just got used to the idea.'

'You are very quick to take sides, considering you're a complete outsider!'

'There are no sides to take,' Alec said calmly. 'I suggest you go and speak with Mr Cole, Edward's solicitor. I'm sure he will help to clarify the position. More wine?' he asked Naomi.

'Thank you.'

Despite the very obvious end Alec had brought to the conversation, the man calling himself Gavin Thame continued to stand beside their table. 'I've not finished with this,' he said.

'Finished with what?' Alec asked frostily.

'Talk to the solicitor, Mr Thame.' Naomi heard the emphasis he put upon the name, the implied query. 'I have nothing to say and neither does Mrs Rawlins.'

'I'm going to contest the will.'

'So I gathered. Goodnight, Mr Thame.'

A drop in the level of background noise seem to alert their unwanted visitor to the fact that he was now the centre of attention. 'You've not heard the last,' he said and walked away. The noise level returned to normal as he stalked out.

'Unpleasant,' Naomi said. 'What's he so angry about? I'm betting it's not the will.'

'I think you're right, the tone was all wrong. Aggrieved relatives who still hope to reach amicable agreements don't come on quite so strong so fast, or with complete strangers.'

Naomi poked at the food on her plate. 'Do I have any more cauliflower?'

'Here, have mine.'

'Sure? Thanks. Local accent but not especially educated. Used to getting what he wants.'

Alec laughed. 'If he's what he says he is, then Edward must have had a brother. So, where's he sprung from and, well, we don't have to ask why now, but why him and not the brother?'

'What did he look like?'

'Six feet, maybe a shade under. Not heavily built, but he's fit, I'd say. Not skinny. Short brown hair, light-brown eyes, a nose that looks like it played rugby.'

Naomi turned her head, aware that they had

once again been joined at their table. 'Well?' Susan asked. 'What do I do?'

'You do nothing,' Alec said. 'You leave it all to Mr Cole and you refuse to discuss any of it.'

'But he's a relative, a nephew. Eddy wouldn't have cut him out of the will, surely.'

'Eddy did,' Alec reminded her. 'And we only think he's related because he's telling us so.'

'Mr Cole said he had letters, photographs, all sorts of stuff.'

'Did he,' Alec said heavily.

'Odd how that sort of thing went missing from Eddy's house just before this man turned up,' Naomi added.

'Oh my God, you mean...?'

'We don't mean anything,' Alec stressed. 'Just that we need to look into this properly and you mustn't allow yourself to be pushed around by some stranger suddenly turning up and playing on some sense of moral imperative. Let your solicitor handle it.'

'But—'

'But nothing, Susan,' Naomi said gently. 'Have a word with Sergeant Dean so he knows what's going on and that you're worried about it. Then let Mr Cole sort him out.'

'Will you talk to Sergeant Dean as well? Please?'

'I'll give him a call,' Alec promised. 'Now, try not to let it get to you. What's important is what Eddy wanted. If Eddy didn't mention a nephew or a brother in his will then he must have had a very good reason. You said that no one turned up at either Martha or Karen's funeral.'

'No, no they didn't, did they?'

That thought seemed to calm her and she went away.

'What do you think?' Naomi asked.

'Same as you, I expect.'

'That he's a phoney with a motive we don't know yet and that he's not going to go away?'

'Ah, the voice of suspicion,' Alec said.

'Voice of experience,' she contradicted. 'Good job you extended your holiday.'

'Is it? You know, the day job is starting to look so much more attractive.'

TWENTY-THREE

The following morning Alec took his troubles to Blezzard and Dean. Susan had already contacted them and Blezzard had spoken to Mr Cole.

'Your feelings are?' he asked Alec.

'That he's got nothing to do with Eddy. Not in the blood relative sense, anyway.'

'But?'

'Well, Naomi put her finger on it, I think. He's angry with Eddy about something, deeply angry, and it has nothing to do with being cut out of a will.'

'Might be.' Blezzard perched on the edge of his desk and folded his arms across his chest. 'I hear there's a great deal of money involved.'

'Playing devil's advocate?' Alec asked. 'Yes, it might be just what it seems to be. Arguments among family can be difficult for an outsider to understand and he might be family, might be feeling genuinely aggrieved about being separated from his uncle's money, but there's been no involvement, so far as we know, between Eddy and any blood relatives for years until now. No siblings, no sign even of a kissing cousin. Not at either of the funerals or when

Eddy fell ill afterwards. None of the triggers you'd figure would have brought about family reconciliations seem to have been pulled. No one turned up before, and it's a terrific coincidence that photographs and personal items should have gone missing just before this man came on the scene. Of course, he may be legitimate, but Mr Cole, the solicitor, reckons he was very chary about giving out the usual personal details, home address and such. When he finally did supply one, and Mr Cole checked, he said the woman who answered the phone seemed very odd, as though she wasn't sure who he was talking about.'

'And did this Gavin Thame say who this woman might be?'

Alec smiled. Blezzard had already had this conversation with Cole; the solicitor had told him that. Blezzard, Alec thought, just wanted to know if Alec had any additional details. 'He said he was lodging with her,' Alec said.

'Hmm, pity we don't have a picture of this Gavin Thame,' Dean said speculatively. 'We might be able to get the locals to wave it around a bit and see if anyone recognizes him.'

'Ah,' Alec said. 'Well, the quality isn't brilliant, but ... Do you have a Wi-Fi link?' He produced his mobile phone and scrolled through the images, showed it to Blezzard. 'I took it last night, when he was in The Lamb.'

'Enterprising of you. Sergeant Dean, find the man a computer, will you? Let's see if this

Gavin Thame really is who he says he is.' Blezzard pushed off from the desk and started to leave.

'Before you go,' Alec said. 'Kevin Hargreaves?'

'Isn't completely off the hook.'

'Right. The other thing is, Karen Thame's accident. Do you know who the lead officer might have been?'

'It was twenty years ago,' Blezzard said.

'But it'll still be on file.'

'He'll be retired.'

'Even so.'

Blezzard sighed. 'Dean, get him what he wants,' he said and Alec knew that curiosity, if nothing else, was getting the better of Inspector Blezzard. Occupational hazard, Alec thought, and he should know. After all, that was what had got him into this.

Brian was not impressed by Gavin's performance so far. Sure, he'd been interested, more than interested, when Gavin had approached him outside of Susan's flat and put his proposal, but it was clear now that Gavin was lacking in the subtlety department.

'You can't go in all guns blazing,' he said. 'That just puts her back up. She's a stubborn woman, is my ex.'

'That why she's an ex, is it?'

Brian grimaced. He shook his head. 'My fault,' he said. 'I got cocky, didn't bother to hide the latest blonde. She took umbrage then took a hike, and next thing I know she's trying to take half the house.'

Gavin glanced around at the rather pleasant house that Susan very clearly hadn't obtained her half of. 'Looks like you won that one,' he said.

'I did and I didn't. She got the money, I got a restraining order. Eddy paid her my share.' He shook his head. 'I didn't realize the old man had money until then, but he said he'd pay me off if I promised never to go anywhere near Susan again. Not to call her and not to let her know where the money came from. I told her I'd cashed in some insurance policies my dad had left me.'

'You went along with it? She believed you? Why didn't you try it on with the old man? Tell him you wanted more if he wanted you to stay away?'

'Because, my friend, our Eddy was a brighter old sod than you give him credit for. He tied it all up tight, got his solicitor to draw up this paper I had to sign. I had to give Eddy a fifty per cent share of the house, didn't I? The same as that bitch would have had if I'd had to sell.'

'So, why'd he do it? What is she to him?'

Brian shrugged. 'I don't know. All I know is I didn't have to sell, didn't have to give her anything so long as I signed this bit of paper. I got a good deal,' he admitted reluctantly. 'She could have got Cole involved and dragged it through the courts and she would have bankrupted me if that had happened. The way I saw it at the time was that he'd given me a get-out clause.'

'So, where did you think he got the money from?'

Brian shrugged. 'Didn't know, didn't care.'

Gavin frowned. 'He was a bastard,' he said. 'He wrecked my life. Killed my father.'

'Yeah, you told me. At length.'

Gavin flushed but he said nothing, just poured himself another drink. That was something else, Brian thought, he couldn't half put it away. 'Look,' he said. 'Go tonight and apologize for coming on so strong. Play on her conscience. She's got more than enough of it, God knows. You don't get anything from Susan by trying to railroad her, but make her feel guilty and we'll both be in the money. Just don't overplay your hand. Don't get greedy. A share, that's all, she'll go for that. I know Susan and she'll want to salve her conscience. She's into all that do as you would be done to you stuff.'

Gavin took a large mouthful of spirit and washed it round his mouth before swallowing. 'She doesn't deserve any of it,' he said.

That evening Naomi and Alec had elected to go back to Wells for the concert they had seen advertised. This time they sat in the main body of the church while members of a local choral society and a string quartet joined with choristers and presented a very mixed programme, from sacred music to something Naomi vaguely recalled came from *The Merry Widow*.

She thoroughly enjoyed the experience, but was aware that Alec grew restless in the second half.

'Are you OK?'

'Hard seats and I'm hungry. They go on a bit, don't they?' he commented as members of the choral society performed an aria from *Madam Butterfly*.

'Alec, you philistine!'

'The philistines were a very sophisticated people.'

Naomi shook her head in mock sorrow. She was aware that the restlessness had nothing to do with hard seats or hunger and everything to do with his anxiety about what was going on at The Lamb. He was sure Gavin would return. Had both wanted and not wanted to be there. Naomi's desire to go to the concert had swung the decision making and she had made certain he had switched off his phone – which he hated doing – and had also insisted he call a restaurant they had spotted earlier in the week and book a table for after the performance.

Bugger Gavin, Susan and even poor Eddy. Naomi wanted a proper night off.

They emerged from the cathedral into a chill but clear night. Naomi didn't need Alec to tell her that; she could feel the frost begin to bite as soon as they stepped from the porch, hear the crackle of already frigid grass as she stepped on to the green. She shivered, but breathed deep of the cold, crisp air, suddenly exhilarated.

Alec took her hand and slipped it through his arm. 'Such a bright moon,' he said. 'And there's a ring around it. Doesn't that mean storms?'

'It means there are a lot of ice crystals in the air.'

'Then how come they all line up and form a circle?'

'How can things line up to form a circle?'

'You know what I mean. So, tomorrow we go and see ex-Inspector Bradford. I'm not holding my breath. As Blezzard said, it is twenty years ago.'

'And as I said, coppers have long memories. Elephantine. You'd remember, I'd remember. He will.'

Alec squeezed her arm. 'Hope you're right,' he said. 'We need something to pull all of this together, and Karen's death seems to be the pivot point somehow. I just don't get the mechanics of it yet.'

He switched his phone back on when they got back to the car, as Naomi knew he would. She sighed, was unsurprised to find that he had three missed calls and two texts. All from Susan. He also had a missed call from Kevin, who was obviously trying on her behalf.

Naomi sighed. 'What do the texts say?'

'Well, Gavin, whoever he is, came back. The locals kicked him out. She wants to know where I am and why I'm ignoring her.'

'Okaay. So phone Kevin, find out what's been happening and then text her back.'

'*Text* her back? That will go down like a lead balloon.'

'Well, call Kevin first. He's likely to be a bit more reasonable.' She could imagine Alec's expression. She laughed. 'And next time we go away anywhere and someone wants to know what you do for a living, tell them you're a chartered accountant or something. Or a zoologist. Anything but a bloody policeman.'

TWENTY-FOUR

Brian had visited Edward Thame's house only on a couple of occasions and had not been made to feel welcome. He was not inclined to return, even though the occupant was now deceased, but Gavin's frantic phone call had dictated that he should.

He'd thought about ignoring it, telling Gavin where he could go; the initial idea that Gavin could force Susan's hand, with Brian's help and information, and that both he and Brian could benefit from the will had seemed like a good one, but increasingly Brian was regarding Gavin as a liability.

'Tell me about her,' Gavin had said at that first meeting, when they'd sat relaxing over a pint, Brian's curiosity piqued by the notion that Eddy had a relative he didn't know about.

At that point, he told himself, he'd actually thought he was doing a good deed. Susan had, inadvertently, denied the true relations of Edward Thame their right to inherit and that just had to be wrong. The promise of a cut, should Brian be able to help Gavin rectify that situation, seemed only fair.

'Think of it as a fee,' Gavin said. 'You know,

like these no win no fee lawyer blokes that advertise on the telly.'

The first warning bells had sounded then. It was the no fee bit that alarmed. But he had chatted about his ex-wife and even indulged in a bit of alcohol induced nostalgia. Susan may doubt it now but there'd really been a moment when Brian had thought she might have been 'the one'.

But, as the conversation meandered and Gavin outdrank Brian two to one, the truth emerged: Gavin was no more a relation than Brian; his agenda had more to do with profit and revenge than it had to do with anything resembling natural justice. The alarm bells had rung again, but Brian had failed to give them the proper amount of attention. It was only afterwards, when he'd sobered up and thought about the deal, that Brian thought to himself: this bloke's mad as a box of frogs.

He had decided to tell Gavin where to go with his ideas and that he wanted nothing more to do with a plan so absolutely doomed to failure, but the Gavins of this world, Brian discovered, don't take no for an answer. He had his mind set and he would not be swerved, diverted or otherwise distracted from his goal.

Driving out to Eddy's, Brian asked himself why he hadn't just put the phone down. Why he was obeying this new summons, which had come so late at night that he'd been getting ready for bed.

'Must be as nuts as he is,' Brian said. He thought about turning round and going home, but something stopped him. Several somethings stopped him, if he was being totally honest.

The first was curiosity. What if the old man really *had* found something worth laying hands on? Compared to Gavin's convoluted game, simply swiping something from the house seemed clean and simple and Susan had plenty coming to her from the sound of it. She'd not miss ... whatever it was.

The second, in a contradictory way, was a faint vestige of loyalty. Susan was essentially a good person and he knew he'd been a fool to muck her about the way he had. She hadn't deserved it and, in his heart of hearts, he knew he'd been the real loser in the situation.

Third was fear. There was something about this Gavin bloke that was feral, vicious and that didn't operate by anything resembling normal rules. Brian, skipping all his life along the verges of dishonesty, recognized the type and knew to be afraid of it. If he let Gavin down now, Gavin would come looking to find out why.

A few more brains and he'd be dangerous, as my gran used to say, Brian thought. She'd used to say that about Brian, actually, but he'd never felt he really deserved the vague insult. Gavin certainly did. So, thinking about it, did Eddy, with the major difference that Edward Thame had had the required number of brain cells.

Edward Thame had shown himself to be both devious and dangerous, and Brian was sort of looking forward to demonstrating that fact to Susan. That particular revenge would be very sweet.

This obsession that Gavin had about Eddy, seemed, to Brian, to exactly mirror that which Eddy had demonstrated towards Gavin's father. 'Twenty years,' he said aloud. 'Twenty frikking years? That's commitment. Boy, is that commitment!'

When Gavin had first told Brian about Eddy's persecution of his father he'd thought he was joking.

'Sent cards and presents. Aw, come on, that's just—'

He broke off, Gavin's face darkened. 'Letters, too, and press cuttings. He kept the pressure on, didn't let my dad get over what had happened. Eddy Thame kept my dad in prison for twenty years, just like if they'd put him away. But if he'd gone to jail he'd be out by now, he'd have served his time. Eddy didn't see there was an end to it. He'd have carried on till the day he died.'

'So, you're claiming he drove your father to suicide. Right. Gavin, why didn't he just go to the police? Tell them what Eddy was doing? There are such things as restraining orders, you know.'

'Oh, you'd know all about them.'

Yeah, actually, he did. Susan wasn't the only

242

woman who'd taken the legal route to separation.

'Why didn't he go to the police? Because he was guilty, man, you can see that. He caused that crash but the police couldn't do nothing about it. So Eddy Thame acted like a bloody vigilante.'

A vigilante that sent presents and cards. OK, so presents and cards for a dead child, which was a bit weird, and Brian could sort of see how that would get to someone after a while – if that someone had a guilty conscience, anyway.

It was to Brian's credit – at least, in Brian's eyes – that he'd been curious enough to ask around and find out a bit about the accident that had killed Karen and her friends. He could sort of countenance leaving the scene of a crime, but what he'd found out actually made him think. At least one of the girls was likely to have survived if Gavin's dad had phoned an ambulance. Even if he'd left the scene, he could have stopped somewhere and got help.

That, in Brian's view, made Eddy's persecution of him more comprehensible and it also made it clear why Gavin's dad hadn't gone to the police. He wasn't sure what crime he'd have been charged with, but something like leaving the scene of an accident and that leading to involuntary manslaughter came to mind.

Driving out to Eddy's cottage, Brian made a decision. He would tell Gavin he no longer wanted any part if this and he'd tell him why.

That his father had not just driven drunk and caused a crash, but he'd probably been responsible for killing someone who might have survived. In some crazy way that Brian couldn't quite justify, that made it all ten times worse: that he could have done something to make the incident just a fraction less tragic than it had been, but he had failed to do so.

He turned into the short drive and saw Gavin's car already there.

'What kept you? I've been here a bloody hour!'

'I'm not stopping. I just came out to tell you I've done with this.'

'Yeah, right.'

Gavin turned away and headed into the house. It seemed he had already unlocked the door, and Brian wondered why he'd waited outside.

Reluctantly, he followed. 'Hey, I mean it, you know.'

Gavin took no notice of him. He walked ahead, going through the house and turning on the lights. He wore no gloves, Brian noticed, and didn't seem to care that someone driving by might notice the lights being on.

'Gavin, what the hell are you doing?'

Gavin paused, turned to face him and Brian knew that if he was wise, he should get out now and go and find the nearest policeman.

'Looking,' Gavin said.

'Looking for what?'

'Whatever there is.'

They were in the kitchen at the back of the house and Gavin turned away from Brian and started to open cupboard doors, slamming them back as far as they would go and peering in. A swipe of his arm brought the contents crashing out and on to the floor.

'Gavin!'

'What?'

'I'm going.'

'No. You're not. You're going to help me look.' Suddenly he was beside Brian, a knife from the block on the counter in his hand.

'What the hell? Oh, you've lost it big time, you really have.'

He backed away and Gavin followed him into the hall.

'Look,' Brian said. 'Let me talk to Susan, she'll see reason. She'll understand what your dad went through, what Eddy did to him. She's soft like that. We can settle this, all come out of it with what we want. Now put the bloody knife down.'

A thought struck Brian and he wondered why it had waited until now to appear, it was so obvious. 'Did you kill Eddy?'

'Old fool tried to fight me so I gave him a shove.'

'Did you want him dead?'

Gavin shrugged. 'Eventually. I'd have liked to make it slower, just like he made my dad die slowly. You should have seen him when he was younger, Bri. Just so full of it. Yeah, he drank, but he was a good dad. He played footie with me, he took me out with him, he didn't take no rubbish from anyone. Eddy took him away from me. He changed after that; died a bit at a time and Eddy made it happen. I wanted him to feel it, to know what he put us through, but I shoved him and he fell. We don't always get what we want, do we?'

Brian wanted to leave. That was what he wanted. He backed away towards the front door, glad he'd not bothered to close it. His hand in his pocket found his keys and he pressed the fob, hearing the familiar beep of the lock disarming.

'I'm leaving,' he said, trying to keep his voice as calm as possible. 'This is over. Now.'

'Not now, not ever,' Gavin said.

TWENTY-FIVE

Naomi dozed in the car as Alec drove. She'd had a bad night – and not enough of it, anyway.

Susan had been hysterical by the time they reached The Lamb, telling them that Gavin had arrived just after eight and that he'd clearly been drinking, but had also clearly decided to try a different tack, buying drinks for anyone that would accept one and asking questions about his Uncle Eddy.

'He was weird.' Kevin's verdict was unequivocal.

'Maybe just because of the drink?'

Kevin shook his head. 'Nah, not drunk weird, just weird.'

Several people had accepted a pint from him – why not? Kevin said. He was paying. But it seemed there were strings. Gavin asked a lot of questions about Eddy, about his research and his treasure maps and what he'd found. The locals, predictably, began to wind him up.

'They were telling him, like, Eddy struck gold.' Kevin didn't know if to be amused or annoyed. 'They kept telling him, like, Eddy was a treasure hunter. I told him that Eddy was a serious historian, but he'd stopped listening by

247

then. He just got mad, wanted to know where the maps were and what Eddy had found, and when Susan said he'd found nothing valuable he accused her of wanting everything for herself.'

'I stopped serving him,' Susan said. 'I let him have one drink, then told him he had to go, but he just got more and more abusive. Ken and Larry threw him out later and Kevin hung on with me and said he'd follow me home.'

Which is what he'd done later, after Naomi and Alec had smoothed the ruffled feathers and told her, again, that she had to report the incident to Dean or Blezzard and to Mr Cole, and after which Naomi and Alec had tried to get some sleep.

'How far is it now?' Naomi asked, rousing to find that the smooth rhythm of motorway driving had given way to the frequent gear change demands of a B road.

'Ten minutes, maybe a bit less. You feeling any better?'

'Not really. Are you OK?'

'When we've seen DI Bradford, we'll find ourselves a café and I'll stoke up on coffee.'

'OK.' She fell silent, listening to the changing note of the engine and the tyre noise on the uneven road. 'I hope he's in, after all this.' They'd been unable to reach him by phone but had decided to come up anyway.

'Well, we'll soon know.' He slowed and she assumed they were now in a village. She heard the satnav tell him to turn right. Moments later, they stopped.

'We're there?'

'Yes. Hang on and I'll help you out; I've pulled on to a verge.'

Naomi waited until he came around to her side, releasing Napoleon from the back seat first and then helping Naomi out on to the soft verge. The air smelt of recent rain and the damp was chill against her skin. She turned her head, catching the scent of winter honeysuckle.

'OK?' Alec led her through a small gate. She heard the latch fall back again as it closed behind them. They walked up a gravel path and Alec knocked on the cottage door. It opened only seconds later.

'My friend Matt Blezzard called,' a voice said. 'Told me I should expect you. I told him it was about time someone came looking. About bloody time.'

'When Eddy had been a much younger man he had felt certain there was a solution to everything. Life had fallen into place for him. Good degree, good job, happy marriage, wonderful child, even though she'd been a little late coming on to the scene. From such a height of grace it seemed inevitable, that the fall should be so heavy and so far.

'Cancer, the doctor said. Then, that it had metastasized. Then, that there were only months – and then weeks, and nothing that had fallen so neatly into place before could compensate for the chaos that those few words had brought.'

'And then Martha was dead,' Alec said.

'Martha died and there was worse to come. I remember breaking the news about Karen, saying to him, I'm sorry, sir, but your daughter, Karen. There was a car accident. I'm afraid ... I'm afraid she's dead. And he just stood and looked at me like the words didn't make a scrap of sense. It was as though he could not comprehend a world in which such a mess of grief could be thrown at him. The fall from grace was complete, and none of it of his making or in his power to change.

'Eddy disintegrated. There is no other word complete enough to explain what happened to him. He dissolved into the morass that was grief and loss and emptiness, and when he finally climbed his painful way back out again, it was as though that man of certainty he had been was a mere shadow of a memory.

'He wrote to me. He said, "I have lost all purpose. I am empty, a vessel that has been spilled out on to the ground." But he found something to fill that space and I'm not saying it was a good thing, just that this is what he did, and if I'd known all of it then I might have intervened. As it was, I knew Eddy now had something that was driving him, something that made it worth him getting up in the morning, and I told myself that it was his research. We joked about his treasure hunts and about what he'd do if he found his millions buried in some muddy field. If I'd known the truth, I think I would have acted.'

'You think?'

'I don't know. That's just it. I really, really don't know. I only realized what Eddy was doing in the few weeks before he died.'

'And you discovered that he'd been persecuting the man he believed was responsible for his daughter's death.'

'Yes, I discovered that.'

'How?' Naomi asked. She shifted position in the too comfortable armchair. The fire was warm and the quiet room conducive to sleep. She wanted to maintain the very opposite of that. The cup she was holding rattled in the saucer and she steadied it carefully. 'Did he tell you?'

'No, the dead man's son, Gavin Symonds, followed the same trail you've done.'

'*Gavin* Symonds? What does he look like?'

'Brown hair. He had his hair cut short when I met him. Just a bit too short. It made his jaw look very heavy for his face, just like his father's was. He's five ten, maybe. Just a bit under the six foot mark, anyway, and not heavily built, but he looks as though he knows his way around a gym. Why?'

'Because someone claiming to be a nephew of Eddy's has turned up. He calls himself Gavin Thame.'

'Ah. And the description fits?'

'Can I show you a picture?'

'Please do.'

Naomi heard Alec get his phone and scroll through the images. 'Here. Is this Gavin Symonds?'

'Yes, I do believe it is. The hair's grown and he has a bit of five o'clock shadow in this picture, but otherwise, I'd have to say yes.'

'Thank you,' Alec said. 'That clears up a lot of questions. Why did he come to you?'

'He found out somewhere that I'd been the officer in charge of the investigation, that at one point I'd taken his father in for questioning. He turned up here one day with a bag full of ... evidence, he called it. Birthday cards and Christmas cards. News clippings, presents all wrapped up in tissue and ribbon. Gavin had opened some. His father had stopped after the first few years, but he'd kept everything and he'd left a suicide note, which the police had found after he killed himself, but which Gavin had seen too, confessing that he'd been drunk on the night those young people died, had been driving too fast and had come up behind them on the bend.

'Apparently the driver swerved to try and get out of the way – accelerated, Symonds thought – somehow rolled the car and then hit the tree. He told his son that he thinks he clipped the back end of the other car; and he probably did, because there was glass from a headlamp found at the scene.'

'Wasn't it compared to the car Symonds was driving?'

'Of course, but that was it, you see. Symonds wasn't driving his own car. It was his wife's car. He dumped it somewhere and walked for a bit and then got a taxi and went and had another drink. Then he got his own vehicle and drove back out to the scene. By then our lot had arrived, and the ambulance, so he turned around and headed for home and that's when he was picked up. But the timing seemed to be wrong and he was in an undamaged car, so there was nothing to tie him to the crash.'

'But you did.'

'Yes, I did. You know when something nags at you? Something you can't put your finger on but it nags and festers until you have to take notice of it?'

Naomi laughed softly.

'Oh yes,' Alec said. 'We all know that feeling.'

'And then James Symonds killed himself by driving into a wall. He drank a skinful first. His GP had been treating him for depression and his marriage had broken up some time before. Cause of death was obvious and so was the evidence of suicide. Case closed.'

'Except that Gavin knew there was more to it.'

'He did, or thought he did. He arrived here very distressed and I believe the distress was genuine. I made him a cup of tea and I listened. I thought I owed him that. There didn't seem to be anyone else willing to listen. His mother, he said, didn't want to know. She'd got herself a new man and a new life, but I think what really got to him was that he now understood something.'

'What was that?' Naomi asked. 'No, no more tea for me, thank you.'

'Well, he said his father changed. Went from being a good dad and his best friend to being a stranger, and he said that it happened almost overnight. Gavin was eight years old when the accident happened and Karen and her friends were killed. He didn't understand why his parents started rowing but he remembered the police coming round and his dad being angry, and then, he said, things started to settle down a bit ... and then it all fell apart. James Symonds became the opposite of what he'd been. The drinking got worse, and he became violent towards Gavin's mother and towards Gavin. He remembered the arguments developing, with his mother accusing his dad of having an affair. The little gifts Eddy sent in his daughter's name could well have seemed like that, I suppose. But the upshot was that Gavin saw Eddy as being responsible for ruining his parents' marriage, his childhood and ultimately taking his father's life.'

'That's a lot of anger,' Naomi said.

'It is indeed. I tried to make him see reason,

but he became angry and I had to ask him to leave. I said I'd call the police if he came back again but I don't think he cared. In fact, I think the only thing that stopped him coming back is that I couldn't tell him any more. My official involvement ended twenty years ago. I'd had no contact with his father after that.'

'Did he know you'd stayed in touch with Eddy?'

Ex-DI Bradford laughed mirthlessly. 'Oh, no. I've learnt over the years to be careful of what people know and don't know. I expressed surprise and shock and left it at that. Truthfully, Eddy's contact with me was sporadic. At first he was phoning most days and then most weeks. After the inquest it tailed off but then from time to time he'd get in touch. About eighteen months before he died he visited. Twice. He said he'd found something new about the case. I told him it was no longer a case and he said he knew for certain now that James Symonds had changed cars that night. That Symonds had actually admitted as much. He wanted me to get it all looked into but I had to tell him the chances of that happening were minimal. So he said he'd have to see to it himself, and he never called again.

'I let the matter go. Then I read about James Symonds' death in the local papers and I called my old friend and colleague DI Blezzard and told him a little of what I knew. Just in case.'

'In case?'

'In case of something, I wasn't sure what. I just had this terrible feeling that things hadn't ended with Symonds' death or with Eddy's.'

'You said you suspected him right from the start. That you had a feeling?'

'I did. The patrol car that stopped him did a breath test and then a blood test when they got him back. He was rambling, they said, as though he already had a story worked out about how he'd been in the pub and would be home late and his wife would be mad. They said he kept repeating that over and over again.

'I saw him later that same night and he was still at it. I asked him if he'd seen the crash. I didn't say what crash or where. He said no, he hadn't seen the car, which you might think is a reasonable assumption. It could have been any kind of vehicle, but a car is a reasonable guess. But then he started talking about what a bad bend that was and how there were too many trees. Only matter of time before someone swerved off the road and hit a tree.'

'And he couldn't have seen any of that when he came back?'

'No. We'd got an officer on point and a car pulled across one lane with the blues on. You couldn't have seen past that. I spoke to him several times after but he said he couldn't remember anything about that night except that he'd been drinking and had forgotten how to get home. And that's the story he stuck to. We examined his car, of course.'

'And the wife's car?'

'Reported missing that same evening. By the wife. It turned up a couple of weeks later, parked up in a side road about four miles from where they lived. By that time things had gone off the boil and we'd no way of proving that the damage done had happened on the night of the accident, especially as by that time some little toerag had broken off both wing mirrors and smashed the other headlight.'

'Convenient,' Alec commented.

'Quite. But,' DI Bradford sighed, 'who knows? Who knows indeed.'

Naomi sat thoughtfully, listening to the cheerful crackle of the fire, questions still bubbling into her head. 'Did Eddy ever talk about his family, apart from Karen?'

'Occasionally. Family was a sore point. There was a brother – Guy, I think he was called – but they parted company a long time before. He got a local girl in trouble then didn't step up. She was engaged, I believe, to someone else, and Eddy said he advised her to keep quiet about Guy, to get married and keep it to herself. Eddy was a much younger man then and I'm not sure the older Eddy would have felt the same. He trusted less, had lost a lot of the compassion I think he had back in the day. His moral compass tightened on the pin, as my father used to say. Tightened and rusted fast. He said that his brother had emigrated and once hinted that he and Martha had paid him to go away, but I don't know any details. I know he kept in contact with the woman and her new husband and they had a little girl. She was born the same year as Karen.'

'Her name was Susan,' Naomi said.

'Yes,' Bradford sounded surprised. 'I believe it was.'

TWENTY-SIX

Alec called Blezzard when they got back to their car but was told he was out at an incident. He left a message, annoyed with himself for not having got Blezzard's mobile. Sergeant Dean answered at the second ring and Alec gave him the news.

'Right. Good. I'm sure Susan will be relieved. Look, got to go. We're at an incident. Give me a call when you get back to the B&B.'

'Will do,' Alec said. He rang off, oddly disturbed by the invitation to make contact. 'What's going on there?' he wondered aloud.

'What's going on anywhere? If I'd sat by that fire any longer you'd have been covering me with a blanket and leaving me there.'

Alec laughed. 'Well, we're a little less in the dark than a couple of hours ago. I suppose that's something to be grateful for.'

Arriving back at the B&B it was immediately obvious that something was seriously wrong. A police car was parked outside The Lamb, Kevin's car just behind it, even though Alec knew he should have been at work. Bethan came out to meet them.

'Have you heard? Isn't it terrible?'

'Heard what?' Alec's brain immediately made connections. The incident Blezzard and Dean were attending. 'Is Susan all right?'

'Well, as all right as you'd expect, I suppose.'

Alec decided to short-circuit the explanations. He helped Naomi out of the car and they headed next door to The Lamb. A female police officer sat with Susan and glared suspiciously at Alec. 'We *are* closed, sir.'

'It's all right,' Susan said, then dissolved into sobs. It was left to Kevin to fill in the details.

'She called me at work. The police were here and she couldn't get through to you – Bethan said you'd gone off somewhere first thing – so she called me at work and sounded so upset I came right over.' He took a deep breath, realizing that he wasn't making much sense. 'The police came to tell her they'd found a car in a ditch. It had been on fire, and at first they thought it was an accident and the petrol tank had gone up or something.' He paused. 'You know Susan's ex? Brian?'

'Only by reputation.'

'Well, it's his car. The fire brigade had put it out and they could just make out the number plate, but Alec, there was a body inside. Brian was in the car.'

'Are they sure it's him?'

'Who else would it be? He's not at home, the neighbours say he went out late last night and hasn't been home since. It's got to be him.'

'They must be fairly sure,' Naomi said quietly, 'for them to have come and told Susan.'

'True,' Alec agreed. 'Kevin, where is the car?'

'You're going out there?'

'Sergeant Dean said to call him when we got back. Likelihood is, he and Blezzard are still on scene. Can you give me directions?'

'You want me to come with you?' Kevin asked hopefully.

'No, best not. I'm pushing the boundaries of professional courtesy as it is. Look after Naomi for me, help her get back next door if she wants to go.'

'Thanks,' Naomi said sarcastically, no keener on staying to face Susan's obvious grief and confusion than Alec was. 'OK, look, I'll fill Kevin and Susan in on what we've found out and we'd better call Mr Cole too. He'll need to know in case this Gavin tries to see him again. He's not turned up here again?'

'No, I don't think so,' Kevin said. 'What have you found out about him?'

Alec took his leave. Glancing back from the door he saw Naomi, her arm through Kevin's, going to sit down beside Susan. The police-woman stood and looked suspiciously in his direction. Kevin's route in his head, he retrieved the car, avoided Bethan's questions as best he could and left, realizing as he did that the course would take him past Eddy's house.

A half mile past the cottage and he saw the police activity. He pulled in and made the belated phone call to Sergeant Dean.

'Where are you?' Dean asked.

'Green car, just down the road. Want me to wave? I thought I'd better get a visa before I tried to cross the lines.'

He heard Dean laugh and then speak to someone he guessed was Blezzard. 'Drive down and park up behind the black car at the farm gate,' Dean told him. 'Stop there and I'll come and get you.'

Alec did as he was told, taking in the scene. Scientific support in their light-blue coveralls could be seen on the verge and down in the ditch. Uniformed officers stood around, some diverting traffic, others waiting for when they could move into the scene and liaise with the CSI. Blezzard leaned against the black car which Alec recognized as Sergeant Dean's.

Alec parked.

The land flattened out, the vastness of the levels obvious. The road was raised a little above the land and wide ditches flanked either side, a reminder that this was once marsh, pimpled with little islands on which the early settlers had made their homes. That salt sea tang Naomi talked about was perceptible here, even to Alec.

'The farm, across there.' Blezzard pointed. 'They saw the fire, realized it must be a car and called out the fire brigade. I figure whoever set the fire expected the whole lot to be burned through.'

'Kevin says you got the number plate.'

'Lucky, that. Whoever set the fire didn't reckon on the ditch being half full of water. Back end went up, front end was scorched, but Mother Nature was ahead of the fire brigade.'

'And the body? You're sure it's Brian?'

'Sure as we can be until we let the coroner loose on him. He's crispy but still recognizable. Lucky for us, our fire starter wasn't that efficient.'

'Eddy's place is just back there.' Alec pointed.

'So it is.'

'Has anyone taken a look?'

'You could say we've been a little tied up here.'

'Right, but maybe...'

Blezzard sighed, but his mouth twitched in a half smile. 'Look, I'll tell you what you can do. You can give me a lift back to The Lamb and I'll stop off with you at Edward Thame's cottage. If there's anything to see then we'll get someone over to see it better. That do? Now, I've just had a very interesting conversation with an old colleague of mine. It seems that we've now got a solid ID on this Gavin. Not Eddy's nephew, then?'

'It seems not.' Alec tried not to feel put out that Bradford had called ahead and spoiled the impact.

'So, tell me,' Blezzard said. 'What was this Gavin Symonds doing and what the hell did that old fool Eddy Thame think he was playing about at?'

Another hour and CSI released the scene to uniform. The body had been extricated from the car and the private ambulance had come to take him away. Alec had seen the body as they'd laid it in the gurney – contorted and twisted but the flesh not completely burned away. Half of the face had been pressed tight against the window, and the window had lain against the mud and wetness of the ditch side. It was strange, Alec thought, and more than a little disturbing, to witness that change from burnt to almost recognizable flesh.

'You must be very certain it's him. To have told Susan that her ex was dead, I mean.'

'We told her that his car had been found, that there had been a fire and a body inside. She made that connection for herself.'

'But you still told her about the car?'

'This is a rural area, Alec. People know one another, people talk. If we'd not told her she'd have found out by the time the lunchtime customers arrived. The Lamb is a pub, if you didn't notice. Pubs are hotbeds of gossip and local knowledge. We thought it was better coming from us.'

Reasonable, Alec thought. They watched the ambulance drive away and the tow truck take up its position. Earlier, it had lifted the car partly free of the mud to allow access for the

CSI.

'Eddy's place?' Alec asked.

'If you like.' Blezzard eased himself carefully into the passenger seat of Alec's car.

'Bad back?' Alec asked.

'I played squash last night with my son-in-law. Big mistake. I'll be paying for it for days.'

Son-in-law, Alec thought. He didn't put Blezzard at much more than ten years his senior and *he* wasn't even at the having children bit yet, never mind son-in-laws. 'Grandchildren?' he asked.

'First one due in March. We started early. Lis and I met at school. You and Naomi...?'

'Don't have kids, met on the job, finally got married a year ago. We've talked about it, but I don't know. I think we're both a bit unsure.'

Blezzard nodded, but said nothing. Blood ties, Alec thought, they were so important to so many people and yet neither he nor Naomi ever felt the binding strength of them that so many seemed to. He loved his parents, but they had never been close, in the sense that they'd want to play squash. The thought of it filled Alec with amusement. His father just wouldn't have seen the point of the game, never mind playing it with his son.

Should he and Naomi actually get around to having children, he couldn't imagine his parents being doting grandparents either. Naomi's were pretty good at it but lived far enough away that they were hands-off most of the time.

Naomi's sister Sam and her family had become important to Alec, and he enjoyed the company of the two boys very much, but apart from that, their closest relationships seemed to be with friends and not family, with people who had come into their lives by mutual choice rather than genetic accident.

'Penny for them,' Blezzard joked.

'Oh, life, the universe ... Right, let's see what's happening at Eddy's. That door isn't shut.'

He pulled up in front of the porch and Blezzard leaned forward to look.

'You're right,' he said. He got out and led the way inside, pushing the door open and standing stock still just inside the hall.

'Someone wasn't a happy bunny.' He took out his mobile and called for backup and the CSI. 'Question is, what were they looking for? Or didn't they care?'

'Both,' Alec said flatly. He headed for the stairs.

'Hey, leave it to CSI, we don't know what...' He sighed, followed Alec up the stairs.

Alec headed straight for Karen's room. The door was open and Alec didn't bother to cross the threshold. The mess downstairs had been bad enough; broken furniture, torn curtains, cushions with their insides ripped out and spilled on the floor, but that was petty and amateur compared to the considered and thorough effort of destruction that had taken place here.

Everything in Karen's room had been ruined. Alec recognized tiny fragments of soft toy and dressing gown and flowered bedcover. Someone had taken a knife to the lot in a rage of stabbing and ripping and slashing. Dust motes from the strata that had fallen so softly for so many years now hung in the air, illuminated by weak sunlight that was now uninterrupted by the yellowed nets.

'What was this?'

'Karen's room. He closed it up and left it as it was when she died. Everything was just as she left it.'

'Well, not now, it's not. You think Gavin Symonds did this?'

'I do. I also think he killed Brian Rawlins.'

'Something of a stretch, isn't it? We don't know the two of them had even met.'

'No,' Alec admitted. 'We don't. Yet.'

TWENTY-SEVEN

Gavin wasn't sure what to do. He wasn't sure of anything much any more, only that he was tired and desperate and wanted to find a way out of the mess he was in.

Above all, he was angry. At himself, at Brian, at Susan and Eddy and, oddly, most of all at his father. All his troubles had started that night when his father had driven the car that had caused the accident that had killed Karen Thame and her friends, and that had ruined everything because that had led to Eddy Thame coming after his father and ruining everything all over again. And Gavin could do nothing.

It was all wrong. All wrong and Gavin wasn't making it any less wrong. But what could he do?

He hadn't meant to kill Eddy; or had he? Gavin couldn't really tell any more. Had he meant to kill Brian? Frankly, he didn't know that either and he didn't care any more. He just wanted a bit of peace.

'You think this is what Gavin Symonds might have been looking for, then?' Blezzard asked as he studied the maps and the coins Alec had

268

found in the little tin box.

'Well, I think he hoped there was more to it. The way I read it is that Eddy wanted Kevin to see all this, to share in it, but for some reason he kept quiet about it.'

'Maybe Eddy knew someone else was after this. Did Gavin threaten him? The way I understand it is that Gavin didn't know anything much about any of this until yesterday evening.'

Alec nodded, realizing he was right. Eddy hadn't hidden the books in Kevin's bag because he was afraid someone – Gavin – was after them. That couldn't be the case because no one *had* been after them. No, maybe Eddy's habit of semi secrecy was the only reason. Maybe... 'Maybe he had just wanted to surprise a friend? Kevin would have found the notebooks, would have understood what they were all about and the two of them would have gone chasing after the rest. I think we were wrong. There was nothing sinister; it was just Eddy being Eddy. Bloody obtuse.'

'Does that fit with what we know about him?'

'It fits. After the first time I spoke to him, Susan told me that in some ways he was sharp as a tack, in other ways he was a bit touched. No, she put it differently, but that's what she meant. Nothing we found out about Eddy contradicts that. DI Bradford said he disintegrated, just fell apart after Karen's death and never really recovered. Bradford seems to think that persecuting Gavin's father gave Eddy back his purpose in life. It focussed him. Gavin seems to have been driven by the same motivation; he focussed on Eddy.'

'They'd both lost people they loved.' Blezzard picked up the coins and examined then thoughtfully. The locket, too, came under scrutiny. 'Anything inside?'

'No. I suppose there might have been at some time. Eddy wrote about the Kirkwoods in his book. He'd found a load of original documents, letters and such, so he was able to find out a bit about what happened to them. Catherine got away, but she had to leave a lot of her treasure behind. Eddy was convinced there was more than this and I think he was probably right. I also think it's long gone by now.'

Blezzard dropped the locket back into the box. 'So,' he said. 'What next? I suppose we go next door to talk to Susan Rawlins again. Dean is tracking down Gavin Symonds' mother, so seeing her will be the next move, and I'm hoping we'll have a positive ID on the body in the car. What we have to do is think what Gavin Symonds' next move will be. Will he go home? Does he have anywhere to be, anyone to miss him?'

'No,' Alec said firmly. 'If he had, then what his father did or didn't do would have faded in importance. The hurt would have been diluted.'

'It wasn't for Eddy,' Blezzard argued. 'From what I've seen, a lot of people cared about

Eddy, but the obsession with James Symonds didn't diminish, did it?'

'Because Eddy only gave a little bit of himself to any one person. No one had it all, not after Martha and Karen. You'd need to talk to an awful lot of people to get a complete picture of Eddy Thame.'

TWENTY-EIGHT

Late that afternoon and much to Alec's surprise, he was driving north again, and with Blezzard in the passenger seat. Naomi had once again been left behind and Alec could see that she was far from pleased, but once Blezzard had suggested Alec go with him to see Gavin's mother, both he and Naomi knew there was no way he could refuse.

'And this is the man who talked about leaving the force,' Naomi said acidly.

'Well, that was the way I felt. Actually, it's still the way I feel, but we're in the middle of this now. I can't just walk away.'

'Of course not.' Naomi sighed. 'Look, go, I'll be OK, just don't be too long and you owe me dinner somewhere other than The Lamb tonight.'

'Anything you say.'

Blezzard had talked to the local officers and had got a little background on the Symonds family, which he shared with Alec on the way. 'Father was well known. Banned twice, lost his licence again three months before he got back in the car and killed himself. Gavin has a record. Petty theft and he got into a few fights.

Nothing serious though, and the last incident on file is back when he was twenty-two. He moved away after that, probably came back for the funeral.'

'Do we know where he moved to?'

'As yet, no. Hopefully the mother will fill in the details.'

'Do we know anything about her?'

'She has no record, that's all I can say.'

A red-brick house on the outskirts of Bristol proved to be the home of Gavin Symonds' mother and her new partner. The house was small, modern, identical to the others in the row and fronted by a patch of grass.

'Housing association,' Blezzard said. 'Some kind of shared ownership thing, if I remember right. It was the biggest of its kind locally so it got on to the local news.' He smiled. 'That's why I know.'

Glancing up and down the street Alec noticed the quiet tidiness of the area. Identical houses, identically mown in front. No sign of kids, but then it was still school time. He guessed the cul-de-sac would be filled with kids playing at the end of the day, but now the sense of desertion and stillness was quite profound. They had called ahead and told Mel Symonds that they were on their way. She had sounded wary but oddly resigned. It was a tone Alec had encountered so often before: oh, no, not *more* trouble...

She opened the door as they turned towards the house, recognizing them for what they were. Another sign that Alec was familiar with. Blezzard introduced himself and Alec, flashing his ID and taking it as read she would not ask to see Alec's. She didn't, which was just as well, he thought. Right now the most official document he had on him was a choice of driving licence or library card.

'Come in,' she said. 'Room at the end of the hall. Go in.'

The hall was narrow, stairs going up, kitchen off to one side. It looked, from Alec's quick glance, to be clean. Long years of being offered tea in other people's houses raised awareness of such matters. It was odd to have the kitchen at the front of the house, he thought, imagining the variety of cooking smells that would waft out on to the street at mealtimes.

The back of the house was given over to a room that ran the full width. Dining table at one end, large telly at the other. Patio doors on to a small square of garden. The floral curtains matched the cushions on the sofa, Alec noticed as he sat down.

'Thank you for seeing us.'

Two policemen on the sofa, Mel in the chair. A pack of cigarettes lay on the chair arm and she fiddled with them for a moment and then sat forward, with her hands between her knees, and studied both men carefully, as though comparing them to specimens she'd encountered before.

She was probably in her early fifties, Alec

thought, but she looked older and more tired than a woman of that age should do. The bleached blonde hair didn't help, too harsh for the rather pale skin. He guessed she had been a blonde in her youth. She was thin and her hands were nervous, clasping and unclasping then sliding between her knees as she rocked forward.

'What's he done,' she said, her tone flat and almost bored, though Alec knew it was more resignation than disinterest. 'I knew he'd bring trouble the moment he came back.'

'He'd been living away, Gavin?'

'Yeah. Went six, seven years ago. It's been just the odd phone call since, the odd birthday card when he remembered. I think he stayed in touch with his dad better, but I was glad to see him go, if I'm honest.'

'You didn't have a close relationship, then?'

She laughed. 'No, he was his daddy's boy, never mine. And then I went off and lived with Malc and he didn't forgive me. He said he understood that his dad was difficult. I mean –' she rolled her eyes – 'difficult. He hit me. He hit Gavin, but Gavin had this idea in his head that it wasn't always like that. That his dad changed, and he was forever trying to get back to this time when everything had been all right. Been good.'

'Before the car crash that killed Karen Thame and her friends.'

Her eyes flickered towards the pack of cigarettes, but she resisted.

'We know your husband caused the accident,' Blezzard went on. 'He admitted as much in the suicide note.'

She nodded, barely. 'I always thought he did,' she said. 'But I didn't want to know. You get what I mean.'

'Four teenagers died that night,' Alec said. 'It's very likely that at least one of them would have survived if he'd called for help.'

'He was afraid he'd get in trouble.'

'He let them die because he was afraid he'd get in trouble? Oliver Bates, Jill Wellesley. Sara Coles. Karen Thame.'

'I know their bloody names, so don't start on me.' The sudden burst of anger was unexpected and intense. 'I didn't kill them. I wasn't driving. I didn't cover it up.'

'Where did Gavin go to?' Blezzard changed tack.

She shrugged. 'He got into building. Labouring. Birmingham then Leeds, I think. I didn't take much notice. He wasn't here, the rest didn't matter.'

'He was your son. Weren't you concerned?'

'He was an adult, supposedly. Old enough to make his own way. Oh, don't you dare judge me. His dad was violent and self-centred and Gavin was the same. I had a second chance at being happy and I took it. I'd done my bit, he couldn't say I didn't.'

'And he came back for the funeral?'

She nodded. 'I thought I'd better let him know, and I sent a letter to the last address I had, but he'd heard from somewhere else. He turned up at the funeral and I told him no way was he stopping here. He could go to his dad's place.'

'That was the family home, originally?'

'If you could ever call us a family, yeah. He said he still had a key so I let him get on with it. He can keep the place, for all I care.'

'And that's when he found out what Eddy Thame had been doing?'

A shrug this time.

'You didn't know?'

'I didn't put it together. Look, I left close on ten years ago. I've not kept track of what his dad did since. He was never an easy man; he got worse as time went on. I took my chance, I got out. Then Gavin left. I don't know what went on with his dad after that.'

'But you've not remarried?'

She shook her head. 'Once bitten,' she said. 'We get on fine. We're happy, but I know men. They get a ring on your finger and that's it. They change. While he still thinks I can walk, he keeps trying to make me want to stay. I know men.'

On that note they left, there being nothing more to say.

'Do you think she knows more about any of this?' Blezzard asked as they settled back into the car.

'No. If she did she'd have closed her eyes and chosen not to see. So, she can't tell us where Gavin might be; let's see what his father's house can tell us.'

Symonds senior had kept the family home. Red-brick again and also terraced, but this time Victorian. Uniformed officers awaited their arrival and opened the door without aid of a key.

'He's not been here in several days, according to neighbours.'

'Any of them talk to him?'

'Only to say good morning, that sort of thing. They said the dad kept himself to himself in recent years. Sullen was the way one described him, which, when you reckon people don't like speaking ill of the dead, probably tells us something.'

Blezzard nodded and he and Alec went inside. The house was cold and Alec was reminded of Eddy's place after just a few days of non-occupancy. It didn't take long for the chill to set in or the sense of abandonment. Unlike Mrs Symonds' place, which was neat and tidy to the point of emptiness, this little house was crammed. Newspapers scattered across the coffee table. Abandoned mugs on the floor. Pizza boxes from the local takeaway on the kitchen counters.

Gavin had been camping here, not actually moving in. Alec wondered what it had looked like before. Glancing at the shelves he noted books and music and films in various formats. An ageing video recorder sat beneath the television, a DVD player resting on top. Cable television, represented by a black plastic box set beneath the video. The books were leftovers from Mel Symonds, he guessed, unless Gavin or his father liked romances and family sagas. He was struck by the same lost-in-time feel that had pervaded Eddy's house. Another man stuck in a time warp, he thought, but with the difference that Eddy's had been because he wanted to record the best of times. Symonds' because, from the appearance of things, he was holding on to the worst.

Blezzard called to him from the kitchen. It was larger than Alec expected, the house having at some time been extended and the kitchen also knocked through into the coal hole and old outside toilet. There was still a fire grate, and that surprised him. In Eddy's rural location the use of open fires seemed appropriate, but he'd rarely seen an urban terraced property that had kept its grate, especially not in the kitchen.

'I'm guessing this is what set the cat among the birds,' Blezzard said, pointing to the stacks of paperwork and the two supermarket bags set on the kitchen table.

Alec looked, slipping on gloves and sifting through one stack, which turned out to be birthday cards. In each one was written, 'Another year, another birthday she didn't get to have.'

Christmas cards had the same message.

'Presents,' Blezzard said, inspecting the bags. 'And letters, newspaper clippings. There's a form of service from the funerals and obituaries for the four kids.'

Alec took the papers as Blezzard passed them to him. He noted the one identical to that which he'd found in Karen's dressing gown pocket and wondered again what made it so unusual that Eddy had been moved to separate it out and keep it from the rest. Skimming the others, he found that it seemed to be the only one that made any mention of a drunk driver being picked up or any real speculation of what may have happened had help been summoned at once. Was that what made it special; added to its potency?

'I can imagine something like this would have worn anyone down,' Blezzard said. 'It would have been easier on him if he'd come and confessed. Served his time, been out of jail again by now.'

'He got locked in,' Alec said. 'Set the course of action that first day and couldn't see a way back out. I think Eddy did the same, though for Eddy this became the thing that kept him going. It makes you think, doesn't it?'

'In particular?'

'Well, if Eddy hadn't died the night. If he'd had to go on living in a world with no James Symonds, no one left to blame or to persecute, how long do you think he'd have carried on?

280

So, what now. Can we take this lot back with us?'

'*I* can take this lot back with me, if that's what you mean.'

Alec chuckled. 'Force of habit. That's what I meant, of course.'

They waited while a uniformed officer listed and tagged the material Blezzard would be taking away, then, armed with a half-dozen evidence bags, they turned back for home.

'You'd better call that wife of yours,' Blezzard said. 'Stop at the next services and I'll get us both a coffee.'

Alec nodded, abruptly aware that he really needed one. He was weary now, as tired as he'd been when he'd first driven down here. The work tiredness he had hoped to leave behind was once more enveloping him, bringing home to him just how much he really was ready for a change.

At the services just outside of Bristol they stopped and Alec tried Naomi's phone, got no reply. He tried Susan's, thinking they would still be at The Lamb, and again received no reply.

Kevin picked up. 'No,' he said. 'They left about an hour ago. Susan was still upset and Naomi suggested she'd be better off at home. The policewoman left and I promised to hang on here until the evening staff arrived. She can't afford not to open tonight, so I'm just holding the fort.'

'So, Naomi is at the B&B?'

'No, sorry, she left with Susan. She said to tell you to pick her up from there when you got back. I think you've got a very expensive dinner to buy,' he added slyly.

'Oh, I'd bet on it. Thanks, Kevin. Give me the address, will you, and do you have the phone number?'

Alec wrote them down, accepted a large takeaway coffee cup from Blezzard, who'd just come back to the car.

'Problem?' Blezzard asked.

'Susan and Naomi have gone to Susan's place. Neither is picking up the phone. Susan's probably driving and Naomi's phone is probably in the bottom of her bag and her bag somewhere on the back seat. I'll try Susan's home phone; they might be there by now.'

No response there either.

'They might have gone for a coffee or a walk or something,' Blezzard said, but he could see Alec was concerned. 'Look, I'll get someone to swing by, just to make sure.'

Alec nodded his thanks and started the engine; the strongest feeling that something was very wrong had settled on his shoulders. 'Here,' he said, passing Blezzard the phone number for Susan's flat. 'Keep trying, will you?'

'Alec, I'm sure they're fine.'

'Are you? Well, humour me. Please.'

Blezzard shrugged. 'Consider yourself humoured,' he said. 'I'll get Dean to call round too,' he added, and Alec looked sharply in his direction.

'So, you're sure they're fine, are you?'

Blezzard shrugged again. 'Doesn't hurt to have a backup plan, does it?'

TWENTY-NINE

'Are you sure you're OK to drive? We can ask Kevin...?'

'No, I'll be fine. You're right, I will be better off at home. Thanks for coming with me, though.'

'You don't know it's him,' Naomi reinforced.

'Well, who else is it going to be in Brian's car? I don't get it, though, he was a good driver. How fast would he have to go for the car to blow up or whatever it did?'

Naomi said nothing. Susan seemed unable to even countenance the idea that Brian's death was not accidental, and no one had pushed the other theory – that the cause was more sinister – but Naomi had heard it in Blezzard's voice. Had felt it in Alec's attitude. Something wasn't right. Something in the way the car had burned, perhaps, which told them this wasn't a matter of a crash followed by the tank exploding.

On the back seat Napoleon huffed and snored. 'At least he's happy,' Susan said, almost managing a laugh.

'He has a contented nature,' Naomi agreed. 'And pretty basic needs really. Uncomplicated.'

'Pity humans can't be more like dogs. Oh,

God, another funeral to arrange.'

Maybe they can do a two for one, Naomi thought, then chastised herself for flippancy and felt relief that she'd not said that out loud. Alec would have understood this need to break the tension; she doubted Susan would. 'Surely this one won't be down to you? Doesn't Brian have family?'

'He has a mother, but she lives abroad and he's not had much to do with her since she remarried. He didn't approve of her choice.' She laughed harshly. 'God, but for a man with the morals of an alley cat, boy, could he be judgemental.'

'No siblings?'

'No, he was an only child, which probably explains a lot.'

'Alec was an only child,' she said blandly.

'Oh, I didn't mean ... Only that...'

'I know. Sorry, couldn't resist.'

'Oh.'

Silence that was suddenly spiked with frost descended and Naomi groaned inwardly, wondering if it was too late to change her mind and to ask to be driven back to the B&B. Maybe she could feign a migraine or something. Instead she took refuge in sympathy again. 'Do you have someone you can call, maybe go and stay with for a few days?'

'Yeah, I suppose that might be a good idea. I'll have a think about it, but there's the pub to run and—'

'And you were telling me what good staff you've got. They'd cope.'

'I suppose they would.' The thought seemed to deflate her even more.

'Just for a few days, anyway,' Naomi added. Lord, her tact seemed to be failing on her today ... or was this just perverseness on Susan's part? Was she determined to take everything the wrong way? She reminded herself that Susan hadn't exactly had an easy time of it lately. She deserved a bit of a wallow.

'We're here,' Susan said, sounding relieved. She waited for the traffic to clear and then made a sharp turn into the car park. 'I'll just park up.' She steered carefully into her space and switched the engine off.

Right, Naomi thought. Hurry up and come back, Alec. I need a good dose of sanity and normality here.

Behind them a car engine sputtered into life. 'Should we get Napoleon out first and then you or ... What!'

'Doesn't matter much. If there isn't much room then it's probably easier if I—'

'Oh God!'

'What is it?'

'It's Gavin.'

The sound of the car engine, Naomi realized, had got louder. She'd registered it behind them, had assumed the car was turning or heading out of the car park. Now, she understood, it was directly behind Susan's car. 'Stay calm, lock the doors and—'

Too late for that. The passenger door was jerked open and a strong, bony hand seized her by the arm. 'Get out,' Gavin said. 'You'd better get out too,' he told Susan.

'Stay where you are and call the police,' Naomi told her, trying to keep as calm as she could.

'I said get out.' A sharp point and the feel of cold metal against her throat.

'Better do as he says,' she said grudgingly. 'Gavin, this is a really stupid thing to do, you know that, don't you?'

'Just do as you're told. I don't need an opinion.'

Naomi got out of the car, telling an anxiously whining Napoleon that he should stay. The last thing she wanted was to risk harm to the big black dog. She could hear Susan, whimpering and fearful, and a sudden wave of impatience overwhelmed her. *For God's sake, woman, I'm the one with the knife at her throat!*

Actually, that qualified not just for impatience but for downright anger.

Naomi had been in tight spots before and against far more experienced and competent assailants than Gavin. She could feel his shaking, hear the tense, short breaths, and knew he really hadn't thought this through. He'd probably expected Susan to come back alone; Naomi was not part of the plan. She knew that what made the likes of Gavin dangerous was that they were totally unpredictable. Scared and overwhelmed, there was no telling what they might do in the heat of the moment.

'Gavin, I'm not going anywhere, how about you put the knife down?' She tried very hard to sound calm; succeeded, she felt, only in sounding slightly strangled. The blade was cold against her skin and the hand that held it trembling so violently there was a real danger he might cut her without even meaning to.

Gavin tugged on her arm. Stretching out her fingers she could feel the glass in the windows of Susan's car. She remembered the care with which the other woman had parked and guessed there was only a small gap between this and the neighbouring vehicle. Experimentally, she pushed back against Gavin, pretending to stumble as he tugged on her arm. He moved, but only a little, barked at her to 'watch it' and confirmed her guess about the small space. If she could get Susan to run, to get help, maybe they could gain back some control. Question was, would Susan take the hint?

Of course, there was always the danger that should Susan flee, Gavin would take it out on her, but Naomi thought it was worth the gamble. She couldn't resolve this alone and she didn't rate Susan as a useful companion in peril. The other woman was crying now; Naomi, uncharitably perhaps, was finding the sound just a bit annoying. She could well imagine that Gavin, nerves already stretched taut, would be even more irritated by it.

Gavin moved crabwise, dragging Naomi with him. 'Get in my car,' he told Susan. 'Get in my bloody car.'

Now or never, Naomi thought.

She reached out for Susan's car, then shoved back against Gavin, jerking her head away from the knife. She felt the painful crack as the back of her head hit his chin, felt him lose balance, just enough. She pulled sideways, against the pressure of his hand on her arm and shouted at Susan, 'Run, dammit, get help, just bloody run.'

'I can't!'

Oh, for fuck's sake. 'Susan. Run!'

Gavin had already recovered, tightening his hold on her and pressing the blade more tightly against her skin. She felt the prick and cut and the blood run, tried not to think about it. Tried to listen out for what Susan may have decided to do. Heard shuffling steps and then running feet, but she knew the moment was lost.

'Get in the bloody car, or so help me I will kill her.' Gavin's voice cracked and Naomi cursed inwardly. She heard the car door open. 'Driver's side,' Gavin barked. 'And you, in the back, and I swear, so help me, you try anything again and one of you is dead. I don't need both.'

He pushed Naomi forward, twisting her arm painfully behind her back. There was a second when the pressure from the knife released as he reached the car door handle, but it wasn't long enough for Naomi to act. He pushed her inside on to the back seat and slammed the door shut. Naomi curled there for a moment, shocked and angry; she heard the front passenger door slam and Gavin snap at Susan to drive. She guessed the blade would now be threatening the other woman. She struggled into sitting position and felt for the door handle, only to find that Gavin had the child locks on. The handle wouldn't move.

Susan stalled twice before they managed to drive away, Gavin's mounting fury destroying what was left of her capacity to think. Somehow, she managed to get it moving on the third attempt and they lurched out of the car park. Hopefully, she'd be stopped for dangerous driving, Naomi thought bleakly. What do we do now? she wondered. Correction, what did *she* do?

Her bag, her mobile, everything was still in the back of Susan's car. She felt around on the back seat but found nothing that might be of use. She worried about Napoleon, also in the back of Susan's car, grateful that at least it wasn't hot weather, but even so; they never left him alone in the car. He'd be distraught. No, he wouldn't, she corrected herself, he'd go to sleep. Wouldn't he?

When would Alec get back with DI Blezzard? Would he come looking for her? Of course he would, but how on earth could she let him know where they were going when she didn't even know?

'Where are you taking us?' she asked as calmly as she could.

'Just drive,' Gavin said. 'And you, keep quiet.'

He doesn't know either, Naomi thought. He really is making this up as he goes along. He's abducted us but now he has no idea where to go.

A call came through to DI Blezzard from Sergeant Dean just as they came off the motorway and turned right towards Bridgewater at the large island.

'Find somewhere to spin us round,' Blezzard instructed. 'We need to be heading back the other way.'

'What happened?'

'A disturbance at the flats where Susan Rawlins lives. A man with dark-brown hair was seen forcing two women into a red hatchback. Susan's car is in the car park; your wife's dog is still inside.'

'Gavin.' Alec spotted the entrance to a factory unit, dived in and U-turned. 'How much of a head start does he have?'

'Fifteen minutes at most. Dean's got the CCTV people involved; we'll pick them up.'

'Not if they head into the countryside, you won't.'

'No, but there aren't many places to hide out on the Levels. You know how flat it is.' Blezzard tried to sound confident. 'You want me to drive?'

'No, I can manage, just don't expect me to keep to the speed limit.'

Blezzard said nothing. Alec put his foot down. Fifteen minutes was a long time at seventy miles an hour, even at fifty. Who was driving, he wondered. Gavin or Susan? Probably Susan; it's hard to keep control of someone when you've got your hands full with steering wheel and gear changes.

'Alec, you're doing eighty. Slow it down; there's a stack of sharp bends ahead.'

Alec slowed to seventy. Took the bends and then accelerated again as the road straightened and rose steeply.

'Alec! We end up wrapped round a tree, that won't help anyone. Slow it down!'

Reluctantly, Alec saw sense. Blezzard was on the phone again speaking to Dean. He was at the flats.

Napoleon, recognizing Dean as familiar, if nothing else, was making a fuss of him, Blezzard reported, and Naomi's bag was still in the car, as was Susan's. Witnesses said the man had a knife, that one of the women struggled with him and the other started to run but then got into the car. She, the blonde one, was driving the car.

Alec nodded. Turning into High Street, past the shopping village and into the town centre. The flats, another quarter of a mile on, were wedged in-between older buildings, their approach a narrow entrance that widened into a car park in front of the modern, purpose built apartments. Alec saw Susan's car parked in a numbered parking bay. Visitors' spaces had been set aside on the opposite wall. Gavin must have parked there.

Getting out of the car and glancing around, Alec noticed security cameras above the door. He pointed. 'Do we have access?'

Dean appeared at the entrance door and beckoned. Napoleon thrust his large head out beside his knee and woofed happily. Alec fussed him.

'The building supervisor arrived a few minutes ago. He's sorting out the CCTV. We've picked them up heading out of High Street and again on the CCTV near the supermarket. One camera just catches them. After that, of course...'

'We're out in open country.'

'I've got six cars out; there's only so many ways they could have gone. He'll be looking for somewhere to hole up.'

'Eddy's place?'

'I've got someone there, and the scientific support won't have finished yet either.'

'Pull them out, fast,' Blezzard instructed. 'Get everyone out of sight, now. He doesn't know the area, so we've just got to hope he heads for somewhere familiar. Where do you think you're going?' Blezzard demanded as Alec started

293

back towards the car.

'Eddy's cottage.'

'Oh, no, you don't. Look, see sense. I've just pulled our lot back so we don't spook him. If he goes there we'll soon know. If not then you'll be running round the Levels like some headless chicken and if I need you in a hurry ... First we look at the tapes, see what we can glean from that. Once we know what we're dealing with we act on it, you understand? You'll do no good chasing shadows out there.'

Alec clenched both fists and then relaxed them, consciously, trying to regain some level of control. He nodded, not trusting himself to speak. Blezzard was right, of course, even though Alec's every instinct to protect, every desire, told him he should be out there looking. The one compensation in all of this was that Gavin didn't know the Levels well. He had a limited choice of where to go and how to get there.

'What if he heads for Bristol, for his dad's place?'

'Then he'll have to head back towards the motorway and we'll pick him up.'

'What if he changes cars?'

'Not easy with two women to control.'

Especially not if one of them is Naomi, Alec added silently. She would not take any of this kindly. He wasn't at this point sure if that was a good thing or not.

'OK,' he agreed reluctantly.

Dean led them through to the office and the supervisor, who was already searching through the digital tapes. It didn't take long for him to pinpoint the incident they wanted. Gavin had waited for almost an hour before the women had arrived. Parked in the visitors' space, he had clearly been settled in for as long as it took.

Alec watched in silence as Gavin's car pulled up and blocked Susan's in, as he dragged Naomi from the car, as she fought back, and then Susan's indecision.

'He's been here before, I think,' the building supervisor said. 'We had complaints about someone in a red car hogging the space. Mrs Rawlins' ex has been here too. She took out a restraining order against him some time ago, so the downstairs neighbour, Mrs Richards, she took it upon herself to make a note if he ever came around. She told me the other day he'd been here.'

'Dean, go and see if she can pinpoint when,' Blezzard said.

'She's the lady who called us,' Dean said.

'Oh, she'll know,' the supervisor told them. 'She'll have a record of the date and time and duration of stay, if I know her. She's a one-woman neighbourhood watch, is Mrs Richards. Bless her, she's on her own and doesn't have a lot else to keep her interested.'

Alec ran the recording again, trying to discern more about Naomi's state of mind and that of Gavin. It was easy to see how Susan was coping.

'He looks nervous,' Alec said. 'Can we zoom in on the knife?'

The supervisor fiddled with something and focussed in on the hand holding the blade. 'Looks like one from the cottage,' Alec said. 'I noticed them because the handles are unusual. Sort of pierced metal. His hand is shaking,' he added. He took a deep breath.

'We'll get to them,' Blezzard said. 'Alec, she'll be all right.'

Dean reappeared with a list in his hand. 'Last Tuesday at about eleven thirty,' he said. 'And Thursday at ten in the morning. Mrs Richards is sure she's seen Gavin Symonds here before too. She's almost certain it was on the Thursday morning and he was talking to Susan's ex.'

They soon pinpointed the dates and times she had specified on the CCTV. Brian, uncharred and still living, walking across the car park. Susan giving him the cold shoulder. Brian again; Susan shorter with him this time. A glimpse of the red car in the background. Then Gavin walking over to Brian as he stood by the car. The two of them leaving a short time after and, as Brian's car left the car park, Gavin's pulling away just ahead.

'So, you were right,' Blezzard said to Alec. 'They did know one another.' His mobile rang and he stepped away to take the call.

'What is it?' Alec demanded, when the call was finished.

Before he could reply, Blezzard's phone rang again. He held up a hand to silence an impatient Alec and listened, then thanked the caller. 'They've been spotted at Eddy's place,' he said. 'I've told everyone to hold back. We'll get the negotiators in.' He nodded to Dean, who went to make the call.

Alec grimaced; he knew from experience that they would take their time getting there. Negotiating teams had to be called, mobilized, briefed, and got to the scene, often from a good distance away. Like tactical firearms units, they were always around but not always where you wanted them.

'And the other phone call?'

'The post-mortem on Brian Rawlins won't be done until tomorrow, probably, but the preliminary examination shows that the fire was not the cause of death.'

'He'd been stabbed,' Alec said.

'Once. Just below the ribs.'

With the knife Gavin was still using, Alec thought.

THIRTY

'Get out of the car,' Gavin said.

Naomi complied. They had driven out into the countryside; she knew that from the way the road surface had changed and the number of bends had increased. It was very quiet now, just birds singing and that faint susurration, born on a fresh wind, that she associated with the Levels.

'We're at Eddy's house,' she guessed.

'So what if we are? Get inside.'

'I can't see,' Naomi reminded him. 'You'll have to show me the way.'

'You, help her,' he snapped at Susan, and Naomi heard the other woman move around the car, felt her take hold of her sleeve.

'Are you all right?' Naomi asked.

'Not really. No, I'm sorry, I couldn't run, I—'

'Shut up,' Gavin said, 'and get inside.'

Naomi could imagine him anxiously looking around. She'd have expected the CSI to still be here now that the cottage was a major crime scene. Yes, it was possible they could already have left, but someone would have been keeping an eye on the place, surely. She heard Gavin opening the door. 'Did you see anyone on the road when we came in?' he snapped.

'What? No, no one.' Susan sounded too distracted to have noticed, anyway.

Naomi tried to imagine what may have been happening. With luck, someone would have seen Gavin taking them away, would have called the police. Someone would have guessed where Gavin would take them, would have officers watching. They would be found, they would be safe. With luck.

Of course, it could be that no one saw, no one acted, that the forensic officers had simply finished and left and Alec would be cross because she wasn't answering her phone.

She preferred the first option, Naomi decided.

'Get in there,' Gavin demanded, and Susan turned to the left of the hall and led Naomi into what she remembered had been Eddy's office. 'Sit down over there.'

Susan led her to the couch in the corner of the room and they both sat down.

'Now, shut up and stay put.'

She heard him leave and the door close, heard something being dragged in front of it. Didn't he realize that the door opened inwards?

She didn't actually think he was aware of anything much any more, not in any logical way, which was worrying in that he may no longer see the logic even in keeping them alive.

'What will he do with us?'

'Nothing,' Naomi told her. 'We're his insurance.'

'You think so?'

'Yes. Are there windows in this room?'

'One, why?'

'So we can get out.'

'Are you crazy? He'll hear us. Where would we go?'

If she was right, then someone would see them getting out and rescue would not be far away. But was she right? 'Is it big enough to get out of?'

'It's small, but I suppose so.'

'See if you can get it open. Just open it and then come back over here. Do it fast.'

'What?' Susan was squeaking with fear now.

Naomi turned to her and reached to grasp her by the shoulders. 'Look,' she said, 'if I could do it I would, but you're the only one in the room with all five senses intact at the moment, so it's up to you. Go and see if we can get out through there.'

'No. I can't. He'll hear and he'll come back.'

'Then you'd better be quick, hadn't you?' Naomi hardened her tone. 'Look, help might be on its way, but we might have to help ourselves. I want to be prepared, and while you're about it, look for anything we might be able to use as a weapon.'

'A what?'

'Susan, get a grip. *Now.*'

She heard the other woman draw a deep and

300

very shaky breath, but then felt her get up and heard her start across the room, pausing at every slight sound. She heard the slightest click as the latch was lifted on the window, the louder metallic scrape. She held her breath as Susan flew across the room and fell back on to the sofa. Both women listened intently but Gavin did not come back into the room.

'I tried it,' Susan whispered, 'but I think it must be painted shut or something. I couldn't get it to budge. I daren't push it any harder in case he heard.' She paused, evidently thinking about it. 'I never saw that window open,' she said. 'But I didn't come in here much. It was Eddy's room.'

OK, plan B. 'Anything we can use as a weapon? Is there a fireplace?'

'Just an electric fire in here. I can't see anything.'

A sound in the hall silenced them. Dragging away whatever he had stood in front of the door, Gavin came back in.

'How long are you going to keep us here? It's cold.'

'I'm thinking,' he said. 'You know, I searched this place. He was supposed to have stuff here, stuff he found. Where is it?'

'His finds are all in that cabinet over there,' Susan said. 'But there's nothing valuable. He didn't find anything valuable.'

'So you say.' He snorted in disgust. 'I mean, look at this place. Not even a decent computer.

The old guy had nothing. Nothing. I reckon that solicitor of yours is winding you up. Look at the state of the bloody house. That's not worth a damn either. He was a fraud, a phoney. He had nothing. Nothing.'

'I don't want anything from him. He was a friend. Whatever he left me, I'd much rather have Eddy back.'

'Right, sure you would. Do you know what that old man was really like? Not just a phoney and a fraud, but a blackmailer. He killed my father, drove him to suicide. He persecuted him and wore him down until he didn't know what to think or how to cope any more and he drove his car into a frigging wall. Your Eddy was a murderer. That's all he was. He deserved what he got. I just wished I could have made it slower, that's all. Slower and more painful, just like it was with my dad.'

'I don't know what you're talking about,' Susan protested, and Naomi realized that was absolutely true. They'd been busy discovering the truth about Eddy Thame but Susan had been out of the loop.

'Don't you? You make me sick, you really do.'

'Eddy was kind. He was gentle. He never hurt another human being in his entire life. It's you that deserves to die. You!'

'Yeah, right. Dear old Eddy, kind sweet old Eddy. Let me tell you what he really was. He was cruel, devious, unforgiving. He didn't give

302

a damn for what he did to me, to my dad, to our family. He hounded and hounded and my father killed himself because of it and anyone that can't get their frigging head around that deserves what Eddy got. And that ex-husband of yours? He thought he was too clever for me, didn't he? Thought he could just turn around and walk away.'

'You killed Eddy and Brian, didn't you?' Naomi said.

'Damn right, and damn right there's nothing to stop me killing you. Who's going to know?'

He left and slammed the door behind him, dragged the useless barricade back across.

'He killed Brian? And Eddy? And what did he mean about Eddy?' Susan demanded. 'You know, don't you?'

Naomi sighed. 'Eddy discovered that Gavin's father had caused the crash,' she said. 'He could not get enough evidence for the police to make an arrest, so he took things upon himself. He made sure Gavin's father never forgot his guilt.'

'And he killed himself?'

'Yes.'

'Oh, my God.'

'Eddy never stopped grieving,' Naomi said gently. 'It stopped him from thinking rationally about some things. He couldn't let it go.' Trouble was, she thought, neither could Gavin.

THIRTY-ONE

Blezzard pulled on to a narrow track alongside a copse of trees, joining officers already assembled there. Someone handed him a pair of night-vision glasses and he looked back towards the cottage before passing them to Alec.

'No movement since they arrived. We don't know where in the house anyone is. Any ETA on the negotiators?'

'No,' Blezzard said.

Alec looked. The cottage appeared quiet and empty, only the red car giving any hint at occupation. Behind the house he could see the garden stretching out into farmland, bounded by stream and hedge. Beyond that he could just see the point at which the path ran from the bend in the road and across the fields. Before coming out here they had looked at computer maps and Google earth and Alec now had a good sense of the lie of the land. They had discussed what Alec had seen the day he had gone to Eddy's cottage; the day Gavin had hit him over the head.

'If there's anyone in the kitchen, then they can see down the full length of the garden if you leave the lights off. So approaching from the rear is difficult. You'd have to stay in the shadow of the hedge and then make your way round to the front through the little gate. From the front you've got cover, but as you get close the hedges block the view from the house. You'd have to be in Karen's room, though, to see the road, so anyone in the house would be as blind to what was going on as anyone trying to get near.'

He thought now about the way Gavin had probably gained entry. Through the landing window. Alec wondered if he could do it, make the climb without alerting Gavin or pulling the downpipe from the wall. Gavin was a good bit lighter and somewhat shorter than Alec.

He kept those thoughts to himself, knowing they'd be met with an immediate negative from Blezzard.

'So, what now?' he asked.

'We wait. We call the house phone and see if Gavin answers. If he does, we try and build up some kind of rapport and then hand over to the negotiators when they get here.'

'And how long will that take?'

'Who knows,' Blezzard said. 'They're on their way, that's all I know.'

Alec sighed and leaned back against the car. It had been a long day. It seemed like forever ago that he and Naomi had gone to see DI Bradford, or even since they had spoken to Gavin's mother. Now the early dark of a winter evening had closed in and cut them off, it felt, from the rest of the world.

Blezzard left his side to go and speak to the officer who'd been on scene when the car had arrived. It had already been dusk, difficult to see much, but he had been able to identify a man and two women, one woman leading the other inside.

Abruptly, Alec made up his mind. A couple of weeks before, he had been ready to blame his friend, Mac, for acting without reference to anyone else. For not confiding or trusting. Now, he knew he was on the verge of acting in much the same way, but he could not just stand by and wait. He'd seen Gavin on the CCTV recording and knew that man was now long past being rational in his thinking. He was past the negotiating stage, Alec was sure of that.

There were a dozen officers standing around in the gathering gloom of the copse, chatting quietly. Content to wait. Another time and Alec might have been one of them. It was odd, he thought. All of this indecision he had suffered lately about his future, his aspirations, his career, and yet, in a sudden moment of clarity, he realized that all the agony had been wasted. It was the next minutes that would decide everything that would happen in the coming years, not just the coming hours, and it needed no thinking about, in the end.

He stepped back, behind Blezzard's car and into the deeper shadow of the trees. No one was looking his way and Blezzard was deep in conversation, poring over a map spread out on the bonnet of a car, scrutinizing by torchlight what they'd previously looked at on the computer screen. He had the images in his mind, fresh and strong and reinforced by the view through the night-vision glasses. He wished, for a moment, that he could have taken them with him, but the officer who'd lent them to Blezzard had taken them back and dropped them on to the seat of the car Blezzard now stood beside.

Alec knew what he was doing was foolish and, on all sorts of levels, that it was wrong, but he couldn't help himself. A few paces and he was out of the woods and on to the road. A solid surface beneath his feet, Alec turned and began to run.

'Do you think they'll have noticed we're missing yet?' Susan seemed to have calmed down a bit. Boredom will do that, Naomi thought. Boredom will take you to the point that you almost wish something, anything would happen, just so you can break the tedium by being scared again. She knew, because she'd been in a situation like this before. A little like this, anyway.

'They'll know. They'll be looking for us. Likelihood is they'll have a very good idea what happened. You have CCTV at the flats?'

'Yes, CCTV and Mrs Richards.'

'Mrs Richards?'

'The old lady who lives on the ground floor on the right as you come in. She sees everything. She lives on her own and likes to sit beside her bedroom window, watching the comings and goings. She can see the street from there. It's not much of a view but she seems to enjoy it.'

'Good,' Naomi said. 'Every crime scene needs a Mrs Richards.'

Susan almost managed a laugh. 'How come you're so calm?'

'Oh, don't be fooled. I'm not, but I've learnt it doesn't help to panic. I'm trying very hard to follow my own advice.'

'What do you think he's doing?'

'I have no idea. He's so quiet.' It was hard, she thought, to build any kind of rapport with your captor when they didn't actually come and talk to you, and he'd not been back since just after Susan had tried to open the window.

Maybe they could try the window again.

'Is it dark in here?'

'Very. Why?'

'Do you think you could switch the light on?'

'Won't that make him mad?'

'I don't know. Is there a desk light or a small lamp or anything?'

'Um, yes, a standard lamp.' She got up and switched it on. It was close to the sofa; Naomi didn't think Susan would have had the nerve to cross the room again to find it.

'Do you want to try the window again?' she

asked hopefully. She felt Susan shake her head.

'No way. I told you it was stuck.'

'OK, it's all right. I won't ask again.' At least the light might be visible, she thought. If there was anyone out there to see then they'd notice the light and know what room they were in. Wouldn't that help?

Sighing and suddenly deflated, she slumped back against the cushions of the sofa and closed her eyes.

'Naomi!' Susan's voice interrupted her thoughts. 'Naomi, I think he's coming back!'

Alec found the path with little difficulty. He followed the bend in the road until the thick hedge gave way to a stile. As his eyes became accustomed to the gloom he could make out the flat field, the hedge and the large bulk that was Eddy's house. Forgetting the actual path, Alec set off across the field, heading straight for the cottage. He couldn't run here, the field being too wet and claggy and his footwear not exactly appropriate for the task. He slid and slipped and felt as though he was trying to run through treacle, or wet beach sand that sank beneath his every step. He wondered if they'd missed him yet.

There were no lights on at the back of the cottage. From what he could remember, there was a low hedge and a bit of fence right at the end of the garden. It was from that point that he'd spotted the path and the stile the day he'd been there. That would be the easiest access point, the downside being that it was also on a direct line from the kitchen window. If Gavin looked at the wrong moment then he could be seen.

Alec struggled on, the reasonable, logical side of his brain telling him to turn back, slip back into the copse, pretend he'd been there all the time. But Alec wasn't really listening to the logical side of his brain. His focus was on Naomi, just on Naomi. Was she all right, was she scared? What was happening to her? And that focus kept him struggling on through the mud and stopped him thinking about what Blezzard would be saying when they realized he was gone, or about the threat to Naomi from a man they knew had already killed twice.

'Naomi!' Susan gripped her hand tightly.

The door opened and Gavin stood on the threshold. 'What the hell do you think you're doing?'

'Doing?'

'The light. You switched on the bloody light.'

'It's my fault,' Naomi told him quickly. 'I told her to.'

'I don't care which of you bloody did it.'

Naomi heard a crash and the sound of glass breaking. Susan cried out, then Gavin grabbed Naomi by the hair. 'Move,' he said. 'Seems I can't trust the two of you together.'

Susan was screaming in panic as Gavin

dragged Naomi, still grasping her hair, through into the hall. She guessed from Susan's reaction that he still had the knife, was waving it at the other woman. She staggered as he pulled her far too fast, heard a door open and then he pushed her, cracking her head as she fell into the small space. Naomi landed heavily on something hard and unforgiving and the door slammed shut.

Naomi reached out, feeling the wooden door, the close walls, the sloping ceiling, and realized the hard thing she had fallen on so painfully was a vacuum cleaner. He'd thrown her into the cupboard under the stairs. She heard Susan shout out and then scream and scream again and Naomi's whole body chilled. Oh God, what if Gavin had killed her?

She heard footsteps in the hall as he walked back towards the kitchen. She tensed, expecting a fresh assault, but he just kicked the door and walked on by. She released her held breath and listened intently, hearing sounds from the kitchen that she couldn't quite define. A chink of crockery, scrape of a chair, others that were vague but which further shredded already too-frayed nerves.

She felt around, finding the vacuum cleaner hose, a leg of what felt like an ironing board, and shelves stacked with what she assumed from the shape were bottles of cleaning fluid and polish and the odd duster. Her scalp was sore from where he'd dragged her by the hair, her back and buttocks now bruised from where she'd landed badly. Naomi realized she'd gone beyond the point of being afraid now. It was likely that Susan was dead and she'd be next. Naomi's fingers explored the range of cleaners and sprays on the shelf beside her and she made up her mind. When Gavin opened that door again, he wasn't going to have anything his own way.

In the kitchen Gavin stared out into the dark. Once he thought he saw a movement. Twice he thought he heard a sound he could attribute to neither wind nor wild things. He glanced now at the blood on his sleeve. He'd sorted that bitch, made her pay, and he'd made up his mind. He'd wait until morning and then he'd leave and head back north, back to where he'd been working and where he had friends. As for that other one, she could stay where he'd put her. If someone came and found her, good for her, but Gavin really didn't care. He thought about killing her, but that was still a thought he hadn't fully crystallized. The blind woman was something he'd not considered in any of his plans; she hadn't figured in his consciousness until she'd forced herself in, and so long as she was out of sight, Gavin was quite happy to put her out of mind. For now, anyway.

Outside of the cottage Alec had heard the scream and his heart had frozen mid beat, but then he knew instinctively that it was not Naomi. He should have hated himself for feeling such relief as flowed through his veins alongside that realization, but all he could feel was profound joy. He was here now and he'd find a way to get inside and he'd find his wife and they would both go home.

A second scream.

Alec shut his mind, focussed on the task of climbing a downpipe that was never intended to take his weight and finding purchase for his feet, still mired with mud, against the brick wall.

That, and praying that no one would have been efficient enough to re-latch the window he had unfastened that day he had been at Eddy's, as he realized belatedly that he was carrying nothing with him that would slide in and release it from the outside.

'When did he leave?' Blezzard was incandescent.

No one knew. Blezzard snatched up the night sight and scanned the fields and the house, saw nothing. If Alec had gone that way then one of the hedges or the line of trees must be blocking him from view. There, he caught a brief glimpse. 'Oh shit!'

'What?'

'Look.' Blezzard handed the night sight over, pointed towards the cottage. Alec was halfway up the wall, presumably hanging on to something Blezzard could not see.

'He's inside.'

Blezzard swore again, much more extravagantly this time. Gave orders for everyone to move forward. Silently, on foot, calling for backup, just in case.

'Ambulance?' someone asked.

'Yes, but make sure they know to hang back. I swear, if Gavin Symonds doesn't kill him, I'll do for him myself.'

Alec stood on the landing and listened, expecting any second that Gavin would come charging up the stairs. He'd been quiet, but not silent enough, he was sure of that. And he was unarmed. Really didn't think this through, did you? he chided himself.

He tried to recall anything that might be useful in the upstairs rooms.

From the hall he could hear a small sound, like a latch or a sneck of a door opening. He had been heard. He was certain now. Gavin had come in that same way, he knew it was possible.

He needed a weapon. He needed something now.

Downstairs, Naomi heard something bump on the floor above her, the enclosed space below stairs amplifying sound. Her hands closed tight around the spray cans she had found. She'd tested both to make sure the sprays worked and

the cupboard now smelt strongly of laven-
der and disinfectant. She was having trouble
breathing as it caught in her lungs.

She waited. Another small sound, less of a
bump this time, more of ... she wasn't sure. Was
there someone up there?

Gavin obviously thought so. She heard the
kitchen door open and the metallic sound of
whatever he'd used to barricade the door being
moved away. This door opened outwards; he
seemed to be getting the hand of barricades.

Naomi took a too-deep breath, tried not to
cough. The cupboard door was flung wide and
she reached both hands out in what she prayed
was the direction of Gavin's face. Pressed both
buttons on the spray cans and kept them pressed
down hard.

Gavin shouted, shocked at first and then
pained. He fell back and Naomi followed, beating him with the cans, yelling and screaming
her anger and frustration. Gavin's flailing hand
knocked one of the cans from her grasp so she
grabbed at what she hoped was his face, her
fingers tangled in his hair.

Now it was pure revenge. Scalp still sore and
her body bruised, to say nothing of payback for
the fear he had caused her, Naomi wound her
fingers tighter and attacked with everything she
had. Teeth and feet and nails and still half-full
can. She didn't know if Gavin had the knife
and, frankly, she no longer cared. If she was
going to die, then she was going down fighting.

Footsteps on the stairs, running. Shouts from outside, the sound of the front door crashing open. Naomi had Gavin by the hair now and the force of her attack had forced him to the ground. Alec caught her wrist as she was about to smash Gavin's head to the tiled floor for a second time.

She screamed with frustration as he dragged her away and then turned and buried her face against him, fists pounding as Alec held her tight.

The hall was filled with people, shouting and exclaiming, and one in particular angry with the man who held her so tightly.

Naomi turned on Blezzard, tearing herself away from Alec and attacking with the full fury she had directed towards Gavin only moments before. 'Don't you dare shout at my husband! Don't you dare to tell him he was wrong! Don't you *dare*!'

And then Alec was holding her again and he was apologizing. Apologizing! For her? For himself? And she was crying and shaking like she'd never be able to stop ever again.

'Susan's going to be all right,' Alec told her as they sat in a police car waiting to be taken back to the station. A paramedic had checked her over and agreed she was fit enough to answer questions and make a statement.

Susan had been taken on to hospital.

'They think she'll make it.'

'My fault,' Naomi said. 'I asked her to switch the light on. I thought if you were out there, you might be able to see.'

'Not your fault. None of it is your fault.'

'What happens now?'

'We get a right royal bollocking, I expect. Or, at least, I do. Then we go home ... and I resign.'

'Really?'

'Darling, do you really think I'll get away with this? Not on top of everything else. I think I'll go before I'm pushed.'

EPILOGUE

They drove north the next morning after saying goodbye to a bemused Bethan and Jim. Kevin had also come to see them off, and Alec gave him the little box containing what was left of the Kirkwood treasure, and also Eddy's maps. He kept one coin back, a memento.

'You'll go on looking?' Alec asked.

'Oh, sure. Susan told me about what Eddy left for me in the will. I don't fancy uni or anything, though. Do you think he'd mind?'

'No, and anyway, I think Eddy forfeited the right to tell anyone what to do in the end.'

'Yeah, I guess so. I loved him though. You know, like he was an uncle or something.'

'A mentor.'

'Yeah.'

Susan was going to be all right. Maybe Gavin got careless or she managed to dodge out of the way, she couldn't remember clearly what had happened, but both stab wounds, though serious, had missed vital organs. Neither Naomi nor Alec had really felt any desire to go and see her, and Naomi doubted Susan was ready to see them either.

'So, what now?' she asked again as they

drove north once more.

'I told you, it's time to change everything.'

'Really?'

'Really.'

Blezzard had been beyond angry, his fury so great that he'd handed over to another officer when Alec was interviewed. Alec was right, Naomi thought, his career would never survive a scandal like this. He had potentially endangered himself, her, and anyone else who had got dragged in, unprepared.

November was over, and she realized with a slight shock that it was now the third of December. It would be Christmas soon.

'We need a bigger tree,' she said.

'A bigger what?'

'Christmas tree. Alec, I want to go overboard this year. Deck-the-halls sort of overboard.'

'Isn't that one of those mixed whatsits? Metaphors.'

'Probably. Let's have everyone over. Your mum and dad, mine, Harry and Patrick and all our friends and have a party. One absolutely major party.'

'Sounds good,' he said.

'What will happen to Gavin now? He's not fit to stand trial, you know.'

'Aerosol poisoning?' He tried to laugh, didn't quite manage it. 'Part of me thinks you're right. He needs treatment not punishment. Part of me just wants to see him hang.'

'Good job that's not an option then.'

'Isn't it, though. Look, there's a lay-by just coming up. There's something I have to do.'

'OK.'

Alec stopped the car and took out his mobile, started to text. Naomi waited until he pressed send before asking, 'You're texting Mac?'

'How did you know?'

'I just knew. What are you telling him?'

'That I'm sorry, that I understand. That it looks like I'm out of a job and does he want to come to the party we're having, to celebrate?'

Naomi smiled, reached out and took his hand. 'Let's go home, Mr Friedman,' she said.